W R A T H

CORALEE JUNE

I hated fire. I hated how the smoke wrapped around my naked body, stinging my skin with defiant embers. I hated the smell of burnt flesh, the ashes heavy on my tongue, my charred soul like splinters deep in my chest.

She's dead, Juliet.

There's nothing else you can do—

Dragging my bleeding feet across the concrete, I walked toward the flames. Heat licked at my cheeks. Sirens off in the distance cursed my ears.

Dead, dead, dead.

All of this started because I made a choice. Because I fell in love. Because I was a lonely girl clinging to dangerous men.

She was dead because of them.

For Laura

prologue
juliet cross

I hated fire. I hated how the smoke wrapped around my naked body, stinging my skin with defiant embers. I hated the smell of burnt flesh, the ashes heavy on my tongue, my charred soul like splinters deep in my chest.

"She's dead, Juliet," Nick whispered. "There's nothing else you can do—"

I shoved him away from me and sobbed hard and recklessly. Dragging my bleeding feet across the concrete, I walked toward the fire. Heat licked at my cheeks. Sirens off in the distance cursed my ears.

"Dead, dead, dead," Anthony whispered while rocking

back and forth on the concrete.

William was the only one to stop me from jumping into the flames. He wrapped his arms around me as I cried out. I hated him for saving me, for loving me.

All of this started because I made a choice. Because I fell in love. Because I was a lonely girl clinging to dangerous men.

She was dead because of them.

chapter one
juliet cross

Rotted, severed limbs coated in a rancid mixture of blood and mud surrounded me. The air smelled unforgiving. It was a stench that danced all around us. Earthy. Deadly.

There was a full moon hanging ominously in the cloudy sky, and Anthony howled like a rabid wolf as he attacked the hole we were digging with a sharp pickaxe. Instead of removing dirt, he just whacked the ground as if he were still chopping up the three bodies we were currently making a permanent home for. "We'll put the living room by the earthworms, Juliet!" he exclaimed excitedly.

My breathing was ragged. Skin slick with sweat despite

the bone-deep chill in the January air, I wiped at my brow with the back of my hand before cutting at the earth with my sharp shovel and tossing rogue dirt into a pile outside the pit. I was a mess. The cotton, blood-stained shirt I wore was stretched across my breasts and riding up my tight, empty stomach. I learned the first time we came out here not to bury bodies on a full stomach. Gnats were caught in the web of my tangled hair.

"How much deeper, boss?" Anthony asked with a chuckle. I looked around the private property that Nick bought two months ago and sighed. It didn't matter how deep we buried the bodies, no one would come to Anthony's new playground and dig up the people we hid here. The Civellas' connections wiped the fear right out of this experience. We didn't have to worry about getting caught. We didn't have to cover our tracks. We could probably put a billboard on I-70 announcing our sins, and no one would bat an eye—no one that wanted to live, anyway.

Murdering someone and hiding their body was supposed to create an intoxicating adrenaline rush. It sent a person into fight-or-flight with the simple snap of a neck. The forbidden act was like a drug to some, but Anthony was seeking a high he'd never get. What we did wasn't dangerous—not really. And when you were palm deep in the clenched fist of the mob, murder didn't feel so wrong. No one went against the Civella family. They were above the law. Hell, some days I wondered if they were above God.

"Not much deeper," I choked out. My muscles were

sore, but I liked the workout. My morbid, weekly exercise routine started a few weeks ago. It was an unprecedented shift in Anthony's mental state. He woke up determined to bathe in blood and gore. Anthony wanted to play with his victims. I'd sit in his dungeon and watch with dulled horror as he dressed them, set them up for tea parties, and spoke to them. And when the decomposing bodies were ready for disposal, he said it was too easy to just drop them off at the morgue. He wanted to work. He wanted to chop them up and hide them like the serial killers in my podcast.

And me? I just wanted to make him happy.

It was wrong and nightmare-inducing. I wasn't sure if I was just so deep in my own disassociation that I couldn't comprehend what was happening, or if my love for him managed to defeat the odds and overcome the horror of it all.

I didn't understand what triggered him. We were all just trying to navigate his moods right now. Anthony had always been this playful, ticking time bomb. But lately I felt like I barely knew him.

I grabbed my water bottle and took a swig. "Who are these guys?" I asked conversationally. Anthony liked to give the dead fake lives. I think it made the entire ordeal easier to handle.

"Dillon was a banker," he replied before walking over to me and grabbing the shovel from my fist. Anthony was too sexy for words. The dark jeans and black hoodie he wore were casual yet form-fitting, and he'd grown more muscular the last couple of months. As usual, he had a beanie on his head and a smirk on his mouth. "He liked to cheat on his wife with his business partner. She thought he was at poker night, but he was really poking Mr. Nelson in the ass with his tiny dick."

I bit the inside of my cheek and grinned. "Dillon sounds fun."

"He's great at parties. Hey, you think he'll want to come to William's birthday party next week?" This conversation might have seemed strange to some, but I was used to Anthony speaking as if the dead were still here. He was haunted by lives long gone. I learned months ago that it was easier to go along with it.

"We can send him an invite. Does this grave have a mailing address?" I replied.

He shrugged. "I think I have it in my address book."

"And what about her?" I asked while nodding at another body.

"You don't remember?" he asked. "Bitchy Bertha was at the luncheon yesterday and had the audacity to complain about your egg salad sandwiches. We don't need that negativity in our lives, babe."

Anthony started shoveling, and it wasn't long before he stripped out of his sweatshirt and black tank. His hot breath against the chilly air cast a deep fog over his skin, and my eyes drank in the sight of his sculpted body. Anthony Civella was an ache I couldn't soothe. The rippled muscles on his torso flexed as he flung dirt and shoveled deeper. I licked my lips, only slightly disgusted with myself. As he worked, I sat beside the pile of chopped up bodies.

It should have bothered me. Some days, I prayed to feel horrified by what we were doing.

But oddly enough, my humanity died when I fell in love. It was the price I had to pay for selling my soul to three monsters.

Despite sitting in a field of fresh plots and staring at one of my psycho boyfriends, I found normalcy in the grotesque insanity of it all. Death, destruction, crime, and control followed me everywhere I went. Even now, I knew that Nick was sitting in a Range Rover a quarter mile away, watching me. He rarely let me out of his sight these days, which made it difficult to have an equal relationship with his two brothers.

Anthony, Nick, and William still fought over me, but Nick? Nick claimed me. He destroyed the competition.

"Is your shadow still watching us?" Anthony asked, referencing Nick. He then scooped another pile of dirt.

"What do you think?" I asked. Anthony had this habit of asking questions he didn't want the answer to. These nights were supposed to be ours.

"I think he's going to stop letting you come with me soon," Anthony grumbled before kicking the wall of dirt in front of him with his sneaker. "He thinks I'm getting worse. Maybe I am."

There was no denying that Anthony had experienced a shift in his personality. Part of me wondered if he was struggling with Vicky's betrayal harder than the rest of us. Before she tried to kill us all, they were very close, and Anthony was the sort of man to let his pain simmer. I first noticed that something was up two months ago when he stopped coming to breakfast with Grams. Then, he asked Nick to find him some land so he could bury bodies. Now, everyone was scrambling to find traitors, rapists, and thieves for Anthony to...play with.

"You're not getting worse," I lied.

Anthony didn't buy it for a second. "Nick wouldn't be worried about your safety if I was okay. He cares more about you than he feels guilty about me, you know. When it comes to you..."

It hurt my heart to see Anthony struggling so much. Maybe it was why I willingly came here with him to bury bodies. I didn't know how to make things better. Sometimes happily ever after was just a state of existence. Six months ago, Nick, William, Anthony and I made the decision to try a relationship between all of us. But it was just the start.

"I don't know why he's got a stick up his ass about this. Nick used to get off on this shit with you, remember?"

I licked my lips as the stark vision of my first murder hit me in the chest. The dungeon. My chained legs. The way my foot stomped on my nameless victim's battered skull until the last breath escaped his bloodied lips. Nick once told me it made him hard to watch. He said he wanted to pull his dick out and stroke himself at the sight of me fighting for my life.

"I remember," I whispered.

"Not anymore," Anthony replied ominously.

"Maybe if you just talked about it—"

"Talk about what? How I'm having nightmares again?

Or how about the panic attacks? You don't just magically get better one day."

"No one expects you to," I argued. "I love you, Anthony."

He looked around and frowned. "I'm sure this isn't the relationship you envisioned."

"Nothing about my life now is what I envisioned. I'm dating three dangerous men. Grams is working with some of the best doctors in the world. I'm going to school for forensic science while working nights at a sex club. All the while, I'm spending my off time burying bodies with the man I love. I'm a killer." The last declaration made my throat close up. I cleared my throat and continued. "My best friend isn't my best friend after all. I think Nick is paying people to download my podcast, because I now have ten thousand subscribers. And Bitchy Bertha is telling me my egg salad sandwiches aren't any good. It's a lot to process, yes, but I wouldn't change it for anything."

After a lingering silence, he spoke. "Fuck Bertha," Anthony growled, making me smile. "I'm going to cut out her tongue."

I shivered and compartmentalized that statement. Half the battle of dealing with this insane, deadly world was by pretending it was all normal.

"You know, just earlier today, Nick asked me if dragging you into these games was really necessary."

I furrowed my sweaty brow. This was news to me. Nick never used to question what Anthony and I did. He understood that his brother had...unique coping mechanisms. "I don't mind coming here with you,

Anthony," I replied softly, desperately trying to keep the pity out of my tone.

"You don't *mind*?" he scoffed. "How benevolent of you. Putting up with your crazy boyfriend and his dead bodies." He dropped the shovel and hoisted himself out of the hole with his strong arms before sauntering over to a pile of limbs. "But how far will you really go for me, huh? Would you let me finger fuck you with Dillon's thumb?" Anthony picked up an arm and waved it at me. Nausea rolled around my stomach as the limb leaked fluid all over the dirt.

I rolled my shoulders back and raised an eyebrow at him. "My gynecologist advised against that," I replied dryly. I wouldn't give in to his anger. Anthony lived a life of chasing flies.

"I could kill my brother. Would you help me hide his body?"

I jolted from the shock of his statement. What the actual fuck? My first instinct was to react with anger, but I calmed down after a steadying breath. I prayed Anthony didn't see the anger in my eyes. "You wouldn't do that. You love your family."

"How far can I go, Juliet? How hard can I push you? What if I killed *you* and kept you forever? Pretty little doll locked up in my freezer. A fuck toy I can pull out whenever I want."

His words were meant to shock me. It was a visual that made me even more sick to my stomach, but still. I was devoted to this man and the demons in his mind. I'd fight to bring him back to me every damn time. Some might think it was pathetic, but I didn't care. If he was trying to push me away, it wasn't going to work.

After brushing off my hands on my thighs, I stood up and walked over to him. Anthony wanted to know how far I'd go. He lived in a world of extremes. And even though I knew he was pushing me away, I wouldn't let him.

"Why would you want to kill me, Anthony?" I asked before wrapping my arms around him for a tight hug.

"So I wouldn't have to share you. I hate hearing how I'm not good enough. My brothers have bad days and no one bats an eye, but I have a bad mind, babe."

I pressed my forehead to his and sighed. I needed to have a talk with Nick and William. It wasn't fair for Anthony to feel like an outsider in this relationship. "If I were dead, I couldn't do this," I whispered before pressing my lips to his for a chaste kiss. "Or this."

My lips grazed his jaw, and I ran my hands down his bare back.

"You do make a very valid point," he groaned. I embraced the sweat on his skin and the death in his scent. I sunk my teeth into his bottom lip and brushed my fingers along the waistband of his jeans before pulling away in a taunting motion.

"I know you prefer the dead, Anthony. The dead can't hurt you. They can't make fun of you or question you. The dead can't judge. But the living?" I paused to whisper in his ear. "The living can please you. The living can love you back."

I ran the tips of my fingers down his chest and along his

abs. I spun around and pressed my body into his, arching my back so that my ass was pressing into his hard erection. I could feel it even through the thickness of his jeans. Anthony licked at my neck before sucking on the sensitive skin there.

"Besides," I continued. "You can't kill me, Anthony."

"Oh?" he asked distractedly while running his palms along my hips.

"You'd have to catch me first."

And with those words, I jerked out of his hold and started sprinting along the property away from him, dodging fresh burial plots and towering trees as I went, all while laughing hysterically. It thrilled me to stretch my legs and feel playful. A rogue branch scratched at my cheek, and I swiped at the beads of crimson blood dripping from the wound. Wind whipped at my hair, and I took a brief moment to look over my shoulder and see if Anthony was still chasing me.

I caught a brief look at him, and a tingle of fear swept across my mind like a black veil. His eyes were animalistic. His form while running was anything but playful. Stiff. Angry. He looked like a predator. And for the first time in a long time, I feared the man I loved.

I thought this was just a joke. Anthony was always playing with me, teasing me. But that single look at him had my heart racing. I pumped my arms hard and pressed my sneakers into the dirt, picking up speed as terror slashed through me. "Anthony?" I gasped before tripping over a root.

Tossing my hands in front of me, I barely caught myself before scrambling to stand back up. Thick fingers threaded through my hair, and I was jerked by my scalp to a standing position. "Don't ever run from me again," Anthony said in a sinister voice in my ear. He shook his head, as if trying to clear dark thoughts from his mind. "You know what, Juliet?" he asked. "The dead can't love me back, but they can't run away, either."

And with that, Anthony slammed his mouth to mine. Fear and lust tangled into this complicated, pulsating knot in my chest as I dragged my blunt nails along his back. He shoved me against the trunk of a rough tree as I cried out. He was demanding and passionate. Anger, lust, and possessiveness flooded his expression as he pierced my lip with his sharp teeth. I groaned and pulled him closer. I could feel every tremble in his muscular body and taste the salty tang of blood on my tongue.

His eyes welled with tears, and I wanted nothing more than to take the pain away from him. How could I possibly help him when I didn't know what to do? This, right here, was all I could give him. My body, my patience, my mind, and my heart. He owned it all.

"Anthony," I whimpered when he shoved my black leggings down my thighs, stopping just above the knee. A brutal chill in the air brushed across my nakedness, and he unbuttoned his pants.

He pulled out his hard, throbbing cock and spoke in a dangerous tone. "You can't leave me."

Poising his body right between my legs, he braced a

palm at my neck. I breathed him in and opened as wide as my restricted legs could go. "I'm not going anywhere."

He thrust inside of me and clamped his hand around my throat, squeezing so hard my eyes immediately watered. I was so shocked by the move that I couldn't even choke out a protest. I squirmed and pressed my hands against his chest as he fucked me hard and raw. My back was scratched to hell from the bark of the tree, and veins built with a pressure so intense I could feel my fading pulse in my head.

"Pretty and dead, pretty and dead," Anthony said over and over. I felt my mind slipping. My sex was aching from each punishing jerk of his cock. Mud and salty sweat covered my skin, the slick heat painting my thighs like a humid summer day. Dewy. Uncomfortable.

"Pretty and dead."

I felt my vision going black. Panic like acid traveled through my thudding veins. No. I struggled against my sense of self-preservation. Certainly, he wasn't going to kill me. My mind ran over his decline. The piles of bodies. The burials. The dissatisfaction. Anthony had been a man on the edge for a while now, but I wasn't ready to jump.

I wrapped my hand around his wrist, trying to tear him away from my throat, but still he wouldn't stop.

Our eyes connected just as I felt my consciousness fall. This was wrong.

And when my mind faded into nothingness, I wondered if Anthony Civella would ever be whole enough to love me.

chapter two
nick civella

My father once told me that in order to survive in this world, you had to have a killer instinct. I latched onto that lesson, digging my teeth into the meaty flesh of violence and shaking my victims until they bled out. It was a thirsty impulse. Do or die. Bleed or flee. It was the same way a predator could sense a weakness in another or how bullets found their target. It took skill.

It was what drove me to protect my family—and to

protect the one I loved.

Everyone thought life at the top of the food chain was strategic and thoughtful. William sure took that approach to life. But a dull blade doesn't cut. And there were plenty of enemies I needed to grab by the throat if I wanted to stay on top.

I had been feeling like my family was on the edge of something terrible for a few weeks now. Every day, I woke up with this itch to eliminate the threat, but also struggled with the fact that I was letting that threat walk through the front door and fuck with my girl. Anthony was behind the enemy lines of his mind and closing in on us all. I didn't know how to help my hurting brother. And it went against every instinct I had to send my Juliet into the line of fire like a sacrificial lamb, ready for slaughter.

My guard, Luca, was sitting in front of me, keeping watch from the front seat. I brought him specifically because I wanted to have a word with him. "Tell me what you observed this week."

Luca, a tall man with murder on his mind and a soldier's spirit, spoke in a low tone. He was good at what he did and kept his opinions to himself most of the time. I didn't really give a fuck if it was wrong to pay someone to spy on Anthony and Juliet. "She didn't stay the night with him this week. He wouldn't put the bodies back in the freezer, and she wasn't comfortable sleeping next to them."

I cursed. Normally, he prioritized Juliet over everything. "Was he mad?"

"She kissed him goodnight before going upstairs, and

he started hacking at someone's leg. Practically minced the sorry son of a bitch with a pickaxe. He's angry, boss."

Anthony had developed quite a tantrum. It was hard for me to pinpoint the cause. Maybe it was Vicky's betrayal. Maybe it was a lifetime of blood and murder. We were all caught up in the madness. It was just too much for him to handle.

"Have you been able to pinpoint any triggers?"

Luca shrugged. "It changes daily. He seemed fine yesterday. Bought Juliet some of her favorite ice cream, and they watched a movie together. Today, he wants to bury bodies. He's worse when she's gone. But…"

His voice trailed off, signaling that he was nervous to say the next part. All my men had come to care about Juliet. She was the queen of my empire, and I demanded respect from them. "But what?" I asked, not sure I wanted to hear the answer.

"But I don't think it's healthy for her, boss. William thinks Juliet needs a break from all of this. I don't want to overstep, but—"

"Then don't overstep," I interrupted him in a dangerous tone. I knew for a fact that my pompous brother wanted to take *my* girl on a trip to London. I couldn't leave Kansas City right now. Things were rocky with our weapons dealers. Our territory was expanding, and the growing pains made it difficult to navigate. I didn't want him to steal her for any extended period of time. "That's not happening," I snapped. If Juliet needed a break, then she could take a fucking vacation on my cock.

I stared at the rearview mirror as Luca pressed his lips into a thin line. He didn't understand our dynamic. Three insane men sharing one woman. It was complicated.

Juliet was mine. Her body. Her soul. Her heart, future, and pussy.

I just shared her because...

Because...

Because I didn't fucking know why. It made her happy, it made Anthony healthy. It made William bold.

Or it had. For a little while. Once again, we found ourselves in a complex mess. It was like putting a tourniquet on a limb that was bleeding out. Maybe it was time to cut off a leg or two.

"I don't have eyes on them, boss," Luca said from the driver's seat. I scanned the dark night for signs of movement.

"Give me your binoculars," I demanded. I made him watch them out here every week because I still couldn't stand to see him kiss her or make her laugh in ways I was incapable of doing. I was built for doing hard things. Trained at a young age to handle loss and disappointment, I was probably one of the few people alive capable of navigating the pain of openly sharing the love of my life. But that didn't mean I wanted a front row seat to it all.

She was mine. Fucking mine. I just let them borrow her heart on occasion.

He handed them to the back seat, and I scanned the plot they were digging, only to find nothing.

"Did you see them move?" I asked. Luca shifted

nervously in his seat. I hated repeating myself. "Did you see them fucking move, Luca? Answer me."

"They started to kiss, so I averted my eyes. You have the rule about seeing her naked, and I—"

I cut him off by getting out of my SUV and scanning the area. Nothing. Not in the pit. Not in the open area. Nothing.

That instinct I had roared to life. I almost grabbed my chest to soothe the ache like a fucking coward. I picked up the binoculars again and scanned the trees. I saw movement at the edge of the property that made me rage.

Dropping the binoculars, I sprinted in the mud in my fucking thousand-dollar Italian cashmere suit and Gucci shoes. The January chill slapped at my cheeks, and naked branches danced above me. The closer I got, the more my instincts pulled at the darkest part of me.

And when I heard my brother's crazed voice, I pulled the glock from my holster and pulled the safety. It was one of those quick decisions that I was groomed at a young age to make. I knew at that moment, I'd kill him to save her.

"Pretty and dead…"

I ran harder. He had his hand wrapped around my girl's slender neck.

"Pretty and dead..." He fucked her against a rough, cold tree. Eyes closed. Head tossed back. There was no awareness on his part.

"Pretty and dead..." Those words in his haunted voice were ringing in my head. I wanted to scrub it from my brain. Without thinking, I tackled him to the ground

from behind, the move ripping him from Juliet. I dropped my gun and landed my fist against his jaw. Then hit him again. And again. I heard his nose crunch, and blood came pouring out of it.

"What the fuck are you doing?" I roared before grabbing him by the neck and forcing him to sit up and look me in the eye. His lip quivered, making him look like the little brother I used to tuck into bed after a nightmare.

"I...I don't..."

I slammed him back into the dirt and nearly puked at the sight of his body. His entire existence made me sick now. I grabbed my gun once more and aimed it right between his eyes. From this range, I knew I'd get his brain matter all over my suit. Wouldn't be the first time. "You ruin everything!" I screamed so hard that my face felt hot. I reared back and pistol whipped him across the temple once. Twice. I then aimed my weapon at him, and that predator deep in my gut begged me to eliminate the bastard—end the torture of his pathetic existence and save Juliet.

A moan at my back momentarily drew my attention. Juliet needed me, but I pressed the barrel of the gun to his cheek. I wanted to crack every bone in his skull. "You should have died when they kidnapped you," I said.

And the asshole nodded in agreement. He looked at me with pleading eyes, begging me to end his fucked up life.

Too bad I wasn't that kind.

Anthony screamed so hard the veins in his neck bulged. I got off of him, and he curled up into a ball, his dick still out and soft but glistening from her soaked pussy. I wanted to chop it off and feed it to a wild bear.

I ignored him for a moment and went to my girl.

My girl.

My fucking girl. I shouldn't have let it get to this point. She had collapsed on the ground, pants down at her knees, hair tangled, wild, with dirt clinging to the strands. Angry bruises in the shape of Anthony's fingers were wrapped around her neck.

I pressed my thumb to her neck and sighed in relief at the sweet thudding of her pulse. Her chest was rising and falling beautifully. She was knocked out, but alive.

I pulled up her pants because not even fucking Mother Nature got to see my girl—MY GIRL—naked. Then, I scooped her up in my arms.

"Is she okay?" Anthony slurred. He was still lying sideways in the dirt, his hands folded under his head like a sleeping child.

"Barely," I grunted before crushing her to my chest. "What the fuck is wrong with you, Anthony? You can fuck up all the bodies you want, but she's supposed to be off limits."

He started sobbing. The emotions made his body shake. He looked like a lame horse. I debated with myself on what to do. Putting him out of his misery would be a gentle mercy at this point. It was a fucked up thought, but murderous rage was on the menu. "Why am I like this?" he asked before coughing up blood. He wasn't bleeding enough in my opinion.

I glared at him. "Because you're fucking weak."

Anthony looked at me. The time for sympathy was long gone. "I…I…"

"You're letting them win," I said before cursing. My girl was shivering in my arms, and I wanted to get the family doctor to look her over immediately. "Every fucking breath you breathe is a victory for them. You've taken a perfectly good life and handed it over to whatever fucked up demons are living in your head. Juliet is normally along for the ride. It's what made me…"

I stopped my speech to look down at the beautiful woman in my arms.

"Love her?" Anthony finished for me.

"Don't speak for me," I snapped before once again glaring at him. "Juliet can handle a lot, but I decide where her time is spent, and I'm not going to sit by and watch as you fucking ruin yourself and drag her down with you. Ever since Vicky left, you—"

"Everyone fucking leaves," he said before crying. "Or dies. Or hurts. Or…fucking flies." I scowled at him. I didn't have time for riddles or whatever the fuck he was talking about. Juliet was the one who navigated his insanity. Not me. And from now on, not her anymore, either.

"Well, now, you're going to be the one to leave," I said.

Anthony sat up and looked at me. "What?"

"You're out. Done. If I see you in my territory again—"

"You're kicking me out?" There was a sobriety in his tone that hadn't been there for weeks. Good. Let it fucking sink in.

"If I see you in Kansas City, I'll put a bullet through your brain."

He looked confused, almost shocked that I'd even suggest such a thing. "But I'm—"

"You're nobody. You're just a threat to my girl now. Get out of my sight. Don't come back. If you so much as breathe on Juliet, I'll kill you in the most boring way possible, have a massive public funeral for you, and bury you in a cemetery with a tombstone that has your name plastered on it."

Dying ordinary was Anthony's biggest fear. I'd deliver death with a casserole and cheap bottle of wine. It would be the most mundane spectacle of the year. Fuck, I'd tell God to make it rain just to piss him off.

I was done. I didn't give a fuck. She was the most important person in my life. I don't share my toys with people that like to crush shit in their fist.

I looked at my pathetic brother, a pang of pain slicing me through the chest at the sight of him. I knew that I was responsible for the mess of a man he'd become, but I wasn't going to let guilt ruin Juliet's life.

I'd already cut off one sibling.

"I don't want to see you in this town ever again," I said before spinning around and walking away from the brother I loved most.

Never again.

My priorities weren't with him anymore.

No, my girl. MY GIRL needed a savior, and that's what I'd fucking be. She wasn't strong enough to push him away, but I was.

chapter three
juliet cross

My eyes felt superglued shut. Ragged breaths and a throaty moan escaped my lips as I peeled back the curtain of my consciousness. I woke up feeling like I'd eaten a bowl of dry sand. My tongue was like a dried-up creek bed, and my throat was sore. I wasn't disoriented, even though I'd woken up in a different place than when I passed out; the room smelled like Nick's cologne and fresh linen. Morning light peeked through the blinds, bathing the space in a warm glow that welcomed me. The room enveloped me in familiarity and comfort. I just wasn't clear how I had gotten there.

I was home.

I was alive.

I was...confused.

I slowly sat up and ran my fingers over my neck, noting the tenderness and throbbing pain I felt. I cleared my throat and winced at the pain. I was in Nick's bedroom, and my naked body felt cold from the chill in the air. "Hello?" I croaked, wondering if anyone was standing outside the door. It was rare that I was alone here.

There was no response.

I tried to settle my mind with my head cradled in my hands. The events that took place last night were still vividly etched in my memory. Carved in metal. He'd fucked me. He didn't wait for consent or even see if I was wet. And then, during a series of pounding, punishing thrusts against a tall tree trunk, Anthony wrapped his fingers around my throat and squeezed hard enough to make me black out.

Anthony almost killed me. It was a jarring thought. Thinking about it felt like betrayal, and I couldn't imagine saying the truth out loud. My allegiance was tattered by the reality of what he'd done. The love was still there, but so was distrust and shame and pain. No one could know what happened. If they did, I wasn't sure what they would do. These past few weeks, Anthony truly lost himself, and I wasn't sure we would ever find him.

Once upon a time, the darkness in Anthony's soul felt cathartic and healing. There was a purpose to his madness. Because he was so good to me, it was easy to compartmentalize the dangerous things he had done. But that goodness felt tarnished now.

I slowly got out of the soft bed and padded my way over to Nick's full-length mirror. After switching on the lamp and flinching from the harsh light, I took a moment to observe myself. It was an out-of-body experience, like watching a ruined character in a movie or play, not my own reflection.

The undersides of my eyes were dark. There was a tangle of hair on my head, twisted into a bun. My ghost-like skin showcased bitter bruises around my throat. I looked skinnier than I remembered. Sicker.

I pinched the skin on my stomach and frowned. My cracked lips were split. The ends of my hair, dull.

Love was a parasite draining me dry.

Anger and brokenness overtook me. It wasn't supposed to be this way. But somehow, I'd stopped taking care of myself in the pursuit of helping Anthony, serving Nick, and building up William's confidence. We were all guilty of dancing with our toxic desires, but this was the first time I had seen the effects of it on my body with clear eyes.

And yet, my first instinct was to go to him—to Anthony. I wanted to make sure he was okay. I wanted to talk about when it happened and try to make sense of it all. I needed his comfort. Why wasn't he cuddling me? Why was I alone?

It was really fucked up. I was a victim, but my traitorous heart had me crawling back to the monster that attacked me last night. In my mind, I had created two versions of Anthony: the man I loved and the man who destroyed himself while seeking sanity.

Deciding not to wallow, I got dressed in one of Nick's button-down shirts and a cozy pair of pajama pants I left here last time I spent the night. The collar of his shirt hid some of the bruises, but when I got home, I'd need to cover them up with concealer. After brushing my teeth, I left the bedroom in search of Anthony. Every tick of the clock made the hurt I felt burrow deeper within me. Was he worried about me at all? Or was he so far gone that he didn't even realize what he did was wrong?

With soft, resigned footsteps, I traveled down to his basement of death. With a shaky exhale, I pushed open the door, bracing myself for the stench of decay. I was paralyzed by fear the moment I inhaled. It reminded me too much of last night. And for the first time in a long time, I didn't shove my experience into a little box at the base of my gut, I let the trembles surface, I let my fear overwhelm me. I let my humanity rear its ugly head and remind me that none of this was normal. This wasn't me.

Somehow, someway, I needed to find myself again. I'd lost too much these last few months.

"I knew you'd come here first," a deep voice said from the darkness. The familiarity and tone of it instantly calmed me. My safe haven was here. I gripped the handrail and descended toward him, thankful for the dim lights of the basement.

Sitting on a folding chair under a fluorescent bulb, Nick had his legs spread wide and a short glass filled with amber liquid resting in his fist on top of his knee. An expression of blankness filled his face. His blond hair was slicked to the side, and rough facial hair cast shadows along his jawline. "What are you doing down here?" I asked before moving to sit on his lap.

Clearing his throat, he chugged his drink before wrapping his arms around me and tilting my head so it was against his chest. His lips found my neck, and I froze for a moment, worried that he'd see the marks there. Perceptive as he was, he paused at my reaction before licking a tender spot there anyway.

"I was looking for Anthony," he said. "How was your night together?"

I wondered if he could feel my pulse racing at his question. I wanted to avoid this conversation for as long as possible. I wasn't ready to vocalize what had been done to me. Anthony and I were hidden by the woods, and if he brought me home, then there was still a chance no one had to know. I foolishly clung to that ideal and replied. "Good," I lied.

Nick turned his head and stared at the wall. Despite the darkness of the basement, I could see him clenching his jaw. "You were asleep when he brought you back. Practically passed out."

I swallowed nervously. I couldn't tell Nick what really happened. He would be livid. Nick loved his brother more than anything, but I wasn't sure if he loved him enough to overlook this. There was only one levelheaded person in this family that I could talk to.

William.

"I'm pretty tired," I said, even though our interaction

was making me wired. I didn't fear Nick, not like I used to, but I found myself trembling. It might have been foolish, but I held the truth as close to my chest as possible. If Nick didn't know, then that was for the best.

"Slept like the dead," Nick said bitterly before putting his empty whiskey glass down and picking me up. I held tightly to his neck as he marched up the stairs, his angry footsteps slapping against the wood floors as he went.

Once in the hallway, I tugged at the collar of my shirt. "Where are you taking me?" I asked.

"I'm making you breakfast. Do you want some tea for your throat? It sounds like you're catching a cold, Juliet."

"That would be nice," I said, trying to make my tone clear.

Once in the oversized kitchen, Nick seemed to reluctantly set me down in one of the kitchen chairs. Then, he bent at the waist until we were eye level. My heart raced, and I lost myself in his brutal stare. "Are you okay?" he asked.

He was giving me the opportunity to tell the truth. I knew it. He knew it. But the trauma I felt was like cement poured down my throat. I couldn't admit it to myself, let alone to Nick. My eyes watered, but I willed myself to be strong. "I'm fine," I lied. "Just tired and hungry. That tea sounds good, too."

Nick clenched his jaw before straightening and walking over to the cabinets. I let out the breath I was holding when he turned his back to me to pull out a kettle and frying pan. I watched as he meticulously started making breakfast in silence. The room smelled of cooking bacon, and I found myself watching the doorway. Where was Anthony? Had he just dropped me off without a care? That didn't seem like him. I needed to speak to William.

"Penny for your thoughts?" Nick asked before cracking an egg.

"Is William home?" I knew he had worked at Eden's Place last night, but he usually woke me up in the mornings with a kiss on the cheek before going to sleep for a couple hours. The night shift made him nocturnal, but we made it work.

"He had some work to do," Nick replied. "It's just you and me this morning. Is that alright?"

I scoffed. "Of course it is. What do you want to do today?"

Once the food was done cooking, he turned off the burner and let it cool for a moment. Nick then poured me a cup of tea and brought it over to me, along with some cream and sugar. It was so domestic and fragile. A few months ago, I would have never imagined this moment, Nick making me breakfast in his kitchen. "I want to take care of you, Juliet," he whispered gently.

I forced a smile and pressed my hand to his cheek. "You always take care of me."

Nick slid the hot drink away from me before picking me up and setting me on the tabletop. Prying my legs apart, he stepped between my thighs and looked me in the eye. "Do you trust me, Juliet?"

"I do."

"Do you love me, Juliet?"

I reached up and kissed him. "I do," I whispered over his lips reverently.

Nick tugged at my messy bun, exposing my neck. I stiffened once more, but he simply hovered his lips over the bruises there while rubbing his hand up my thigh. I winced when his fingers pried apart the lips of my pussy. Was I bruised there, too?

"Then why, my love, are you fucking lying to me?" he asked before sinking his teeth into my neck painfully and sucking on my tender skin. I cried out in pain as he started rubbing my clit with furious circular motions.

"Nick!" I cried out. It hurt so fucking bad. My body felt broken and abused. He pulled away from me and glared at his handy work. I was certain there was a bloody blister left on my neck from his angry mouth.

"You think I wouldn't notice? I was there last night. I know what happened—I saw what happened." Fuck. Of course he knew. Why was I pretending otherwise? Was I so wrapped up in saving Anthony and protecting the fragile peace the four of us maintained that I couldn't see the truth three inches from my face?

"Nick—"

"Don't call me that. It's Malice now."

It was as if he'd punched me in the gut. I gasped and pressed my hand to my mouth to stop loud sobs from pouring out of me. "Malice? We're back to that now?"

He stood mere inches from my face. "You think I don't know every hair on your head? The color of your skin when it bruises? The fear in your eyes? The way you tremble when you're scared? I know every fucking nuance of your body, Juliet. I know your mind. In fact, I've crawled inside every fucking crack in your soul and built a home for myself there. Not only did you lie to me, but you insulted our relationship by pretending I couldn't see how much you're suffering right now."

Tears streamed down my cheeks in hot, angry streaks.

"I'm not suffering—"

"Don't fucking lie to me, Juliet!" he roared. "You've lost weight. You're covered in bruises. You have bags under your eyes. You lost that fire."

I shook my head, denial washing over me like a burning blanket.

"I'm not sharing you anymore," Nick—Malice—said. "It's killing you."

I snapped my gaze up to him. "You can't do that."

"I would agree," another voice said from the kitchen entry. I looked over Malice's shoulder and stared at William, my entire body filling with relief at the sight of him.

William stalked over to us and placed a hand on Nick's shoulder, shoving him away from me with brute force that made my mouth open in shock. "Are you okay?" William asked me.

I trembled and stared at him through bleary eyes. William was wearing a button-down shirt and a loose tie. The tattoos on his neck pulsed from the raging veins there. He took off his sunglasses—the ones he always wore back when I worked at the diner—and peered at me with stormy brown eyes.

"I'm taking care of her," Malice snarled.

"Are you? Because from what I saw, you were making her cry."

"At least I'm not choking her!"

I flinched and William zeroed in on the movement. I couldn't handle all the anger floating around me. The energy was like a rope tied around my body. He reached up and pushed a fallen strand of hair behind my ear, his eyes taking in every detail of my face. I leaned into his touch, making Malice huff.

Then, William positioned himself between Malice and me. "Anthony's tracker has been disabled, Nick. Where is he?"

"Fuck Anthony," Malice spat.

I hopped off the table and tried to move around William so I could see properly, but he blocked me with his outstretched arm.

"I get that you're mad. I'm pissed off, too. But he's a liability out there. We need to get him help."

"I've given him more than enough help," Malice yelled. "Do you want to know where he is? I sent him away. I banned him from our territory. Anthony is dead to me, and if he so much as looks at Juliet again, I'll rip his spine from his body and hang it above the front door like a Christmas wreath."

I stood there in disbelief. "You sent him away?" I asked.

Malice ignored me, addressing William instead. "And

if you want to join him, be my guest. Juliet is no longer communal property. Look at her. She's wasting away trying to save us all."

"That's not for you to fucking decide, N-Malice," I argued.

He took a step closer to me, but still, William positioned himself between us. Malice looked down at me. "I am in control of everything that happens here. Get used to it."

"Anthony needs help," I pleaded.

"So do you!" he screamed.

William remained levelheaded, something he'd mastered over years of dealing with Nick. "I agree that something has to change," he began. My heart felt like it was being ripped in half. "Anthony went too far. I don't want to see Juliet hurt any more than you do."

"You weren't there," Malice said before running his hand through his hair. His veins were bulging. His eyes were crazed. "You didn't see the way he wrapped his hands around her neck. You didn't see how he fucked her while she was passed out."

William reached out and tightly held my hand as Malice spoke. I melted into the silent solidarity and comfort he offered.

"Where is Anthony?" I whispered. I still couldn't wrap my head around it. Maybe if I kept asking, this would all make sense.

Malice glared at me. "He's gone, Juliet. And he won't be coming back."

chapter four
juliet cross

I was nothing more than a darling little casualty. Malice was constantly at war with his need for control. I started this fight on the frontlines, and he used me to mend his broken little family but got mad at the bullet holes in my chest. He couldn't have it both ways. He couldn't orchestrate this epic love affair between us all, then rip part of my soul away.

It wasn't until William tugged on my hand that I moved. My aching feet were practically cemented to the floor. I was a distressed woman. Everything that had happened had left me completely disoriented, almost in a daze. "Where do you think you're going?" Malice asked.

It was strange how easily my mind slipped back into calling him by his predatory nickname. The man I loved wouldn't have sent Anthony away. He was back to his mob boss mentality. The enemy. The man that made me piss myself with fear.

Ever my protector, William answered for me. I wasn't really in the right state of mind to respond. "I'm taking her to rest, Nick," William said. "Look at her, she's trembling. Barely standing up." Malice shoved past William to get to me. But the man I once considered a bodyguard stayed solid as stone in front of me. "Back off. You're making things worse."

"If she needs taking care of, then I'll be the one to do it," Malice growled.

William clenched his fist as if preparing to go to blows with his brother over this. I might have felt at my lowest, but I refused to kneel at Malice's feet. I wasn't just a docile, desirable little toy. Not anymore.

"No. I don't want *Malice* to take care of me," I said out loud. My neck was stiff. Forearms strained.

"Too fucking bad," he snapped quickly. Too, too quickly.

I took a step back. Then another step. William matched every stride. "I said no!" I shouted. A choking noise escaped my throat. "You don't get to decide everything, Malice. You don't get to control my life. You can't just send people away because they piss you off. That's not how this works—that's not how love works." I straightened my spine and glared at him, determined to get past his hardened shell of hate. "I'm

34

sorry for lying to you. I should have been honest. I guess I was just scared that you'd punish Anthony. I don't want to lose him." He slammed his eyes closed in frustration, so I quickly added, "I don't want to lose any of you."

Malice looked down at the ground. "Anthony was lost weeks ago. I just shut the door behind him. I did it to protect you, and I refuse to apologize for that."

"I don't need an apology, Malice. I need you to include me in these decisions. I don't want someone to make sweeping judgments on my behalf. We could have talked this out, but you completely removed me from the equation. That's the problem."

Malice's downturned mouth had me itching to smooth his expression with the pad of my thumb. "You were passed out cold on the hard dirt with your pants around your knees. Not only were you incapacitated, but I wasn't sure you'd make the right choice. I stand by what I did. And I'd do it again."

Tears like heavy weights fell down my cheeks, making every drop weigh me down. I let out an exhale. "Right now, I really need to process this all. I'd like to go with William for a bit. You're really volatile and..."

"You'll go bury bodies with Anthony and let him choke you out, but won't let me take care of you?" Malice asked before pinning his arms against his stomach, as if putting a barrier between us.

I let out a sigh and walked around William to give Malice a hug. His skin felt hot against mine, and the smell of his bodywash filled my nose. Spicy. Warm. Sensual and inviting. He was stiff against my soft touch, but I tried anyway. "I love *Nick*. But right now, I'm angry with *Malice*. I'm also hurting. Anthony..."

At the crack in my voice, whatever concrete anger Malice was clinging to chipped away some. He wrapped his arms around me and squeezed as hard as he could. His arms were like a metal cage. I found his hug to be less comforting than it usually was. If anything, it just made me feel claustrophobic.

I exhaled shakily before speaking. "I just need William right now, okay?"

When he released me almost immediately, I feared I had said the wrong thing. "You never need me anymore," he said bitterly before dropping his arms to his sides. I'd expected him to talk to me more, but he spun on his designer shoes and left the kitchen without another word.

I stared at his back as he walked, feeling both uncertain and relieved. I wanted Nick back, and I needed him to be more understanding before I tried to talk to him about this. Right now, we were both angry, and he was on edge. We couldn't move past this until he calmed down.

Maybe it was a double standard. I expected more from Nick than I did from the others. Perhaps it was because he was the leader of this strange relationship dynamic we all had. I put a lot of trust in him to navigate this fairly and to do whatever was in everyone's best interest. I couldn't really comprehend why he thought sending Anthony away was a solution.

Overwhelmed by all of my emotions, I started to sway.

I was functioning on adrenaline and sensitive thoughts. Every impulse I had was tearing me in half. Go after Anthony. Bow to Malice. The only person not pulling me in any direction was...

"Shhh," William cooed. "It'll all be okay." He swooped me up and cradled me to his muscular chest.

I drenched his soft shirt with emotional tears. The devastation I felt was almost too much to process. Nick, Anthony, William and I fell apart so easily; how was that even possible? I knew it would be hard when we started this relationship. I had no road map to follow in this situation, and it felt as if I was failing everyone. But I thought we were stronger than this. My men were ruthless and invincible. So why were we letting this roadblock completely derail us?

There was just so much fucking hard work involved. Since I had to be everything for everyone all the time, there was seemingly nothing left for me. Love was supposed to be this magical thing that kept multiplying, not this twisted jealous thing we'd become—men fighting for the scraps that made up my heart. I felt used. I felt selfish. I was running on half a heart with full intentions.

"Miss Cross, it kills me to hear you cry." William brought me to his bedroom, a luxurious oversized space with ornate furnishings, silk bed sheets, and a four poster bed facing large floor-to-ceiling windows.

He set me down on the bed and pulled a bottle of Evian water out of his mini fridge and handed it to me. "How are we going to get Anthony back?" I croaked, already switching my mind to *fix it* mode. Just because Malice sent him away didn't mean I wouldn't go chasing after him. "Maybe you should go look for him some more? How far could he have gotten?"

A sigh escaped William's lips as he sat next to me. I rested my head on his shoulder while thinking of ways to make this right. "I'm not going to go looking for him," William whispered. "Not right now, at least."

I sat up and twisted to look at him, betrayal slashing through me. "Why not?"

He stared at me. "Because you need me right now. Because I'm angry with him and I'm not sure what I would do if I were to see him."

I struggled with his answer. I understood their anger toward Anthony. I had my own issues with what happened last night that I needed to process. But that didn't mean I was going to completely write him off. It wasn't as bad as Malice made it sound.

Or maybe it was.

No. It wasn't that bad. Anthony wasn't that bad. We could work through this.

"I'm fine," I lied.

"No. You're not. You can lie to everyone else, Juliet. But you're not going to lie to me."

I unscrewed the top off the bottled water before taking a gulp. It felt refreshing on my throat and bought me some time to navigate this. I needed to convince them that we were stronger together. William patiently waited for me to speak again. "We have to find Anthony, William. He's not stable. He could hurt someone or himself."

"And if he did, none of that would be your fault," William replied pointedly. "You can't keep taking responsibility for everyone. Not only is it impossible, but it drains you."

A frown crossed my face, and I shook my head in disapproval. "What are you talking about? Malice is the control freak. I'm not taking responsibility for anyone."

The corner of William's mouth tipped in amusement, and I wondered what had got him grinning at me, especially in a moment like this. "Miss Cross, I watched you nearly kill yourself working minimum wage at a diner to pay for your grandmother's medicine."

That had nothing to do with this. "What other choice did I have?"

"Vicky was—is—this broken little thing grieving her parents. You took her under your wing and cared for her. And when she tried to kill us all, you blamed yourself."

My shoulders slumped. "She wouldn't have been pushed over the edge if—"

"If she wasn't selfish, self-centered, and fucking crazy," he finished for me.

He was right. I knew he was right. As a result of spending all this time observing me, William knew me better than anyone else.

"You've been trying to fix Anthony since that first night you saw him at Eden's Place," William said in a whisper. "Do you remember that night?"

How could I possibly forget? Anthony looked so broken then. Despite the pain he was in, he let the world use his body for its own purposes. Sometimes, when I closed my eyes before bed, it wasn't all the dead bodies we'd buried that haunted my mind. It was the sight of him on stage at Eden's.

Taking a deep breath, I asked him, "Is it wrong to want to help the people you love?"

I felt William pulling me closer against him and wrapping his arm around me. "No. But as Nick displayed downstairs, sometimes love and the best of intentions can get warped. I might not always understand my brother, but I feel the fear he feels. Part of him feels guilty for using you as a Band-Aid on Anthony's mind. He's terrified of losing you. Anthony has been abusing the privilege of Nick's guilt for far too long to get away with far too much. This confrontation is painful, but far overdue."

"He's just pushing me away," I whispered. "They both are, and it pisses me off."

"It's okay to be angry with Anthony. And I understand why you would feel upset with Nick. But you should know that I agree with his decision."

I *was* angry with Anthony. I fully felt the weight of that anger with every swallow. My throat burned from his betrayal. I'd been simmering in distress since last night. And as far as Malice was concerned, I was tired of being bossed around, manipulated, and controlled. It was time for things to change.

I waited another moment before speaking again. "You really aren't going to help me find Anthony?" I asked.

William kissed my forehead. Even though I was

practically shaking with rage, he didn't seem to mind. "Anthony needs to fight for himself. I think time is the best thing we can give him right now. Would you rather drag a broken man back to his dungeon, or welcome a healed man back into your arms?"

I cried and wiped a stray tear on William's shirt. He was always so poetic with his words and knew just what to say to both break me down and build me back up. "But what if he never comes back?" I said with a shudder. The idea of no longer having Anthony in my life made me sick to my stomach. I wanted to puke from simply vocalizing those words.

"It's impossible to stay away from you, Miss Cross," William cooed while rubbing my shoulder. "And if he does, it's still not your responsibility."

I got up from beside William and then straddled his lap for a full hug. I needed all the strength and comfort he offered. He wrapped his arms around me and pulled me close. Nuzzling into his neck, I softly cried while breathing him in.

Moments passed, and William held me the entire time, letting me cry, letting me rage, and comforting me.

"You don't think Nick is serious about not letting us be together, do you? I told him off downstairs, but I wouldn't put it past him to lock me in a room somewhere for the sake of keeping me safe," I said with a sniffle.

William laughed. "I'll fight my brother for you, Juliet." I sat up and looked him in the eye, drinking in his determined gaze. "Don't look so shocked."

Biting my lip, I contemplated the words I wanted to say. "You don't usually go up against him," I finally settled on.

"I never had a reason to fight before," he said before kissing my forehead and pulling me back in for a hug.

"I don't want anyone to fight, William. I just want us all to be okay."

I held William tight for what felt like hours, while slowly letting go of Anthony.

chapter five
william civella

I once met a man who made his first billion dollars before he was thirty years old. He was some kind of tech god, who developed an app that now had a permanent home on every cell phone in America. I admired the man. He came from nothing. He wasn't brought up with people frightened of his name or with a silver spoon glued to his tongue.

I had a handful of advantages dropped in my lap. I'm successful because I was born to be. He became successful because he cut his way to the top with a blunt axe.

He was a nice enough man but had some particularly annoying quirks. He drove a flashy car, dated only beautiful women, and flashed his cash around as if he was begging to be robbed. His mansion was impressive, and every second of his day was spent convincing everyone that he belonged in the billionaires club—an elite segment of society that didn't really care for or even accept new members. He didn't even enjoy his success. He was too busy trying to convince the world he deserved it.

I called him the great pretender.

He had made one fatal mistake. Everyone knew he was nothing but a fake the moment he walked into a room. The bastard stuck out like a sore thumb for one simple reason: His suit didn't quite fit.

Any man worth his dollar had their suit professionally tailored. No matter what jacket he wore, it swallowed his shoulders just enough to give him the look of a little boy trying on his father's wedding suit. It was something simple that put a massive sign over his head that said NOT WORTHY.

The rules of the rich were ridiculous but did a great job of gatekeeping.

I hadn't spoken to him in years. He probably had his second or third billion by now. That was the thing about large stacks of cash, they had a tendency to multiply.

In the end, he taught me a valuable lesson.

Money was just another word for power.

The powerless scream. Wealth whispers.

My brother utilized the finer things in life, but it wasn't

an indulgence. He had a reputation to uphold, and while he enjoyed the perks our unique life offered him, he didn't go out of his way to impress anyone. Nicholas Civella built his empire on fear. His power came from a deep well of intimidation that he drank from so regularly I was certain it would soon become dry, but it did him a grand disservice.

We lived in a modern world, and the only thing that was eternal was a good suit and a fat wallet. Loyalty was fleeting. Blood dried up when it hit the concrete. But money? Money lasted forever.

I marched down to his office, not really sure what the fuck I was going to do but feeling determined regardless. For as long as I could remember, I let my brother run my life. But he went too far this time.

"Sir?" Matteo, one of our men who worked a few of our laundering schemes, stopped me in the hall.

"What?" I grumbled. I wasn't really in the mood to deal with whatever problem had come up. It wasn't even in my job description, but everyone came to me when there was a problem, Nick when there was a solution, and Anthony when there was a dead body to play with.

"The travel agency at the mall has a thief. I was looking at the books, and it's not adding up." We had quite a few travel agencies in our pocket as fronts for money. The mall location had their hands on the most cash.

I rubbed the back of my neck and felt my eye twitch with anger. "Does Nick know?" I asked. My brother liked to eliminate the problem before fixing it, but it made for more problems down the road. You had to establish loyalty and make sure every leak in the pipes was fixed before demolishing the entire fucking bathroom.

"No, sir."

"Don't tell him. Send me the books, the work schedule, and background on all our workers there. I'll work on it. Thanks for letting me know."

Matteo squirmed a bit. "Yes, sir. Can you be the one to tell Malice, sir?"

Ah, I'd forgotten. Matteo was still earning Nick's trust and wasn't allowed to use his real name. It was such bullshit.

"I'll tell him when the thief is found. Go on."

Matteo disappeared quickly, and I made a mental note to have him followed. Everyone was a suspect. Hale's betrayal six months ago proved that. More and more, Nick's position here felt ceremonial. He might be sitting on the throne, but I called the shots.

When I walked into Nick's office, he didn't look up at me. His face was buried in his laptop, likely typing threats to whichever asshole pissed him off today. "Why isn't Juliet allowed to leave the property?" I demanded. If Nick was surprised by the anger in my tone, he didn't show it. However, he finally tore his eyes away from whatever he was working on to look up at me.

"I don't normally have to explain my decisions to you, brother," he snapped before adjusting his tie.

I ignored his comeback. Maybe it was about time he started explaining himself. "Juliet tried to go visit her grandmother today. The moment she got to the gate, a handful of guards stopped her and made her turn back around. The only reason she's not in here ripping you a new asshole is because she's too angry to even look you in the eye. You can't lock her up here."

Nick slammed his fist on his desk, and I had to resist the urge to roll my eyes at him. These temper tantrums were ridiculous. "I can do whatever the fuck I want where she's concerned," he yelled.

Whatever he wanted? Fuck that.

Blinding rage coursed through me. I didn't even realize my feet were moving. My hand wrapped around his throat and lifted him out of his chair on its own accord. It was a thrilling out-of-body experience I wanted to revel in.

For years, I dreamed of doing this. He'd been taunting me our entire lives, daring me to show him just what I was capable of.

He widened his eyes in fascination as I threw him against the wall. He was too cocky to feel the terror I wanted him to feel, which only made my anger grow more. His hand reached for the glock strapped to his hip, but I intercepted him and pinned his wrist to the wall.

"You finally grew some balls, I see," he croaked in a snarky tone. I had to force myself not to squeeze tighter.

He did not understand. There was no way I would be able to restrain myself anymore. My brother wanted me to step up and be a man. He groomed me, dangling the love of my life in front of my face like she was some kind of treat I could nibble on if I was a good little dog that did his bidding. And it worked—until now. Now, I'd bite the hand that fed me if necessary. I'd kill the brother that controlled me if I had to.

I no longer feared going against my family. I had grown to accept that in order to earn a place in this world, I had to fight for it. Nick was a joke. The man was in a metaphorical suit too big for him. I was the better businessman. I was the one building a thriving empire with the help of good sense and hard work. He was nothing but psychotic muscle, and I knew for certain that everyone in our organization respected me ten times more than they feared him.

"What are you going to do? Fight me for her? We both know you're too weak to take me on. And you know that what I'm doing is right. You *saw* her." Nick had spit collecting on his lip as he spoke. I resisted the urge to pull out a handkerchief and dab at it.

I shook my head in disgust. "That's the thing, Nick. I don't think you're handling this the right way at all. You think you can keep everyone safe and contained as long as you control their every move." I smiled at him. "Juliet's safety is my utmost priority, but her happiness is what's going to make her love me more than she ever loved you."

Those words made the veins in his neck bulge. The rage that was simmering behind his dark eyes surfaced, and he shoved at my body, almost strong enough to push me back, but not quite. "You don't know what the fuck you're talking about," he grunted.

"I don't?" I asked in a taunting tone. "Because Juliet didn't want you to comfort her last night—she wanted me. And the more you try to lock her up, the more she's going to run straight into my arms. I guess I should be thanking you." I let him go and straightened my tie. He hovered his hand over the weapon at his side, as if debating on shooting me. He could try. I'd have a bullet lodged in his skull before he could have his mind made up. I'd grown stronger these last few months. Wiser. Faster. More dangerous. "You got rid of Anthony. You're pushing her away. You might have owned her in the beginning, but she's mine now."

Nick stared at me for a long moment. My heart raced from the adrenaline of standing up to him, and then finally, he tipped his head back and laughed. "You sound just like me. I should be proud, I suppose. Finally stepping up to be a Civella instead of a coward."

I wasn't a Civella. I was a man deeply, irrevocably in love with Juliet. Whatever the fuck that meant, that's what I was.

Nick shook his head. "You're lucky I'm willing to be the bad guy," he spat. "You talk a big game, but when it comes down to it, you wouldn't have been able to make the decision I made. You wouldn't have banned Anthony. You're just benefitting from my difficult decision." I felt my eyes twitch at his words. I couldn't even argue with him. The truth was, I was glad that he was the one to send Anthony away to get his mind straight. That didn't mean I wanted him gone forever, but he needed to figure his shit out before he ruined Miss Cross.

"You can pretend to be big and bad. Go ahead and walk in here and try to intimidate me. You're nobody. You're just a temporary fix. It's me that makes the hard decisions. It's me that has her best interest at heart. And at the end of the day, when shit hits the fan, it'll be me she runs to. I fix problems. You hide from them. Anthony creates them. That's how it's always been. That's how it's going to be."

Fuck Nick. Fuck him for finding my biggest fear and exploiting it.

"I'm not hiding. Not anymore."

Nick looked down his nose at me, his lip curled like I was trash stuck to the bottom of his shoe. "You know how I love a good challenge." He pulled out his phone and dialed a number. It was so like my brother to stop mid-conversation to do whatever he fucking wanted. "Little Fighter," he purred while holding the phone to his ear. He had some balls calling Juliet. She was really pissed off at him. What was his game? I stretched my neck, desperate to hear her side of the conversation.

"I heard you wanted to go visit Grams. I'm sorry for the extra safety precautions. I suppose I was a bit aggressive on that front. How about I go with you and we can talk? I know you're mad, but—"

Juliet cut him off, but I couldn't hear what she was saying. Fuck! Time passed. He occasionally said things like. *I understand. You're right.* And my least favorite, *I love you too.*

Then, he smiled before speaking again. "Of course. I'll have a car take you now." He hung up, then grinned at me. I straightened my spine, preparing for whatever ignorant and cocky thing he had planned to say. "Thanks for the advice. I guess as much as it pains me to say, you were right about one thing. Locking Juliet away won't make everything better. She needs a taste of freedom. Like when you clip a bird's wings but open the door to their cage on occasion." I was boiling with rage. He leaned closer to whisper threateningly to me. "You'll have to pry her from my cold, dead hands before I let you have her all to yourself."

chapter six
juliet cross

Sometimes you had to dance with the devil to survive the song. Malice and I were playing a sophisticated game of cat and mouse. I knew that I had to play nice if I wanted my freedom, and he kept me on a short leash out of fear I'd run away for good. I constantly had a shadow lurking behind me. Armored cars. Guards following my every move. The only person not lingering in my presence was Malice. In the four days since Anthony had left, we only spoke in passing or through surface-level text messages that were shallow in nature.

It both terrified and hurt me. Despite his sending

Anthony away, I still loved Nick. I still craved the comfort he offered me. It felt weird not running to him with this problem. Unnatural. Malice was demanding and forceful. He'd run through concrete walls to get to me—even if I was the one building them up. So the fact that he was giving me space felt wrong on a visceral level. I wondered if it was a trick. He'd starve me of his presence until I was crawling back to his bed, begging for whatever leftovers he'd give me. And considering I no longer had Anthony to talk to either, I was feeling surprisingly lonely. Thankfully, William was going above and beyond to support me while I navigated it all.

Malice was giving me space to lick my wounds and navigate our new normal. But my time was limited. Soon, he would make us both face this. He'd claim me eventually. He always did.

I dug through my messenger bag and pulled out my laptop, prepared for a long night of studying. I attended KC University part time, something that made Grams so incredibly proud. It was so strange to me that when this all started six months ago, it still made my skin crawl to think of owing Malice anything. Now, he paid Gram's medical bills, her utilities, my tuition, and anything else my heart desired. He wholly owned me, mind, body, and soul. I guess I'd allowed myself to give in these last few months. It didn't feel wrong since we were so happy and in love. I convinced myself that his support didn't come at a cost.

But now that things felt shaky again, I couldn't figure out why I allowed myself to become so codependent on all of the Civella men.

"Are the boys coming for dinner? I was thinking about making Anthony's favorite—key lime pie," Grams said while staring into the refrigerator and taking inventory of the food we had. Of course, it was fully stocked thanks to the grocery delivery William had coordinated for her. None of the guys liked the idea of Grams walking to the grocery store.

Grams looked so good. She had a healthy glow to her skin that hadn't been there for ages. Her hair was perfectly permed, and she was wearing a soft pantsuit that William picked out for her at Bloomingdales on his trip to New York. She still had that slight tremor to her movements, but the experimental medicine was working. I felt like I was straddling her home and the Civella Mansion. I didn't really have a permanent place to stay. I was this wayward woman dating three guys and taking care of her Grams, but it worked—for now. It might've been part of the reason I felt so exhausted. I wasn't really sure where my home was.

Gram's place had gotten a major face lift. The guys replaced the roof and the windows, painted the wood paneling out front, and set up a wheelchair ramp for Grams in case she had a bad day, which didn't happen often but was still good to have. I didn't have a bedroom at the Civella Mansion. I just sort of hopped from room to room. I kept clothes everywhere, but the lack of routine was getting to me.

I hadn't told Grams that Anthony was gone, mostly because I wasn't quite convinced that he was. In my mind,

I pretended like this was nothing more than a vacation. It wasn't real. He'd walk through the doors at any moment, and we'd go back to normal—whatever normal was for us.

"No. William is at work and Mal-Nick has a meeting. Anthony is..." I couldn't even force myself to come up with a lie.

Grams stopped scanning for ingredients and slowly turned to face me. "What's wrong, baby?" she asked. My chest felt like someone had taken a hammer to an icepick at the center of my breast bone. Every inhale was this slicing sort of pain that made me sick to my stomach. I wasn't very good at lying to her. She had this way of seeing the truth even when I didn't want to admit it. We'd never discussed it, but she knew what my men were involved in. Just because I evaded some of the more gruesome parts of my life, didn't mean I didn't open up to her.

"Dating three men is hard, Grams," I whispered. "I don't feel like I'm enough." I never imagined that we'd have a conversation like this, but thankfully she'd had plenty of time to get used to our unique relationship dynamic.

She furrowed her brow before slowly moving to sit next to me. "You aren't supposed to be enough, baby," she said softly before reaching out to pat the top of my hand. "The measure of a person isn't what they can give in a relationship. It's how they love. Not how much."

I averted my eyes and wiped a stray tear. "Anthony is..."

"Troubled," Grams finished for me. "He's going through it lately, doesn't even come over to check on Jeffrey anymore." At hearing his name, the all black fur ball lifted its head up from where he was snoozing on the kitchen floor and meowed. I still remembered when Anthony got her the cat. It seemed like such a happy time so long ago.

Troubled didn't feel like an adequate way to explain what Anthony was. "Nick sent him away. William thinks Anthony needs some time to work on himself before he can handle a relationship with me."

"S-sounds reasonable," Grams replied with a slight stutter, likely from the stress of our conversation. "Even though Anthony has a very special place in my heart, your happiness and wellbeing is my priority. William is a very smart man, and if he thinks Anthony needs time, then he's probably right. And as for Nick, that man is terrifyingly charming but a little impulsive. He'll come around eventually."

Impulsive was a nice way of putting it. I didn't want to tell Grams about what happened at the burial ground. She loved Anthony something fierce, but when it came to my safety, she didn't pull punches. Maybe I was brainwashed, an abuse victim conditioned to forgive for the sake of love. Maybe I still had hope that he would somehow get better. Regardless, I didn't want another person I cared for hating Anthony for what he did when he wasn't in his right mind.

"I have a feeling something happened to make Nick and William come to this decision," she noted while scanning my skin with her gaze. I slouched slightly, hiding my fading bruises with the collar of my jacket. "I have a feeling this is another one of those things you don't want to tell me."

I shrugged. "Anthony loves me," I choked out with all

the conviction I could muster. I wasn't sure if I was trying to convince myself or Grams. "They all love me."

"But they have to love you in a way that's good for you, okay?" Grams said, her tone sterner. She pressed her lips into a thin line, and I watched her fingers shake on the tabletop. I didn't mean to upset her, but talking things out was good for me. Grams had this way of helping me feel centered.

I cleared my throat. "So, key lime pie, huh? I've been craving it, actually."

She graciously let me change the subject. "I just need a can of sweetened condensed milk. Feel like running to the grocery store for me?" Grams asked.

I let out a sigh of relief. Going on a walk was just what my brain needed before diving into a night of studying. "Yeah. I can go get that," I replied. "Need anything else?"

Grams scratched her chin. "I would kill for some boxed wine, but my doctor doesn't want me drinking with this medication. Do you think half a glass would mess anything up? Oh, I guess you're not twenty-one yet." She rolled her eyes playfully.

I had Dr. Fulbright's number on speed dial, and thanks to my terrifying boyfriend, the poor physician always answered on the first ring. "I can ask the doctor?" I didn't mention that, thanks to the Civella men, I didn't need an ID for alcohol anymore. I practically walked into the store and was handed whatever I wanted.

Grams beamed. "Wine night!"

I got up and grabbed my wallet. "Be right back."

—

When I walked out the front door, I saw that the guard usually parked outside the house was asleep in the front seat of his car. I almost went to knock on the window to let them know I was leaving, but then I realized this was too good of an opportunity to pass up. I could go somewhere alone for the first time in days.

So I snuck out.

It was a quick trip. I just needed to get back before he woke up, and no one would be the wiser.

The chilly January air wrapped around me as I walked. It had been unseasonably warm this winter, but I expected a few snowfall days to hit soon. The grocery store was about a thirty-minute walk away, and as I passed parks, pedestrians, and dilapidated buildings, my mind wandered to thoughts of Anthony, Malice, and William.

I tried to feel hopeful. I wanted Anthony back. I needed Malice to tell me everything was alright. I was thankful for William's strength in all of this.

It wasn't until I got to the grocery store that my phone started ringing. I rolled my eyes when I saw Malice's name on the caller ID. I'd never changed it from back when he bought me the phone. I'd switched between his two alter egos, but in the back of my mind, he was always Malice, always teetering on the edge of madness and wickedness.

"Hello, Malice."

"You're at Cosentino's Market without a guard. Why?"

I smiled a bit to myself. It was the first time he'd sounded angry since our fight. Admittedly, I was tired of the coddling. I was ready for this boil to come to a head—metaphorically speaking.

"Grams is making me some key lime pie but needed some ingredients."

"And you just went there alone?"

"Yes."

"Without telling your guard."

"Yes."

He went silent on the other end. I heard a car door slam on the line as I marched to the baking aisle and grabbed what I needed. Since I was here, I decided to get some snacks for a late night of studying, too.

"Malice? Are you done with the inquisition?" I asked before biting the inside of my cheek. Let's see if he could pretend to be the good guy now that I'd broken his rules.

"Stay on the line, Little Fighter," he growled, the sound sending a thrill through me. I felt like a boxer warming up for a fight. Adrenaline had me salivating for his anger.

I ran my finger along the shelves, staring at the various packages of cookies, treats, and cakes. Chips. I needed chips, too.

My hips swayed as I walked down the tiled floors, perusing the aisles while listening to him huff on the line. "I'm craving cheese puffs, Malice. And chocolate. Should I get something healthy while I'm here, you know, to balance it all out? Good with the bad."

"Stop talking, Juliet."

Oh, he was thoroughly pissed.

Wonderful.

I was staring at a long line of junk food when he came storming toward me. The man was efficient, I'd give him that. It was at least a forty-five minute drive from his house to get here. He must have been notified that I'd left about two minutes after I walked out the door, then broke every traffic law there was to intercept me.

His hair was disheveled. He glared at me as he stomped on the tile in my direction, with two bulky men flanking both his sides. "When was the last time you went grocery shopping, Malice?" I asked casually before dropping some Twinkies into my cart. He stood in front of me, arms crossed over his broad, muscular chest. Nostrils flaring with angry huffs. No words escaped his mouth at my snarky words. "Do you realize how ridiculous it is to be angry with me for going to the grocery store?"

"I've been very reasonable, Juliet."

"In some ways, you've been uncharacteristically reasonable, Malice," I replied back before mirroring his stance with a bit of defiance and anger of my own. "And yet, you're also following me to the grocery store. Limiting where I can go and when. You're avoiding this. Have you been afraid of me, Malice? Scared that if I look you in the eye, I'll decide to leave you?"

He laughed. "You can't leave me," he growled. His cocky response was expected but also made my skin buzz. It was fucked up, but fighting with this man made me hot.

Malice then crowded my space, and I looked up at him,

making sure to keep my mouth secured into a frustrated scowl. I was daring him with my body language to do something about the scalding tension between us. It was January in Kansas City, but I felt like I was wading through an angry, melting pot of desire. "Tell me what you want, Little Fighter," he snapped. The sentimental nickname was like a balm on my heart.

"I don't know."

"Yes, you do. You always know what you want; it's something we have in common."

My eyes prickled with tears. "I want Anthony back."

If my words affected him, he didn't show it.

"What else?"

"I want you back."

He reached out and cupped my jaw with his tattooed hand. "What else?"

"I want me back? I want to feel like myself again."

He kissed my forehead before speaking. "And who are you, Juliet?"

I didn't know how to answer his question. Was I the girl that killed a man to save herself? Was I a student? A lover? A sex club worker? A hardworking granddaughter willing to sell her soul to help the ones she loved? Was I a victim?

No. I knew I wasn't that. I was never a victim. I survived, adapted, and overcame.

"I'm a fighter," I whispered, the admission felt both comforting and overwhelming.

"Block the aisle," Malice said to his guards. "Turn your

back to us." I was confused by what he said, but quickly understood the instant his strong hand landed on the waistband of my yoga pants. I gasped when his cold fingers brushed along my stomach, finding skin under my jacket and sweater with ease.

"What are you doing?"

"Rewarding you," Malice purred.

I gasped when he plunged between my thighs with his fingers. Wrapping my arms around his neck to steady myself, I nervously looked around, worried someone was going to see us.

Chips fell off the shelf and crashed to the floor. He used his free hand to grab my hair. Pulling my hair back, he exposed my neck to him and softly kissed me. I couldn't resist the feel of his mouth on my skin. I clung to him, the scorching hot need making me arch my body to get closer to him as he stroked my needy clit.

"I love how you feel against my palm, Little Fighter. Hot. Wet. Needy." He punctuated each word by circling my clit with the pad of his finger. My body spasmed from the intense pleasure.

"Fuck, Malice," I rasped while holding onto him for dear life.

There was a certain thrill in knowing anyone could walk by at any moment. Were there cameras? Could people see the way my plump lips parted on a gasp? Could they see his tattooed hand slipping between my thighs and massaging my slick cunt?

Malice shoved the collar of my shirt down, ripping the

soft cotton in the process and exposing my light pink bra. His hot mouth traveled the length of my neck, grazed my collar bone, and sunk lower until he was scraping his teeth against the swell of my breast.

I heaved, each thrusting motion of my inhales surging my tits into his scruffy face. He licked and sucked at me before pulling my bra down and exposing my hardened nipple.

"You are better than any fantasy, Little Fighter. I love exploring your body. My body. Every inch of you is mine." He wrapped his soft lips around my mound and sucked hard, the sensation sending a zing right through my core.

Not once did he stop stroking me. That pleasure kept building, building, building.

"Malice," I groaned as my eyes locked on movement at the end of the aisle. A man with salt-and-pepper hair and glasses tried walking by, his mouth agape as he adjusted himself and stared. One of the Civella guards shoved him away.

I gasped. It was so wrong how turned on I was.

Malice demanded my attention once more by skillfully finger fucking me harder. We started making out like rabid animals. Slamming our lips together. Dancing our tongues. Pressing our bodies as close as we could get them. He licked my bottom lip like it was a treasured treat.

A whimper escaped my lips, and he swallowed it whole before speaking against my mouth. "I love the way you sound when I touch you, Little Fighter."

His strokes became faster. Harder. The pressure kept

building within me, and my legs trembled. His teeth nipped at me, and the sting seemed to make everything feel even better.

I stopped kissing him to hiss in his ear, my mouth hovering over it as I panted so loud I was certain the entire grocery store could hear us.

"Yeah, Little Fighter. Come for me. Say my name. My real name."

My orgasm was a wild, blazing inferno that tore through my senses. "Nick," I cried out before biting his shoulder to muffle my screams. I arched my spine, and my thighs shook. He rubbed me throughout the entire orgasm and coaxed every ounce of pleasure from my body.

I nearly collapsed right there in the middle of the snack aisle. I wrapped my slender arms around him, and Nick pulled his hand from between my legs and held me in a sensual hug, cupping my ass as he held me tightly.

"Such a good girl," he praised me before pulling away to taste my pleasure. Seeing his lips slowly wrap around his index finger and suck my juices had my eyes feeling heavy. I wanted to strip him out of his suit and fuck him.

But just as I was about to suggest this, he pulled his finger from his mouth, making a popping noise as he did. "I'll buy your groceries. Get in the car."

I blanched. "What?"

Malice reached forward, as if he were going to wrap his hand around my throat, but stopped. I wondered if he was imagining how Anthony choked me. Instead, he moved my bra back up and covered me with what was left of my shirt.

"Go back to see Ruthie, Juliet."

"What about..."

Malice grinned, as if my confusion pleased him. "We still have a lot to work through, Little Fighter. I just wanted to give you a taste of what you're missing by keeping your distance."

And with those parting words, he spun around, grabbed my cart, and strolled toward the checkout counter like he didn't just finger fuck me on aisle nine.

chapter seven
anthony civella

"Zahau was found nude with her wrists and ankles bound by thick rope. Her hands had been tied behind her back, and she was gagged. But that wasn't what made her gruesome death so memorable. Allegedly, written on her naked body was the haunting phrase, "She saved him, can he save her?"

Juliet's voice paused, letting the words linger in my headphones for a few beats while I paced the Miami streets. I held my breath, waiting for her to speak again. Listening to her true crime podcast was all that brought me joy these days.

"She saved him, can he save her?"

Something told me he couldn't save her. Not when he was the monster she had to run from.

I let Juliet's voice wash over me as I continued to pace. I hated Miami. It was flashy and loud and kind of beautiful but plastic in that permanently temporary kind of way. Miami embodied the fleeting nature of youth. Beautiful people. Beautiful lives. Beautiful 1980s architecture that looked tacky now.

It was dirty—people left shit on the sidewalk wherever they went. Beautiful women with overwhelming confidence and silicone breasts wore floss over their pancake nipples and grinned at me as they skated by on their retro rollerblades. It was a city full of main characters and selfish narcissists.

I probably would've liked Miami more had I been able to enjoy the delicious food trucks that lined the streets. Juliet and I used to go to an authentic Mexican restaurant every Taco Tuesday. If she were here, she would want to stop at every truck and sample something. But right now, I couldn't stomach much of anything. I wasn't even sure I deserved the nourishment, because I was a walking, talking, breathing, fly-swatting psychopath.

A man wearing high top sneakers and a speedo shoulder-checked me on his way to wherever the fuck he was going, and I imagined slicing him across the jugular and letting him bleed out on the concrete. Reckless despair flowed freely through my veins. I was a man on a mission with no clue what the fuck I was doing. I let my body follow my mind in its wander.

When your madness grew legs, you had to let it run. Escaping was like a tourniquet around the neck. To save the heart, you had to cut off the head.

"Thank you for tuning in. Next week, we will discuss Manuel Pardo, better known as the Miami Mutilator, an ex-police officer turned mass murderer. Until next time, lock your doors!"

Juliet signed off and I skipped to the next episode. Thank fuck she had dozens of these recorded for me to obsess over. These podcasts were the only thing I had left of her. I picked Miami because of this specific episode. It was one of the first ones Vicky made me listen to, back when I didn't know who Juliet Cross was or that she was my soulmate.

I was tempted to go on a killing spree just so she would dedicate an episode to me. It gave me chills to think of her saying my name. Hearing it through my cheap headphones and jacking off while she talked about the piles of bodies leading straight to me.

It was fucked up. I wanted to see her again but
I didn't want
to see her
again.
I didn't want to
see her again.
I really didn't want to see her again
but I also wanted to see her again but I didn't want to

see her again but I also really, really, really, really wanted to touch her, and kiss her, and hold her tight against me— but not too tight, because that's what got me into this motherfucking mess in the first place.

She saved him. Can he save her?

"Hey guys, thanks for tuning in," she said with a grin.

I spoke back, because talking to myself on a crowded Miami street wasn't even on the top ten list of crazy things I'd done. "Hey, beautiful. How are you?" I greeted her.

"I'm so excited for this week's podcast!"

I smiled. "Wish I could be there with you. Remember that time I ate you out mid recording? I was very disappointed to find out these things weren't live."

"Before we dive into our discussion about the Miami Mutilator, I would like to remind you that you can always reach me at crimegirl22@gmail.com."

Her voice was soothing. Inviting. Tempting.

"I wish it were that easy," I replied. "I just want to know that you're okay. Every time I close my eyes, I just see my hands around your neck, and your eyes rolling into the back of your head."

A woman walking her prissy Chihuahua stepped to the very edge of the sidewalk to avoid me. I couldn't blame her. She had good instincts. I was a monster. I ruined every good thing I had. The voices in my head—the souls of the dead—made it hard for me to function like a normal human in society.

I wanted to go home. But I couldn't go home. I wanted to go home. But I couldn't go home. I couldn't ever go home. Home. Home. Juliet was home.

I sounded like a tweaker. My burner phone sat heavy in my pocket as Juliet continued to speak. I debated about pulling it out and looking up a cemetery I could hide out in for a little while. There was something soothing about the silence of tombstones. If I couldn't go home, then I'd at least let the dead welcome me with their crypts and worms.

I didn't trust the living. Miami was too vibrant. Every inhale made me feel alive. I continued to walk aimlessly, pulling my beanie over my ears to try and block out the sounds of people living their lives like they didn't have madness on their minds. Oh, no, that's me.

"What's most interesting about the Miami Mutilator is that he didn't consider himself to be a criminal. He was an ex-police officer and a military veteran. He genuinely thought he was doing the right thing." Juliet's voice was cute when she was passionate about something. It would go up an octave, and her words would start bleeding into one another. She always made me feel normal because, like me, dark and deadly things intrigued her. Hell, sometimes it even comforted her.

I thought maybe it was because her mother was abducted when she was younger, but the more I got to know her, the more I realized that it was just who she was.

"The Miami Mutilator called himself a hero."

"Fuck heroes, baby. You like the villains, don't you?"

Go back, go back, go back.

The fact that Juliet was capable of loving a man like Nicholas Civella was proof enough that she wanted the bad guy. He was the ultimate villain. I was bad because I was a troubled soul. I struggled to control my impulses. I—gave myself a lot of excuses. Nick was pure evil. He enjoyed causing chaos and ruining lives. He didn't bother with petty emotions like guilt. Thinking of him made my blood boil. I was not mad that he sent me away. I wasn't even mad that he wanted to protect our girl.

I was mad that he had enough power and influence to stick to his word. What he said was law, and there was no way around the fact that I was banned from Juliet's life. Showing up was a death sentence, and even though I'm obsessed with the idea of being buried—with the idea of being empty—I didn't want to exist in any form where Juliet was not.

She gave me purpose. The further away from her I got, the more I realized how much I had fucked up. It was clarity that made me sick.

The longer I went without talking to them, the more I wondered why the hell William hadn't come after me. I mean, I knew why. I just thought he and I were in this together. We were like the fucked up *B team* in this group relationship. Was he so desperate for scraps of Juliet's heart that he'd forget the one person that was on his side?

I had to do better. I had to be better. Nick couldn't hate me forever. I wasn't about to let either of them win. He would let me back in, eventually. He always did. But I would never forgive myself if I put Juliet in harm's way again.

Which is why I was here. In Miami. Pacing the hot concrete. Losing my mind. Because I wanted to go back, but I couldn't go back—go back, go back, go back. Not until I was better. And the terrifying thing was, I wasn't sure I was capable of ever getting better.

So I had to join the living. Miami was like the pulsing heart of America. If I wanted to pull myself out of the grave, here was the place to do it.

I turned the corner onto a less populated street that was shadowed by towering buildings above. Out of my peripheral, I noticed an oddly dressed woman. She had a sweatshirt on. Even though it was January, this was Miami. It was fucking eighty-five degrees outside. I'd been considering ditching my signature beanie to give my sweaty scalp a break.

Maybe I was a paranoid asshole. Maybe I liked the drama—maybe I wanted someone to be following me.

Scratch that.

No, I wanted Juliet to be following me. I wanted her to chase down my demons and force me to come back because I wasn't strong enough to figure my shit out and come back on my own. I couldn't go back, back, back.

I sped up. The girl with the hoodie over her head matched my pace. I turned right at the end of the street, and so did she.

Maybe Nick or William sent an assassin after me. Maybe I'd have to defend myself. Maybe I'd get to find some random ass item on the street and use it to murder her with. It probably wouldn't be as epic as Nick with the curling iron, but I was crazy enough to outdo him.

I made it to another street, and the moment I turned

the corner, I pressed my back against the hard brick. I listened. I waited. My pulse battered against my veins with adrenaline and excitement. I wondered if I would get to kill someone today. It was not like Kansas City. The police were not in the Civella pocket. Here, there were consequences. Here, I was free.

She rounded the corner, and I reached out and grabbed the loose fabric of her hoodie. Gasping, she tried to pull away, but I slammed her into the brick wall faster than she could fight me off.

Her blonde hair covered her face, but I got a whiff of expensive perfume, and my stomach dropped.

"Hey there, brother," she said in a rough voice, those blue eyes peeking through the curtain of her hair. "Are you still mad I tried to kill you?"

No fucking way.

Vicky.

I grinned.

chapter eight
juliet cross

Eden's Place trembled as underground music thudded from the walls. As I applied a dark shade of red lipstick to my swollen mouth, I felt shivers run down my spine. My lips were raw from being pulled between Nick's teeth, and I had to cover a light bruise on my neck with concealer.

As William stood behind me, fiddling with his cufflinks, he stared at my exposed back. The lingerie I wore was the same shade as my rouge lipstick on my mouth, a lace corset that dipped low on my spine and tightly clung to my body.

"You are the best birthday present," he murmured reverently while licking his lips in appreciation. I blushed at his comment and applied more bronzer to my cheeks. Anthony and I had planned a massive celebration for William. We wanted him to feel loved. Important. William needed more assurance than the others, and tonight was supposed to be that for him.

But without Anthony, the gesture felt lackluster. I kept expecting Anthony to pop his head in and chuckle about all the wild sex acts he'd coordinated on stage for William. We'd gone with a sensual *Cirque du Soleil* theme at the club. Everyone wanted an invite.

I wanted Anthony to be there to see our hard work come to fruition.

William didn't ask for much for his birthday. I struggled finding a gift for the man who had everything, but it turns out I already had what he wanted:

Me.

William asked to watch me get ready. He set up a chic vanity in his office just so he could have a private exhibition. I made a show of it, slowly rolling up the fishnet stockings on my smooth legs. Straightening my hair with gentle movements. I lined my eyes seductively like a cat.

Not once did he tear his eyes away from me. I captivated his attention, entrapping him in my presence. I felt treasured. I felt powerful.

I wanted to please him.

Not only because it was his birthday and I loved him,

but also because I had a favor to ask.

I had a plan to find out where Anthony was.

The idea formed in my mind and plagued my soul. I couldn't stop obsessing over it. I knew without a doubt that Anthony was within reach, and I needed help to get him. It had been almost two weeks since he left. Every day he was gone, I felt him slip further and further away. It was impossible to get *Malice* to cooperate. No matter how much I begged, he refused to give in.

"I got you something," William rasped, drawing me out of my dark thoughts. I almost felt guilty for thinking of Anthony when I should have been celebrating him. I was being pulled in so many directions it was hard to focus.

I stared at William through the reflection of my vanity mirror. "I thought it was *your* birthday," I replied coyly. One of the things I had grown to understand about William was that he loved to give more than receive. It was a trait he possessed in and out of the bedroom. For a man determined to be selfish with my heart, he wasn't actually that selfish at all.

"Believe me," he began before walking over to me while digging in the pocket of his pants. "This is just as much a gift for me as it is for you."

His reverent face lit up as he pulled out a velvet box and handed it to me. I slowly stood from my seat and stepped closer to him. The smell of his cologne made my mouth water. "What is this?" I asked instead of opening it. The shape and size of the box looked suspiciously similar to an engagement ring. We weren't there yet, were we? And why would he do this now, when things felt so broken between all of us?

William smiled a bit before taking the box back and opening it. A beautiful yellow diamond ring set in platinum and yellow gold stared back at me. It was a huge emerald cut, and I had to blink from all the sparkles dancing in the dim light of his office. "Nick got to give you a necklace," he began before pulling the ring out of the box and reaching for my hand. My left hand. Then, my ring finger. My heart started to pound. "I want you to wear something for me, too. I'm not going to put you in an uncomfortable position and ask you something you don't have an answer to yet."

I looked down as he slid the ring onto my finger. Perfect fit.

"William…"

"I just need to know that a part of you belongs to me, too," he whispered before gently reaching for my chin to tilt it up. With misty eyes, I stared at him.

I was equally nervous and flattered. It was so thoughtful, and I did want William to feel like our relationship was just as important as the others. He knew me first. And in some ways, he knew me best. He was a solid rock of support that I desperately clung to. Malice was so determined to control me, but the truth was, my heart was evenly shared between all of them, and William needed to know that I belonged to him just as much as he belonged to me.

"I love you," I said. The words felt inadequate for such a beautiful moment.

"I love you too. Now ask me what you want to ask," he

78

replied.

The sudden change in the conversation made my brows dip. How did he know I wanted to ask something? "What do you mean?"

"You've been quiet all evening. I can always tell when you have something storming in that beautiful mind of yours." He reached up and ran his thumb along my brow. "Something's bothering you. Let me fix it."

I chewed on my lip before looking back down at the beautiful ring he'd given me. It felt wrong to ask for his help after such a thoughtful gift. Especially on his birthday. This ring, and the finger he put it on, felt like a declaration. What kind of woman was I to ask him to help me rescue my other lover?

"Tell me, Miss Cross," he insisted.

The words poured out of me like water from a spout. "Malice has Anthony's tracking info. Remember? It's not like he removed the device from his ass—he just made it where you don't have access to see where he is anymore. What if we broke into his office, stole his laptop and—"

William's face fell, and I instantly regretted what I said. Maybe now was the wrong time. But the fact William didn't expect me to ask about Anthony just proved that this sharing dynamic still had some wrinkles that needed to be ironed out.

"I know you still miss Anthony," William said.

"How could I not? I love him, William. I'm not just going to forget about him."

William's frown deepened, and I felt a crack form in my

heart. I thought between him and Nick—Malice—William would be the most levelheaded and supportive about this. "Are you going to help me?" I asked tentatively. I had to try.

"Let's just go enjoy the party, okay?" he replied. "We can talk about this later."

I crossed my arms over my chest and glared up at him. "You and Nick keep pushing this back. I'm trapped in the city, a prisoner stuck between the two of you. But it doesn't matter if weeks, months or years pass by. I'm still going to fight for Anthony. And if that means I have to run away to track him down—"

"Don't say that," William replied, his voice threatening—almost sounding like Malice. "You're not going to run away. We both know that *Malice* won't let you get five steps off this property."

I arched my brow at him. "Is it Malice keeping me here? I feel like you have just as much to gain from his possessiveness."

"I'm not discussing this tonight."

Fair enough. I didn't want to fight on his birthday. "Fine. But I'm not dropping this."

"I didn't think you would," William replied bitterly before pulling away from me and stalking toward the door.

The jealousy simmering around me was going to boil me alive, and I had no idea how we could possibly get to a place where we were okay again.

—

Sex. Sweat. Flashing lights and music that mimicked

the beat of pounding fucks in the back of a Mercedes Benz. The vibe at Eden's Place was tantric and erotic. Naked women on stilts sauntered around us. Fit men experienced in gymnastics lifted up their partners and molded them to their bodies. I saw one woman holding a handstand while getting her pussy licked.

I was sitting in a leather chair, my legs crossed so tight that I was squeezing the need building at the apex of my thighs. It was impossible not to be turned on by all the sex and debauchery, despite my tense conversation with William earlier.

Nick was in a mood again—Malice had come to the party and left his kinder alter ego at home. William had pushed his chair so close next to mine that he was practically in my lap, arm swung over my shoulders in a possessive move that echoed our earlier conversation. It didn't matter how hard he pressed into my side, I felt Anthony's absence like a brick wall between us. I couldn't have one without the other.

It was tense, despite the celebration. A woman with clown makeup wearing a leotard that dipped low between her breasts delivered a round cake with sparklers for candles, and the entire club cheered for William, making Malice sneer.

William was the center of attention. Club patrons waltzed by to pat him on the back. Women with sparkling eyes rubbed his neck and pressed their breasts against his arm as they leaned in for awkward side hugs of congratulations. A few men even came up to ask him about business, which surprised me. I knew that William ran the club and sometimes made financial decisions for the business, but shouldn't they be acknowledging Malice if they wanted a deal?

The sexy women and attention didn't bother me. William was an enigma. But for some reason, it absolutely bothered Malice. As the night continued, more men who I knew were business associates for the Civella empire barely spared my Mafia boss a second glance as they spoke with William about things I wasn't familiar with but still sounded important. Hedge funds. Shipments. Traitors.

While William spoke to someone about a mysterious shipment in Louisiana, I picked up a glass of champagne and went to drink the sweet concoction, but Malice ripped it from my fingers, nearly spilling the expensive bubbly all over my lap. "Nice costume jewelry," he said before running his thumb over the shimmering ring that William had given me. I knew that this particular piece of jewelry would send Malice into a pissing match. I snaked my hand back and hid it under the table, but Malice reached out and grabbed my wrist. "It's beautiful," he growled in a sarcastic, angry tone. "I'm not sure it fits you, though," he said. He looked me in the eyes, daring me to say something. My heart practically galloped from the tension.

I felt William lean even closer. He'd obviously finished his talk with the other men to focus on what Malice was raging on about. "It fits perfectly," William said before grabbing my other hand and kissing the tips of my fingers.

Malice nodded before examining the ring with his

skeptical eyes. "Oh, it's the right size, yes, but it doesn't feel right, no? It's too flashy. Tacky, almost."

William scowled. I didn't want to ruin today. "I like it," I replied. I tried sounding as confident as possible, even though a massive amount of emotions was threatening to burn up my throat.

Malice snapped his gaze to my face. "You like it?" he asked, though the question felt weighted with a meaning deeper than the simple words.

"I like it just as much as I like my necklace," I replied pointedly before looking down at the dainty chain and single diamond resting on my collarbone. The one Malice went to hell and back for.

"I think the two pieces clash," Malice growled. "One seems to shout its importance. It's trying to prove something. I'm sure everyone will first look at your ring. It's this needy sort of statement. Almost pathetic in the way it begs for someone to sit up and notice it."

I swallowed. William reached out and brushed the diamond at my neck, making my skin break out with goose bumps. "And what of this archaic, understated muzzle around her neck?" William asked, breathing hard. Though his tone was even, there was a severity to his words that clung to my senses.

"It might be simple, yes. But it's an heirloom. Father wanted *me* to have everything. It's something you would be wise to remember."

William cleared his throat. "Just because someone is heir to the throne, doesn't mean they are the most qualified man for the job."

"But it still makes them king, no?"

I opened my mouth to speak, but a curtain on the stage set right in front of us was pulled back. A single king-sized bed was poised in the middle. Seeing soft white bedding and handcuffs mounted on the headboard, I wondered what William had arranged for his birthday. Watching the shows put on at Eden's Place was always fun for me. I didn't get jealous knowing that my men were watching other performers. Because at the end of the day, they were coming home to me.

I was thankful for the distraction.

William motioned for a man standing in the corner to come closer. I watched as he whispered in his ear. Malice gripped my thigh sensually. Within mere moments, the entire club was cleared out. Unfinished drinks sat sweating on tabletops. Half-dressed, giggling women scurried out like mice being chased with a broom.

Kelsey, my coworker and friend, stopped by the table on her way out to wink at me and hand over a silk blindfold. "Girl, you're going to have one helluva night!" she hissed excitedly before escaping.

"What's going on?" I asked while watching a group of performers slip into the dressing room.

"I was thinking we could have some fun, Miss Cross." William's seductive voice washed over me. "I wanted to enjoy all that Eden's Place has to offer—minus the crowd. I didn't want anyone seeing *my girl*."

Malice took a harsh gulp of his drink and then drowned

deeply in his frustrations. The scowl on his face was almost painful to see. I looked around. Sure enough, the only people here were Malice, William, and me.

William took off his suit jacket before loosening his tie, the excitement reverberating through his large hands and forcing a slight tremble of anticipation in the tips of his fingers. "Feel free to leave, Nick," William said in a taunting tone. "I plan to fully indulge in all the festivities my birthday has to offer." William held out his hand to me, and I took it.

Malice, sensing a challenge in his brother's words, spoke with firm determination. "I love a good show. Wherever Juliet is, I want to be."

My heart stopped, and I became suddenly overwhelmed with nerves. Up until now, we had kept the physical aspects of our relationship strictly separate. Aside from that one time in the conference room back at the Civella Mansion, we hadn't done any...group activities. I felt nervous to have a jealous audience watching over William and me.

William grinned, as if this was his plan all along. "Suit yourself." He tugged on my hand, but I resisted. Malice and I were still healing from everything, but that didn't mean there wasn't love between us. Sometimes struggle was just a wall you had to climb over to get to the heart of a relationship.

I pulled out of William's grip and hovered over Malice. He'd conditioned me to ask permission for moments like this—his possessiveness was overwhelming at times, and I wasn't sure if I needed to ask him now.

But I didn't *want* to ask him. Was it so wrong to love him, make sure he was okay, while still making my own decisions?

I wanted to be in control of my own desires. My own body. My own wants, needs, and relationships. If I wanted to find Anthony and build a life for myself with each of these men, I needed to cut the chains Malice had over me.

He waited patiently, waiting for me to ask him permission like I always did.

"I love you, Nick," I whispered before leaning over to kiss him on the cheek. Just because I wanted to change our dynamic didn't mean the burning adoration I had for him suddenly evaporated. We were stronger together. Our bond was something that outshined the others, but it was time to pull William out of the shadows. It was time to find Anthony in the dark.

His spine was rigid with anticipation. There was an expectation hanging in the frigid air between us.

But I would not ask permission. Not this time. Not ever again. I was the girl who murdered a man to save herself. Not the girl that allowed someone to claim every part of her.

William was grinning like a Cheshire cat when I spun around to follow him up on stage. My next order of business would be to work on his vindictive side. Just because I was making a show of choosing him, didn't mean I wasn't choosing Nick. I was choosing myself and finding equal homes for each of the men in my heart.

The speakers kicked on, and a haunting song started

playing through them. The lights on the stage turned on, bathing the bed in bright red light and drowning the seating area below in darkness. I couldn't see Nick sitting there, but I could feel his intrusive eyes dancing over my skin.

I stood at the foot of the bed, anticipation rising in my gut.

"Get on the bed," William ordered. I swallowed. Malice's eyes were heavy on my back. I felt awkward and uncomfortable—two feelings no woman wanted to experience while fucking. William waited patiently for me as I closed my eyes and took a steady breath.

Inhale.

Exhale.

It was in that brief moment of clarity that an idea came to me. If Malice wanted to watch, then I'd make him an active participant.

I slowly looked over my shoulder at him and felt a rush of adrenaline and confidence at the sight of him sitting at the cocktail table. His legs were spread apart, the dim lights of the room cast shadows along his face, and he was gripping his upper thigh like he was trying to force himself to keep still.

I then turned back to William, who seemed uncertain for the first time. He had shifty eyes that kept bouncing between me and Malice. He was trying to make a statement about our relationship, but so was I. We were all in this together.

With my back facing Malice, I slowly, slowly, slowly

bent over to unclasp the buckle on my heels. I rubbed my legs while doing so. My wide stance gave my little show a splash of eroticism that emboldened me.

Then, I stepped out of my shoes and kicked them to the side. William ripped his tie from his neck and started to unbutton his dress shirt with methodical movements. I crawled onto the mattress, arching my back as I moved toward the headboard. Slow music with a heavy beat filtered through the speakers, and I rolled onto my back.

"So beautiful," William whispered before crawling over me. He wrapped his large, veiny hand around my wrist and lifted it up to the handcuff. He kissed my soft skin with his demanding lips before locking me up. He then did the same with my other wrist before slipping to my feet and wrapping leather around my ankles.

I was fully bound, and it didn't escape me how this was a metaphor for my relationships. That familiar sense of anxiety made me wonder if it was the feeling of being trapped that had my heart racing, or the desire. Perhaps it was both. Perhaps this was the trade-off for love. Leather bindings, handcuffs, and a metaphorical collar pulled tightly around my neck.

I lifted my head up but, from this angle, could no longer see Malice. "Focus on me, Miss Cross," William demanded. I locked eyes with him in a defiant sort of way. He grinned.

Settling between my thighs, William unhooked the clasps at my cunt, revealing my pussy with ease. His hot breath sent a shiver down my spine, and I watched as he brushed his plush lips over me. I grew wet with anticipation. Sparks of need shot through my entire body, and I wondered how long he would make me wait until he tasted me—teased me—tongue fucked me.

"I love the feeling of your body enjoying everything I do," he said before kissing my inner thigh. "There's something about the way your legs shake when you come that feels so..." He paused to lick a long line up my slit. "Satisfying."

I squirmed on the bed against my restraints as William wrapped his arms around my thighs and pried them open as wide as they would go. Cool air from the vent overhead mixed with his heady breath.

Anticipation.

Anticipation.

Anticipation.

Anticipation.

Inhale.

Exhale.

"Please," I begged.

"Because you asked so nicely, Miss Cross," William replied before diving in with his hot, wet tongue. He circled my clit. He moaned at the taste of me. Every move of his talented mouth sent a thrill ricocheting through my trembling body.

I watched him in a hungry sort of way. Dewy sweat collected on his brow as he lapped me up, savoring every taste as he brought me closer and closer to that peak. He was praying at the altar of my cunt, worshiping my pleasure, drawing out every offering of my slick need with swift, intense licks of his tongue.

He had to hold me down with his muscular arms. I was certain I'd fly off the bed if it weren't for him and these handcuffs.

I'd almost forgotten about Malice, with his dark, broody presence watching the spectacle.

But he made his presence known. I knew him. I knew that he wouldn't watch in the shadows. He wanted to take credit for every drop of bliss wrung from my body. I saw him approach the stage before William did. I looked up at him, my mouth parted in ecstasy. My eyes were hooded.

Malice's shadow made William freeze, and I hissed at the loss of building tension at my clit. "No, no," I begged. "Don't stop."

William and Malice had a silent standoff. I waited for them to fight. Or for William to tell him to fuck off.

But I wanted this.

I needed this.

"I'm not really the sort of man to sit by and watch," Malice said in a deathly tone.

William wiped his lips on my inner thigh before responding. "I'm not really the sort of man to share."

Malice slipped out of his suit coat and let it carelessly fall to the floor. He wore suspenders that I wanted to reach out and pull until they slapped against his chest. He undid his cufflinks and set them in his pockets. William resumed kissing my wet pussy while Malice rolled up his sleeves. I sensed the fading enthusiasm in Malice's movements but refused to let this derail us.

"I want you, Little Fighter," he whispered before reaching for his belt buckle and undoing it. With nimble fingers, he undid his button and then reached behind the waistband of his boxer briefs to pull out his hard, heavy cock. Malice then got up on his knees on the mattress and bumped my lips with the head of his dick. "Taste me," he demanded.

I glanced down at William, who was watching my every move. I felt like this was a test, somehow. I knew what I had to do.

Dragging my attention back to Malice, I slowly opened my mouth, and he thrust until it struck the back of my throat. I gagged a bit but was determined to get Malice off. In and out he moved while using one hand to brace himself against the wooden headboard and the other to fondle my breast. Spit and moans tumbled out of my mouth. I felt so good. So filthy. So desired.

William increased his speed on my clit, and when I came, it was hard and fast. I stopped sucking Malice's cock just to scream at the pleasure of it. Wave after wave of the rush raked across my body. William preened as I writhed, my entire body weakened from the damning pleasure of it all.

William made quick work of getting up and stripping out of the rest of his clothes. I wanted to watch him undress, but Malice had completely stolen my attention. He was thrusting in and out of my mouth like he wanted to bruise my throat so I'd wake up with the reminder of what it felt like to have his cock on my tongue.

He moaned and moved faster. William positioned himself between me, then pressed against my entrance with his cock. "Do you want me to fuck your needy little pussy, Miss Cross?" he asked.

I nodded. I wanted it more than I could articulate. This was what we needed.

"Say it," he then demanded.

I blushed. It was hard to talk with my mouth full. Malice didn't let up, either. This felt like a pissing contest of sorts, and I didn't want to mess up.

After a few moments of indecision, I finally gave in. I wanted them too much. I stopped sucking Malice's cock to respond to William. "I want you to fuck me, William," I moaned.

The indecision in his expression made me briefly wonder if I had fucked this up. But eventually, he inched inside of me, slowly, dangerously.

Malice grew impatient and started fucking my mouth more venomously. Tears started to stream down my cheeks, but I wasn't uncomfortable. I felt powerful. Needed. Used up and—

"Tell me you only want me," William demanded while thrusting in and out of me. He was hitting that deep, penetrative spot within me that made my legs shake. I was close to coming again. And if Malice's twitching cock was anything to go by, he was close too. William looked like he was on the edge.

But I couldn't force myself to say it.

William started to move slower. It made me cry out. I

wanted him harder, rougher. I wanted all of us to come.

"Say it," William demanded. I looked at him. Each muscle in his torso was flexed from pulsing in and out of me. I was starting to lose that tether of thrill. If he stopped now, I'd lose this moment forever.

I moaned. Malice cursed. I quickly paused, feeling desperate to move past this. "I want you, William," I groaned.

I didn't say exactly what he wanted to hear, I couldn't. I'd long surpassed the idea that I could only settle for one of them.

William went wild, jolting in and out of my body like a mad man. I moved to continue sucking off Malice, but he was gone.

I blinked twice.

The handcuff around my right wrist fell away.

William's eyes were closed.

My left wrist was freed.

William came hard, hot ropes of cum surged through me, and his entire body stilled from it.

My ankles were freed.

And Malice grabbed the gun holstered to his side, pulled back the safety, and aimed it at William's head.

chapter nine

juliet cross

William grabbed the sheets and wrapped them around his waist before snarling at Malice. "What the fuck are you doing?"

Malice's pants looked like they were about to fall off of him, since the belt was still undone. His hands shook with adrenaline as he aimed the barrel of the gun at his brother. It was strange to see him so disheveled, though I was familiar with his unhinged nature. I'd pushed them too far.

"What the fuck are you playing at, William? You think you're suddenly important? Better than me?" Malice asked.

I curled my legs to my chest, my nakedness and the sharp stab of tension making me feel too exposed for the moment. "You are fucking insane!" William screamed.

"I'll show you how fucking insane I can be. I don't need you. I'm done sharing. I'm done playing this game. You're dead to me, you hear? Dead. You can stop pretending like you run the place, too."

William replied before I could intervene. "Pretend? Pretend! You think I'm pretending to run things? While you're off killing people and making enemies, I'm the one actually making us money. I'm the one cleaning up your messes. I'm the one people actually fucking respect. And you know what?" William asked, spit flying from his mouth.

"What?" Malice replied, his tone dripping with wrath.

"I'm who Juliet wants, too. You just heard her. It's killing you, isn't it? To know that I'm the better choice for her. To know that she could be happier with me—"

"I'll kill you," Malice growled.

I'd been stunned into silence for the majority of their fighting, but I managed to find my voice. "Enough!" I yelled, making them both turn to look at me.

Malice finally lowered his weapon, and I breathed a sigh of relief. He then spun on his expensive heels and marched over to the bed. "We're leaving. You're coming home with me. Enough is enough."

"Don't you fucking touch her!" William yelled.

I was fucking done with this metaphorical game of tug-of-war.

I got up, cum spilling down my leg from the abrupt movement. Malice grinned, likely thinking that I was going to go with him, but I shook my head.

"I'm done," I said, somehow miraculously keeping my voice steady. "I'm done with this. I'm not going to be fought over—"

"We don't have to fight. Just come home with me—us, I mean," William grumbled.

I let out a scream of frustration that bounced off the walls. It was raw and angry and full of pain.

"We've already been through this. You tried to make me choose when you told Vicky. I'm tired of the games, William."

Malice gave a triumphant smirk that made my skin crawl. "And you! You're going to push away every person in your life until it's just you in that big, empty house. You can't control everything."

"Like fuck I can't!" he sneered.

"You can't control me. Not if you want to be with me. You can capture me. Lock me up in your bedroom. Fuck me. Ruin me. But it won't be love. It won't be real. It'll just be you and a warm body."

I scurried over to the wall where a black silk robe was hanging up, and I put it on as tears streamed down my cheeks. "I let Nick be in charge of this relationship because I suppose I wasn't confident enough to say what I wanted. It was easier to let him call the shots, because I didn't want to hurt anyone. I never meant to hurt anyone..."

I furiously swiped at a tear before bending over at the waist and letting out a frustrated sob. All the emotions that had been building up within me had overflowed. The levy I had built around my heart had officially broken. There was no going back now.

"But now Anthony is gone," I choked out before crumbling into a ball and sitting on the floor. Both Malice and William moved to comfort me but stopped when they noticed the other trying to do the same. This was the problem. Their hatred for one another would always get in the way of their love for me. This was no way to live.

"Let's go home, Little Fighter. We can talk this out. Okay?" Malice said, using his softer, kinder voice that soothed my soul just a bit.

"No. Can you please call Kelsey?" I asked before resting my cheek on my bent knee. "I want to go home with her."

William immediately pulled his cell phone from his pocket, desperate to do whatever I wanted. Malice cursed. "I don't think running from us is the answer. I would prefer you come home, Juliet."

"We're done, Nick." I used his real name to really drive the point home. I was so exhausted, there was no point dragging this out. It wasn't working. Maybe it never worked.

He let out a bitter laugh. "We're not done."

He could think what he wanted, but my heart needed space—maybe even permanently.

"I probably couldn't stop either of you from making me stay. I've been chained up in your basement, remember? I know what you're capable of."

William started getting dressed. His silence was like a scream. I wanted to know what he was thinking.

Malice continued his threats. "I'm paying for Ruthie's doctor appointments and medicine. Hell, I'm paying for your schooling. Your food."

"If you took all of that away, you'd just be confirming what I'm feeling right now. You'd be well within your right to stop. I can't force you to care about me, Nick. I'm just done letting you hold the world over my head in exchange for love."

"Kelsey is here," William said in a soft voice. "But I agree with Nick, you should come home."

I looked at his solemn face and felt the stabbing guilt at the pain in his expression. But William would always want me to himself. Malice would always want to control me. Anthony would always lose himself to his demons.

"I am going home," I whispered before pulling myself up off the floor and walking across the stage, past Malice, and down the steps leading to the floor. Kelsey was standing there, waiting on me. The poor girl looked terrified, and I felt bad for putting her in this position, but I didn't have anyone else. She was probably my only friend these days aside from my men, and even then, we only spoke when we were on shift together.

"Thank you," I whispered.

She tenderly looped her arm through mine and started guiding me to the door. "Mr. Civella isn't going to murder me for taking you, is he?" she asked, her tone slightly teasing, but there was an edge to her posture as she quickly moved us out the door.

"He won't," I assured her. I was the person they were mad at. I was the person ending this. I was the person walking away from our relationship. I was saving myself.

———

I wrapped myself up in the cozy blanket Kelsey gave me and sipped tea on her plush couch as the news blared on her flat screen television. Staying here felt like the best option. I didn't want to go to Grams, because I wasn't sure how I was going to explain to her that I had broken up with them. I couldn't look her in the eye and tell her that the doctors' appointments, the financial security, and my schooling were all done. There was a lot to process.

Kelsey walked through the front door carrying a paper sack filled to the brim with bagels and juggling two cups of coffee from the cafe down the street from where she lived. "So, not to freak you out, but Mr. Civella has two cars parked outside our building. One of his goons insisted on paying for breakfast."

I shook my head. Maybe Malice and William thought that this was just a fight. Just a night of anger that they could sweep under the rug later.

I ran a finger over the necklace Nick had given me, then reached behind my neck to unclasp it. "Thank you for letting me stay the night," I said softly while averting my gaze.

I felt the couch dip beside me and looked up at Kelsey's

concerned expression. Her sweeping blonde hair was pulled into a ballerina bun on top of her head, and she had on a crop top and yoga pants. I hadn't actually ever seen her outside of the lingerie we were forced to wear at Eden's Place. "I know we've never hung out outside of work, but you can talk to me. It seems like you need a friend."

I let out a puff of air before reaching for one of the coffees and taking a sip. If I was going to talk about my feelings, then I needed a hit of caffeine first. The hazelnut cream hit my tongue, and I closed my eyes for the brief comfort.

"We broke up," I said once the hot liquid had traveled down my throat and warmed my gut.

"Who? You and Nick? William? or Anthony?" I'd never really been ashamed of our dynamic. In the sinister Mafia world, anything was accepted. Social norms didn't bother me so much, considering I was a murderer. But hearing them all listed out like that made the massive hole in my chest grow in size. I wasn't just mourning the loss of one relationship. I was mourning three.

I tucked some hair behind my ear, then frowned at the sparkling ring on my left hand. I took it off and set it on Kelsey's coffee table beside Nick's necklace. "I ended things with all of them, I suppose," I answered, even though my breakup felt like Anthony's doing.

"And how do you feel about that?"

"Sad. Relieved. Hurt."

Kelsey pulled out a blueberry bagel and tore off a piece of the sweet bread before plopping it in her mouth.

I watched her chew for a moment and couldn't tell if she was trying to think of something to say or if she was just hungry. Usually, Kelsey was quick on her feet and in charge. Off the clock, she felt more...normal? Laid back?

"What's the best way I can help you right now?" she finally asked before swallowing her food.

I smiled at that. "Tell me how I'm going to get my life together and move on from this."

"Do you want to move on?"

I licked my lips. "Yes? No? Maybe?"

"Sounds like you should figure out what you want first."

I nodded. "I want to take control of my life. I need to figure out how I'm going to pay for my school and for Gram's medicine. I want my own job. My own space. I want to call the shots in my own life again." I stopped to look at Kelsey. "And if, after I figure my shit out, they can find a way to love me without fighting over me or controlling me, then I'd like that too."

Kelsey nodded. "Sounds easy enough. I'm assuming you want to quit your job at Eden's Place?"

I gave her a guilty look. "It's going to be too hard to see them every day. I'm already struggling with not running to the Civella Mansion and begging them to take me back. I don't think I can work there and stay strong."

"I'm devastated to lose you, but understand. You need a decent paying job, though. Especially if you want to become more independent."

I chewed on the inside of my cheek. "I used to work in

a diner. The tips were shit though. It would be hard to go from Eden's Place back there, but I guess I have options."

Kelsey scrunched her nose up and furrowed her brow. "No. You have experience at one of the most elite clubs in the city. I'll be a reference for you, too. We could easily get you a bartending job or—"

"I'm not sure I want to work at a club," I replied sheepishly. "I won't turn down work, but if I had to choose..."

Kelsey pulled out her phone and opened her notes app. It was so like her to be organized and helpful. I suddenly became filled with overwhelming gratitude that she was the one with me while I navigated this. "Let's think," she said while typing. "You're going to school for forensic science. You have that creepy murder podcast that gives me nightmares."

"You listen to my podcast?" I asked in shock.

"Duh. I'm a modern woman trying to find a husband in a world full of psychos. It's pretty much a handbook on how to spot red flags. Plus, I like supporting you. Anthony got me on to it."

My heart pounded at the mention of Anthony. Kelsey sensed the switch in my behavior and patted me on the shoulder. "I don't know what happened with him, but he'll be back eventually. That man can't stay away from you."

"Thanks," I mouthed, too emotional to vocalize it.

Clearing her throat, Kelsey continued. "So you like murder and dead bodies. My brother lives next door to a mortician and mentioned they were hiring recently. He's been trying to get me to quit Eden's Place for a while."

She started typing before pulling up the listing. "Here it is. Funeral Assistant. Thousand bucks a week." She then scanned the job listing. "Basically a secretary for the place. Not too bad. Would probably look good on a resume for your future career goals. I think you could easily score it, and I'll talk to my brother's neighbor about you. The dude is always checking out my tits."

She typed some more, and my phone pinged. "Just sent you the posting. I would have your application done by tonight, though. He wants to hire quick."

Kelsey was efficient, that was for sure. "Wow. Thank you," I said. A thousand bucks a week wasn't that much, but it would at least help with Gram's meds.

"Now let's figure out your school situation. It's the beginning of the semester, yeah? I'm assuming Mr. Civella already paid your tuition in full."

Shame rocked through me like a hurricane. "Yes."

"Great. So you have an entire semester to look at financial aid options and apply for scholarships. It's not like he can take the money back, and something tells me he won't be asking for you to pay him. I mean, you could always sell that ring William gave you and probably have money left over."

I wasn't sure I liked that idea. I wanted to figure this out on my own. "You're right. I have time to figure out my school stuff. The rest of this semester and all summer."

Kelsey preened. "Sounds like you're on the road to independence."

Yeah. It did. I could totally do this. She continued, "You

just really need to cut ties with the Civella men."

Yeah. Easier said than done. Malice might be letting me lick my wounds here now, but he'd come for me eventually.

Or at least, I thought he would. The alternative would mean that he didn't really love me. That I was just a blip in his life, someone not worth the fight. Was it pathetic to want him to want me back? Did it make me even more selfish than I already was?

"The guards outside my apartment building are a little alarming. Those men are not going to make it easy on you, that's for sure. Although, my naughty mind can't help but think of all the delicious ways they could win you back."

I picked up a nearby pillow and playfully tossed it at her, making her squeal. "I was just kidding!" she insisted.

We both laughed for a moment, and it struck me how much I missed this. Laughing with a friend—with someone I wasn't fucking or trying to fix. It almost felt like chatting with Vicky, except Kelsey was intuitive and more on my level. She was understanding. Vicky was always too wrapped up in her own life to really listen to me. It was something I fully realized after she tried to kill me.

I looked at the jewelry on the coffee table, and my decision suddenly became very clear. If I was going to focus on myself, then I had to set a precedent.

"If they ask, though, tell them I tried to convince you to go running back to them. I like living and having a job, thank you very much," Kelsey added with a wink.

I stared at the ring and necklace for a moment longer before deciding to be incredibly reckless. I wasn't sure if it was courage spurring me forward or the desire to taunt my men into doing something about their ridiculous behavior, but once the idea hit me, I knew that there was only one option.

I grabbed them in my fist, slipped on my sandals, and marched to the front door. "What are you doing?" Kelsey asked.

"Pissing off a monster," I replied easily before opening the door and waltzing through it.

I moved quickly, knowing with complete certainty that if I slowed down or stopped, then I would lose whatever courage I had and run with my metaphorical tail between my legs back to Kelsey's apartment and back to the scary in-between world where the men were still mine. If I wanted to take charge of my life, they needed to see how serious I was about this.

Outside, the brisk air assaulted me like a slap. There was a winter storm expected by nightfall. My thin sweater and exposed skin felt like ice against the rush of wind. I found the Civella car standing watch over me and jogged over to them.

I was expecting to see one of Malice's men clutching their coffee and staring at me in annoyance, but no, there was none other than Nicholas Civella in the front seat. I gasped as he pushed open the door and stood in the chilly street.

"Have you come to your senses?" he asked, his tone bitter and yet vulnerable at the same time. I noted the dark circles under his eyes. The weary way he looked at me. The overwhelming defeat in his posture, despite his words.

"No," I replied, some of the bravado seeping out of my body like a leak in a tire. Slow but still damning. "I wanted to give you this."

I handed out the necklace and ring for him to take. He looked down at my outstretched palm and then back at my face. "Is this supposed to make you feel better?" he asked in a calm tone. "Is this some symbolic gesture that helps you cope with the lie that we're done, huh?"

Even though he didn't sound angry, the words he spoke rocked through me. "I just want you to understand how serious I am," I stuttered before jerking my hand out farther, nearly bumping the tips of my fingers into his abs.

"Be as serious as you want, Little Fighter. This isn't over."

"It doesn't have to be over," I replied. "I'll put this necklace back on when you stop trying to control my relationships. When you bring Anthony back. And when you are Nick again."

"Is this a bribe?"

"A compromise," I argued.

"And do my brothers have to compromise, too, or is it just me that's being subjected to this?"

A rush of wind whooshed around me, and I shivered. With a sigh of annoyance, Malice shrugged off his coat and wrapped it around me. "You're going to get sick."

I inhaled the scent of his cologne. The masculine, warm smell wrapped me in comfort. "The expectations I have for William and Anthony are none of your business," I said, my voice shaking from the cold.

Malice leaned in closer. "We have a fundamental difference of opinion, Little Fighter. You seem to think that is none of my business, and I think every bit of your existence on this spinning rock in space is my business."

I averted my eyes so that I wouldn't have to see his determined stare. It was hard to look at. "Take it," I choked out before holding the necklace close to his chest once more. "Just take it, Malice."

He angrily curled his hand around mine. "No."

Deciding that this was pointless, I quickly opened the driver's side door and dropped it in the front seat. Breathing heavily from the anxiety of it all, I finally forced my gaze to take in his expression, but was shocked to see that he was smiling at me.

"Go inside, Little Fighter. You'll catch a deathly cold."

I nodded, mostly because I wasn't sure what else to do. The last thing I saw before spinning around and running inside, was him licking his lips. I couldn't help but feel like he was plotting something.

Something told me that I won this battle, but he would win the war.

chapter ten
juliet cross

"Thank you all for tuning in. Be sure to listen next week, I've got an interview with a private eye that worked with the Smith family on Francesca Smith's disappearance almost a decade ago. Until next time, lock your doors."

I hit stop on my recording and leaned back in my chair with a heavy sigh. I'd recorded six episodes this week. Since breaking up with the Civella brothers, I'd been experiencing this strange rollercoaster of emotions, teetering somewhere between anxiety, fear, and disappointment. The first day, William sent over a box of my belongings. It made my decision feel final. The silent treatment was making me sick to my stomach, but it was also oddly familiar, too. It reminded me of the days where I thought he was just a broody bodyguard for Vicky. I didn't know how to navigate it. His quick dismissal of me was like a swift punishment and made me feel guilty for handling things the way I did.

I called him once and left him a message, letting him know that I was available to meet if he wanted to talk about everything. I made sure to include that I was willing to work through this if he made some changes, but the depressing silence that greeted me was answer enough. To say I was devastated would be an understatement, but I had to keep strong. I had to choose myself first.

Malice and I had become pen pals. Except we weren't writing letters, we were just mailing a necklace back and forth. Every night, I'd drop it off in his mailbox, and every morning, it would be back in mine.

I knew it was only a matter of time before things escalated. This game would entertain him for only a little bit, but pretty soon he would level up and I'd have to navigate his vindictive nature.

I got the job at the funeral home, thanks to Kelsey's tits and the owner's determination to win a date with her. It was weird not going to Eden's Place every night. And aside from classes, I was mainly keeping to myself at

Gram's house. Luckily, I hadn't had to talk to her about what was going on with the guys. She was in Oklahoma with some friends at one of the largest bingo tournaments in the country. She'd been doing so well with managing her Parkinson's disease that I felt good about her traveling with friends, and apparently, she was on a pretty big winning streak.

I was lonely. Perhaps that's why I was pouring all my attention into my podcast. I had enough episodes to get me through the month stored up.

I went to open up my editing software, since I didn't really have anything else to do, but an instant message pinged on my Google chat, making me pause. It was my podcast email. Now that I had ten thousand subscribers, it wasn't unusual for them to send me emails or articles, but I'd never had a chat request before.

I prayed I wasn't about to see an unsolicited dick picture and clicked open the window.

Pest92: Have you heard about the new serial killer in Miami?

They sent me a news link, and I clicked on it. Four murders. Female victims in their early thirties. Their bodies were mutilated. Missing chunks of skin. Teeth marks on their flesh...I quickly printed it out, then went back to the chat. I was equally as disconnected from the horror of it as I was drawn to the mystery.

Crimegirl: Do the police have any leads?

Pest92: None. He's leveling up, though. Started about three weeks ago.

Wait. Three weeks? That was about the time that Anthony left.

Crimegirl: Thanks for the tip. I'll look into it.

I went to close out of the chat, but Pest92 replied before I could.

Pest92: Of course. I love your podcast. Look forward to it every week. Though you sound sad lately.

I stared at the message for a long moment, that stormy sadness building within me. I didn't want any of my listeners to hear how upset I was.

Crimegirl: I'm sorry. Been having a rough few weeks. I'll be back to my normal self soon.

Pest92: Want to talk about it?

I smiled. With a random stranger on the internet? Pass.

Crimegirl: And make murdering me easier for you? Have you NOT listened to any of my podcasts? Rule one, don't open up to strange men on the internet.

Pest92: Who says I'm a man? I could be an innocent grandmother that spends her days playing bingo and her nights watching crime television.

Crimegirl: So can I call you grandma?

Pest92: No, it would hurt my frail masculinity. I'm a dude. And your instincts are right. You probably shouldn't tell me all your secrets.

I debated what to type next for a moment. I was enjoying the human interaction and wasn't ready to go back to the mundane, lonely silence.

Crimegirl: I guess we can chat as long as you promise not to be stupid about hiding my body when you kill

me. At least give the authorities a proper challenge.

Pest92: Deal. It'll be the crime of the century. So tell me what's wrong.

I should probably go to a therapist about this, but being vague couldn't hurt. Kelsey had been working all week to cover my shifts, and I just needed someone to be a little pathetic with for a moment.

Crimegirl: Going through a bad breakup.

Pest92: Those are the worst.

Yeah, and I was going through three at the same time. It was a clusterfuck of massive proportions.

Crimegirl: It's given me lots of time for podcasts, though. I've recorded six this week.

Pest92: Lucky me. Although, what does it say about you that you like talking about dead people when you're heartbroken? Should I be afraid?

I giggled.

Crimegirl: I know how to hide bodies where no one will find them.

Pest92: Does your ex know this?

We might have been joking, but the irony wasn't lost on me. I'd buried bodies with my ex—although the term *ex* didn't feel accurate for what Anthony was.

Crimegirl: He does. Maybe that's why he left.

Pest92: He'd be crazy to leave you. A girl that can hide a body and talks about true crime? Be still my beating heart.

Crimegirl: I also work at a funeral home.

Okay. I really needed to stop chatting with this guy. It

was harmless, but I felt like an attention leech—latching onto whatever I could get.

Pest92: A funeral home? How long have you worked there?

Crimegirl: Start on Monday. I'm excited.

Pest92: I hope it goes well for you.

I cleared my throat before typing my goodbye. I had a lot to think about. This serial killer development had my wheels spinning. It was something to latch onto and keep my mind busy for a moment. I was looking forward to the distraction from the pain in my heart. But also, something kept nudging at the edge of my mind. The timing was odd. I was probably making connections where none were, but it was worth looking into regardless.

Besides, I needed to drop off the necklace at the Civella home before bed anyway.

Crimegirl: I'm off to bed, Pest. Thanks for the tip. I'll look into it. Feel free to send me info if it comes up.

Pest92: Sweet dreams.

I closed my laptop and let out a sigh. It was next level pathetic to be at home doing nothing on a Saturday night. Normally, William and I would be at the club, fucking in his office or dancing in the main area. Or Malice would be taking me to a fancy dinner. Or Anthony and I would be burying bodies in the dark.

I caught a glimpse of my reflection and decided I needed to at least look like I wasn't miserable while going through my strong independent woman phase should I run into any of the guys. I wasn't going to go crazy, but clean hair was at least the bare minimum for looking like I had my shit together.

I padded across to the bathroom and quickly bathed, then shaved every inch of my body. Don't ask me why. Once I felt smooth and clean, I turned the water off, wrapped myself in a soft towel, and brushed out my wet hair while walking back to my bedroom.

Where I saw a fucking man standing over my desk.

A scream ripped through my throat, and I pressed my back against the wall in shocked horror. I almost went to grab a nearby textbook to toss it at his head, but when the stranger spun around to face me, I realized it was Malice. Or Nick. Whatever the fuck his name was these days. I couldn't keep up with my own mind's decisions and his altering identity.

"What the fuck are you doing here?" I screeched while gasping for breath and clutching my chest.

"It was getting late. I didn't want you walking over to the mansion in the dark and figured I would save you the trouble of delivering the necklace."

"You fucking psycho. You terrified me."

"Your front door wasn't even locked. Seems like an invitation if I ever saw one."

I knew for a fact that my front door *was* locked. The asshole probably still had a key. I needed to get the locks changed. I had a little nest egg saved up from working at Eden's Place and had plans to get a new cell phone on my own plan and make sure Malice couldn't just show up at my house unannounced anymore.

"You need to leave."

Malice put his hands behind his back and looked me up and down. He was devilishly handsome in his suit. His blond hair was styled perfectly, while those emerald eyes of his dared me to say something—do something. The tension between us had grown tenfold in the time we were apart. I felt weak and needy.

His gaze caressed my skin.

"Where's the necklace, Little Fighter?" he rasped.

I glared at him before dropping my hands to my side. Luckily, my flimsy towel stayed firmly in place. If he wanted to play this game, then fine, I'd play it. Slowly, I walked over, feeling sultry and terrified all at once. I was self-aware enough to know that I was playing with fire. I hated feeling so needy, so in between two extremes. Part of me wanted to move on from this toxic cycle. Part of me craved him like a drug.

"It's right here," I said before reaching for my nightstand, bending just enough to give him a healthy view of my ass. I heard him hiss as I straightened. "Happy?" I asked before holding it out to him. At some point, this game would have to stop. I wasn't sure I was ready for that.

He smirked at me, the warning clear in his expression. "Yes," he replied smoothly. "I'm very happy."

Malice tackled me to the bed in one easy move. My cheek hit the mattress, and my towel was ripped from my body. "Malice!" I screamed.

He snaked his hand up between me and the bed to wrap his hand around my throat for a split second before snapping his hand back as if my skin were poison.

I struggled as he pressed his muscular body against mine. I groaned as his lips brushed the shell of my ear. "I've missed you, Little Fighter."

"Get the fuck off and don't call me that," I grunted. I was so incredibly turned on. The feel of his hard body. The deep, addictive nature of his words. I could feel my heartbeat in my cunt, and slick desire painted the inside of my thighs. It was embarrassing and thrilling.

Malice thrust his hand between my thighs. The harsh intrusion of his finger made me moan. It shouldn't have felt as good as it did. "How long must we play these games, Juliet? You love me."

I bucked as he stroked my clit. My cheap bed frame squeaked beneath me as he spoke cruel truths in my ear. "Tell me you love me, and I'll make you feel good, Juliet. I need to hear it."

His demand made me pause, despite the decadent movement of his fingers. I slowly looked over my shoulder at him. "Love was never the problem, Malice," I croaked out. "I do love you, I just need you to love me back in the way I deserve, not just on your terms."

Malice stared at me, biting his lip to hold back whatever thoughts were swirling around his beautiful brain. We were suspended in time for only a moment, but I saw tender sensitivity there.

But as quickly as the moment happened, it passed.

He flipped me over on my back, pulled at my wet hair, and forced me to arch until his hot lips were on the shell of my ear again.

I was panting, completely spent from the tension between us. I'd never wanted him more than I did in that moment. And perhaps that's what he wanted. "Don't take that necklace off, Juliet. I won't tell you again."

I looked down, straining against his hold on my hair, shocked to see the tiny diamond resting on my skin. How did he even put it on me?

I opened my mouth to say something—anything. But he let me go and walked away from me.

chapter eleven
nick civella

I learned that my threshold for staying away from Juliet was three days. The night I almost had her in her bedroom, I immediately went home to wash the weakness from my skin. It bothered me how hard it was for me to hold my ground. It was frustrating to feel out of control of my own needs, body, and mind. I couldn't stop thinking about her. I couldn't stop aching for her. I couldn't stop desiring her.

I refused to give in, partly because of my own pride and

partly because I had something to prove to myself. I was born and raised to be independent. I needed to know that not even Juliet Cross could hold me hostage.

I was sitting in my office, pacing the floors like a caged lion when her text came through.

Juliet: We need to talk. I'm coming over.

The second I read her message, I raced downstairs and sat in the living room, waiting eagerly because apparently I was incapable of playing it cool. I glared at my watch while listening for the front door.

It only took about twenty minutes to get from her house to mine. Unless you were a god and could tell the police to switch all the red lights to green, then it only took twelve minutes.

The door rattled, and I forced myself to pick up yesterday's newspaper. I was pussy-whipped. My dick wanted to live inside of her. It was a needy bastard desperate to have her in my heart, head, and bed.

I heard a deep voice clear its throat and rolled my eyes in disappointment. "I thought you moved out. Why are you here?" I asked, not bothering to turn around, because I already knew that disgruntled huffing and puffing was William. He had perfected the art of always sounding like someone took a shit on his windshield.

The day Juliet told us both that she was done, he packed up his shit and moved to a loft downtown, taking some of my men with him. I knew we'd eventually stop living together, but the division of resources and the unspoken division of loyalty made my skin crawl. He was doing it on purpose, drawing a line in the sand to make me squirm.

I'd always hoped he'd grow up and be a man. The challenge both thrilled me and infuriated me. William Civella finally found something he wanted enough to fight for.

"Juliet asked me to meet her here to talk," he replied in a cool tone. I glanced at him over the top of my newspaper and chuckled despite the venom in my pulse. Why the fuck did she want to talk to him? I thought she was on her way here to beg, not to have a group therapy session.

"You've let yourself go. Sweats and a wrinkled shirt? When was the last time you shaved?" I asked. He had dark circles under his eyes and scruff on his jawline. I'd never seen him look so...normal. It didn't sit right with me.

"And you look like your usual unaffected self," he grumbled in response. "Cold. Heartless. Uncaring."

I ground my teeth before standing up. "For the record, I don't have a reason to be bitter and pathetic. Juliet and I are working through our differences. I saw her a few nights ago, and I guess you could say we reconciled."

It was a low blow. And a complete lie. Bragging about fucking the girl we both loved was beneath my pay grade, and if I were being honest with myself, it belittled our relationship. But William and I would always be in a pissing contest. And I knew in my gut that he hadn't reached out to her once since our fight. William was the king of mastering the silent treatment. Sometimes I would piss him off just because I enjoyed the week after of complete silence.

Again, I should be happy. It just felt wrong, too.

William scoffed. "She's not staying here, though, is she? And you're waiting in the living room like a pathetic, abandoned puppy. I'm sure whatever physical reunion you shared was temporary and meaningless."

I balled my fist at my side, wanting nothing more than to beat the ever living shit out of him. Mostly because he was right. I thought that leaving her wanting would send her crawling back to me, but instead, it just made our distance feel more intense. I was punishing myself, and it was fucking frustrating.

I cleared my throat. "Whatever Juliet needs, I can handle. You can leave."

He looked at me, then went over to the sofa to sit down, his own wordless protest. Fine. I sat in my recliner, and the two of us silently waited for Juliet to show up, because she had us both by the balls, a fact that made me rage.

Time passed slowly. We glared at one another. He huffed and puffed with annoyance. I imagined all the creative ways I could kill him.

Slamming his head between the toilet and the seat over and over and over again.

A bonfire in the backyard with him on a spit roast, cooking over the open flame.

A knife in the back.

Dragging him with my car along the highway.

When the front door opened, we both jolted out of our seats and stood there like men about to be ambushed. I guessed in some ways we were. William pulled at his shirt and scratched his jaw. I straightened my tie.

And Juliet walked through the door like she owned the place, wearing a black pencil skirt, a button-down white shirt, and her long hair was up in a tight bun. She looked like the most fuckable librarian I'd ever seen. I immediately started daydreaming about bending her over a desk and spanking her until she screamed.

William was obviously having the same reaction as me, because he went and adjusted himself. He was wearing gray sweatpants, which was basically him begging Juliet to look at his junk. Desperate motherfucker.

She swallowed nervously. I had the sudden desire to sink my teeth into her neck.

"Hi," she croaked.

We didn't reply—our silence was the only solidarity we shared. We were both against her and for her. Fighting over her and resenting her. It was complicated as fuck, but at the end of the day, she was mine.

William ran a hand through his hair, the move making the hem of his shirt lift a bit. She licked her lips like a starving street cat staring at a bowl of cream and sugar. Fucking gray sweatpants at it again. I made a mental note to buy a pair.

"Thank you both for chatting with me today. I don't have much time to talk because my shift at the funeral home starts in an hour."

William's finger twitched. It was killing him to know that she wasn't under his thumb anymore at Eden's Place. I may or may not have reached out to the owner of the funeral home and provided a little incentive for him to hire her. If she needed to feel independent, then I'd give her that. I just had to control how she felt independent, because I had issues. I was man enough to admit that the world spun a little better when I was the one doing the spinning. Part of our issues stemmed from how much I controlled her life. I supposed that just meant I needed to be a little more secretive about it. My next order of business was to get her a scholarship at school so she wouldn't feel weird about me paying her tuition.

"Well, let's talk then," I said coolly before sitting down. I immediately regretted picking the recliner, because that meant she had no other choice than to slide onto the loveseat next to William.

She looked beautifully uncomfortable, shifting from side to side, squirming under our intense gazes and pressing her creamy legs together. I knew she was turned on. I knew she missed us.

William remained silent but spread his legs so that he was touching her. I wondered how hard it would be to saw off all of his limbs. Anthony used to complain that bones were difficult to cut through.

"I'm worried about Anthony," Juliet blurted out. Of course this was about him. "There is a new killer on the loose in Miami."

I tilted my head to the side and schooled my face into a neutral expression. I knew for a fact that Anthony was hiding out in Miami. I'd been keeping an eye on him because old habits die hard. I told myself that I kept track of his location to make sure he didn't come back here, but...

nope. I couldn't even admit that I cared.

"What does that have to do with Anthony?" William asked. Juliet looked like she was hanging on to every word he said. It made my chest seize with an unfamiliar emotion. Maybe the silent treatment was the way to go, it obviously affected her. I wanted her to look at me like a starving woman.

She pulled out a cell phone that looked cheap as fuck. What happened to the one I bought her? Fucking independence. I needed to call the phone company and make sure I had a tracker on this one. "Because in one of the articles, there's a photo. He's at the scene of the crime."

My phone vibrated in my pocket, and I checked the message she just sent me—a link to a news article about a serial killer on the loose. I scanned the image at the top of the web page for my brother's annoying as fuck smirk and frowned when I saw him in the far right corner. Face downcast. Crestfallen expression. He stood behind a police line like a statue.

"So, he's in Miami. And the killer has a pattern of..."

"Mutilating innocent women," William finished for her. "The latest victim was strangled to death."

Juliet ran her delicate fingers over her throat, and I instantly was brought back to the night at the mass grave. My eyes glazed over as I imagined Anthony fucking her against a tree and choking her until she collapsed. I squeezed my phone in a fit of rage, and the screen cracked immediately.

"That's not all," she whispered. "Look at his latest

victim."

I couldn't scroll, so I waited for William to solve her ominous request for me. "No shit," he cursed. "This lady looks just like—"

"Cora. He killed Cora," Juliet answered.

With all the shit going on with our relationships, I hadn't even had time to properly hunt that bitch down these last few weeks. Last I heard, she was in Cuba hiding like the coward she was. I got up and grabbed the cell phone out of William's hand and stared at the photo there. Sure enough, Cora's mischievous smile taunted me through the screen. I wanted to throw something. I'd been searching for months for the rat that ruined my life.

"Are you sure she's dead? It's on brand for the bitch to fake her own death," I gritted.

"I have a friend looking into the autopsy report, but it all adds up," she replied.

Friend? What kind of friend? Did this friend have a penis? I made a mental note to kill this friend.

"Who?" William asked. Oh, so he was curious too. *How's that silent treatment working for you now, asshole?*

"Someone that sends me tips for my podcast. He is the one that sent a lead on this case, and I'm really fucking worried that Anthony is spiraling. We need to go get him. This killer is messy." She pulled her bottom lip between her teeth and looked over at William. "Anthony is in Miami," she then whispered. "We know where he is. We could—"

"We could do absolutely nothing because I'm not letting him back in the fold," I replied, my tone leaving no room for debate. Obviously, Juliet—my little fighter—wasn't so easily dismissed.

"I'm bringing him back, Malice. I don't care what you say," she pressed on.

I scoffed. William leaned forward, his eyes locked onto the screen of his phone. Quiet little mouse looked like he wanted to vomit or punch something. "You could try," I replied with a shrug. "But it would be incredibly easy for me to have you put on a No Fly List. I have men stationed on every highway leading out of here. Please, feel free to test the boundaries I've put around you. Just because you think you're free doesn't mean you actually are."

She scowled at my words, and I instantly regretted them. So much for secretly controlling her life. One step forward, forty steps back.

"If this is Anthony, he could be a liability," William said. I hated him for ruining my speech. Juliet had the most exquisite look of anger on her face, and I really wanted to commit the expression to memory so I could jack off later while thinking of her.

"He's his own liability now," I growled.

Juliet shook her head and looked up at the ceiling, likely trying to keep the tears forming in her eyes from sliding down her red cheeks.

"You honestly believe that?" William asked. "If he's arrested and captured, what do you think will happen? They'll start looking into his past. It would only be a matter of time before every single crime he's ever committed comes to light, and any accomplices would go down in flames right alongside him. You might have control over the Kansas City Police Department, but you aren't even remotely prepared for a federal investigation."

William's haughty tone had Juliet nodding enthusiastically.

Yeah, so he had a point. I didn't exactly want the feds digging into my life. I had enough dead bodies on my soul to spend eternity in hell, and I didn't want to spend my precious years of living rotting in a cell.

"I'll handle it," I replied. I wasn't exactly sure how I was going to handle it, but I would. Maybe letting Anthony live was the mistake.

That rogue thought made my chest constrict with pain. I was like Frankenstein. Could I honestly kill my own creation? Anthony was like this because of me. Because I let him get captured. Because instead of therapy, I tossed the woman I loved into his lap and expected her to fix him. Because...because I was fucking everything up.

"You cannot possibly be saying what I think you're saying," Juliet yelled while standing up. Her legs shook from rage. "You can't kill him, Malice. I would never forgive you."

She looked to William, expecting him to back her up. But once again, in a painfully predictable move, he remained silent. Even though she misinterpreted me—I wouldn't be killing Anthony; if I was going to kill him, I would have done it back at the graveyard—I let her think that. Anything was possible moving forward. Just because I was letting both of my brothers breathe now didn't mean

I'd continue to allow them the privilege of life.

"You came to me with a problem, and I will solve it however I see fit, Little Fighter."

She whirled around and glared at William. "Are you going to talk to me? I came here for help and—"

William stood up and rolled his neck before looking down at her. "You called me to fix my brother's problem. Not because you missed me. I've been chasing you since day one, Miss Cross. If you want me, you know where to find me."

He got up and headed for the door. I had to admit, it was a bold move—a gamble I wasn't sure even I would take. I'd never admit it to the bastard, but I wasn't sure if given the opportunity, she'd chase us down.

"William," she called at his back. "William!" She looked at me for a moment before running after him.

Interesting.

chapter twelve
juliet cross

My skintight pencil skirt and heels made it difficult to chase William down the concrete drive. He marched ahead of me, a destroyed man on a mission. I felt the buzz of anger deep in my veins.

"William!" I yelled as he jerked open the back door to a Mercedes Benz and slipped inside. I made it over to the car before he could drive off, and I slapped the window with my palm. "Fucking open this door right now."

He rolled the window down slightly and spoke to me in a detached, emotionless way that made my skin crawl. "Get away from the car, Miss Cross."

"Not until you talk to me. I've called you. I sent you texts. Ever since your birthday, you've been giving me the silent treatment. You obviously still give a fuck about me, because you showed up today. But that's not enough."

Through the crack in the window, I saw him shake his head. "Back off."

"Talk to me!" I screamed. He went still, like a marble statue carved and timeless. He didn't know any better but to be still and pose. "Do you want to love me, William?" I croaked out. "Or do you want to be loved? Because there is a difference. A huge difference." A fat, furious tear dropped down my cheek and caught on my upper lip. I licked it away. "I will probably never love you the way you want to be loved, William. You want me all to yourself. I get it. But it's never going to happen. You can ignore me as long as you'd like. But it won't make you okay with this. It won't win me back."

I waited for him to respond, but it was like waiting for answers about my mother's disappearance. It was all pointless. This was his line in the sand. It was the hill he would one day die on. I couldn't force him to fight for this. And I didn't want to anymore.

Silent. He was silent. He didn't say a single word about my declaration. He was gatekeeping his thoughts because he knew the lack of resolution was a slow and steady torture for me. I cried harder and begged, but he ignored all of it.

William then rolled up the window, and the driver sped off, leaving me in a metaphorical cloud of dust. It made me sick to see him drive away. It felt like William and I had been fighting since the day Vicky left. It was exhausting, and perhaps a smarter woman would have given up by now.

But despite his jealousy, his moody behavior, and selfishness, I loved him. I just didn't know how we'd ever meet in the middle. As I walked the rest of the drive and exited the Civella front gate, I thought about how much of a clusterfuck that meeting was. It was stupid of me to expect a different outcome, I suppose. Malice was still so vengeful and willing to let Anthony get himself killed.

And if I was right, Anthony was on a killing spree in Miami. How was I going to track him down and stop him without Civella help?

I couldn't help but feel guilty about it all. I'd become this massive wedge between all the Civella siblings. One by one, I tore them apart.

I walked across the affluent neighborhood toward the bus stop, acutely aware of the men standing at the top of the hill, watching my back. Malice couldn't let it go. His men might have gotten better at hiding, but that didn't mean they'd stopped following me. I wasn't stupid. I knew his game.

I passed a woman wearing black glasses, a beanie, and dark clothes. She was inspecting a rose bush, but I couldn't help but feel like she had her eyes on me. An instinctual shiver traveled up my spine as I passed her.

"You're going to get frown lines," her raspy voice said. It was a familiar tone I could place anywhere. My feet were practically glued to the sidewalk, and I slowly turned to look at her.

Black choker necklace. A familiar tattoo of wings. "Vicky?" I burst out as she lowered her sunglasses in a teasing way and winked at me with her cobalt gaze.

"In the flesh," she replied. "But don't say that too loudly. We have an audience."

I immediately flinched. Was this another ambush? Cora was presumably dead. Vicky sold us out the last time we saw her, and if she was here now, it was bad news for everyone. I knew if I screamed, the men at the top of the hill would come running. But from their vantage point, it probably looked like I'd just stopped to chat with a neighbor.

Curiosity was the only thing that kept me from alerting them.

"You're not supposed to be here," I rushed out.

"Believe me, I never wanted to come back, but I don't have much of a choice."

Her words shouldn't have hurt me. I knew that we were done. She tried killing me. But it still stung like a wasp in my shirt.

"Leave," I said.

"No. We need to talk."

I eyed her up and down, deciding that something felt off with her. In a split second, I decided to take a deep breath, preparing to scream for help. But she quickly reached for my elbow, her dainty fingers squeezing so tightly that I was certain it would leave a bruise. "Let's not call in the cavalry yet. I just wanted to chat."

I shook her off and pulled away. "Last time you wanted to chat, I was thrown into a white van and woke up in a warehouse surrounded by bodies."

Vicky waved her hand nonchalantly and spoke. "And I tried to blow you up. Yes. I know. But I'm in therapy now. Working on myself and whatnot."

I gaped at her. "That's great. But I'm still not talking to you."

I took a step back toward the Civella Mansion. At least there I was safe. Malice and I might be in a weird phase, but he was pretty clear about where he stood with Vicky. She was dead to him, and if she ever came back, she'd be dead to the rest of the world, too.

Vicky smirked. "We both know you can't run in heels. And even though you have some eyes on you right now, I also know that you and my brothers are in a bit of a rough patch. I mean, do you really want to go crawling back to those assholes, or do you want to catch up with your bestie?"

I felt like I was in some kind of alternate universe. How in the hell was this actually happening? "You have a terrible understanding of what it means to be a best friend."

"I guess you could say the same," she said while twirling a rogue section of blonde hair peeking out of her beanie. "You dated my three older brothers and broke girl code."

I blinked twice. Was she being serious right now? "That's not even remotely on the same level as what you did. That night at the warehouse really messed with Anthony. He hasn't been the same since."

I shook my head free of thoughts about Anthony. He was too painful to talk about. Especially to Vicky. "He seemed fine when I left him two days ago?" Vicky replied before polishing her nails on her sweater.

I scoffed. "You saw Anthony two days ago?" She was totally bluffing. There was no way in hell.

"I did," she snapped back. "He's in Miami—but you already knew that, didn't you?"

I gaped at her like a fish, opening and closing my mouth so many times I thought I'd catch a fly. Vicky ignored the incredulous look on my face and started digging through her purse. "I really think we should catch up. I know you have work today, but afterward, let's meet at our place, yeah? Come alone, please," she quickly added before eyeing the guards—who were now walking toward us.

She scurried off before I could make up my mind about going. It pissed me off that she had information about my greatest weakness, Anthony.

We both knew that breadcrumb of information was enough to get me to talk to her. It might have been stupid, but I'd go to hell and back for him.

—

Walking up to Dick's Diner was like tiptoeing through a dream. My life had changed so much since the last time I'd stepped foot on these sticky floors. Not much had changed here. The same blue-collar townies still sat in the booth.

The air smelled like syrup and bacon, and despite the chill outside, it was hot and muggy the moment I waltzed through the front doors.

I saw Vicky almost immediately. Her petite body barely filled the booth. Had she lost weight? She was staring at a plate of fries, a vulnerable look on her face. Left freely to examine her in the dim lighting, I openly stared for a moment at her withdrawn expression. She had an untouched cup of coffee beside her, and I could see her unmanicured nails tapping on the tabletop nervously.

She looked like a dimmer version of the bright light that used to be my best friend. I guessed both of us had changed in the last year. My problems seemed bigger, and my world view more tainted by the sins I'd committed.

Our eyes connected, and she immediately plastered a fake smile on her face. She casually looked over my shoulder, as if searching for any followers. I had to work hard to ditch my security detail today. I snuck out the back of the funeral home and took six different busses to get here. And on the off chance Malice was tracking my phone, I left it at work.

Slowly, I moved to sit across from her, a strange sense of sad nostalgia rolling over my skin as I did. It felt weird to sit here with her without William. "You came," she said breathlessly.

"What do you know about Anthony, Vick?" I asked. I didn't come here to reunite and have a pleasant conversation. This was about Anthony. She lost the right to be my friend when she tried to have us killed.

She tucked her pale blonde hair behind her ear. "I guess I deserve that," she replied. "It's never been about me, hmm?"

I wasn't about to play into that martyr bullshit. "My entire life was about you, our entire friendship. You were the only person, aside from Grams, that I could trust and confide in. I broke your trust, but you *destroyed* us. Don't sit here and play the victim, because I will leave and not look back."

Vicky's eyes flared with anger, a look that reminded me of Malice. In that instant, I saw how closely they were related. "Looks like someone grew a backbone. I bet it's driving Nicholas absolutely crazy." She smirked before licking her glossy lips. "He loves defiance but hates not having control."

She wasn't wrong, but that didn't mean I liked her commentary on my relationship. I sensed that she was bitter and still struggled with everything, regardless of her nonchalant attitude.

I sighed. "Vicky, I'm here for Anthony. Either you know where he is or you don't."

She pressed her glossy lips into a thin line and nodded. "He's staying at my condo in Miami. We sort of ran into one another there. Seemed fitting that the two excommunicated siblings would find one another."

I felt a small sense of guilt about Vicky being kicked out of the fold, but this was what she wanted, wasn't it? She wanted freedom from her brothers and the opportunity to live a life on her own.

"Where is your condo?" I asked, although I could probably find it somewhere.

"I'll tell you," she whispered. "But I need your help first."

I frowned. Of course she needed something. Why else was she here? "What do you need?"

She wiggled in her seat, seemingly uncomfortable. "I need protection, Juliet."

I wasn't expecting that response. Money, maybe. Power. Influence. I thought she'd gotten a taste of freedom and realized it wasn't all it was cracked up to be. But protection? She didn't sound cocky. She shook with fear, and I found myself feeling legitimately concerned for her wellbeing. "What's going on, Vicky?" I asked. "Who is after you? Cora's dead. I saw it."

Vicky scoffed before plucking a french fry from her plate and taking a bite. "Oh she's dead alright. Dead as it gets, I suppose. Anthony even broke into the medical examiner's office to steal himself a little souvenir."

My throat felt incredibly dry at her words. "So it's true. Anthony is going on a killing spree," I murmured while staring at the tabletop. I leaned back in my booth helplessly. Fuck. Maybe he was too far gone. I wasn't sure if it mattered to me. Could I love a serial killer? Would I?

Vicky let out a brutal laugh. "He wishes! God, he moped for days when the news broke. I gave him a strict *no killing people* rule when I said he could stay with me."

I snapped my head up to stare at her. "Anthony isn't the one going on a killing spree?"

She shook her head. "Not unless he decided to have a

little fun while I'm here."

I let out a sigh of relief. There was still hope for Anthony. I looked up at the ceiling to collect my thoughts. Vicky kept speaking while I reveled in my relief for a moment. "You're aware of the killer roaming the streets of Miami. Anthony said he's been emailing with you about it—"

"What?"

Vicky waved her hand dismissively, letting me figure out what that meant all on my own. She continued speaking all while I took cover from the bombshell she just dropped in my lap. My anonymous informant was Anthony? Pest92... All this time I'd been worried about him and wondering if he was okay, and he'd been the one messaging me?

I frowned. Vicky rambled. "I started getting threats around the time Cora and I went our separate ways."

I arched a brow at her. "Threats?"

"Cora might be a puppet, but the real villain of this story is alive and well, my friend."

"We're not friends," I blurted out. I wanted to make that line in the sand clear as day. We'd never be friends again. "And I beg to differ. Cora tried killing us. And she was pulling the strings on a lot of other deaths, too."

Vicky rolled her eyes. "She's a nobody. The second Malice put a massive ass bounty on her head, she went running for the hills. I can't hang with cowards. She was nothing but a means to an end, and she couldn't even get the job done. Sure, she had followers and cash, but she's no Civella. Her brother, however..."

"Brother?" I searched my memories and suddenly

remembered the one time I saw Cora. She'd tried connecting, i.e., manipulating me by talking about her brother and how she was a caregiver for him.

"Didn't Malice shoot him five times? Cora made it sound like he was bedridden," I replied.

Vicky had a faraway look in her eyes. "He's healed up, I suppose. His body, at least. His mind is a whole other story. He's a monster, Juliet. He makes my brothers look like teddy bears in comparison."

"You know him?"

"I saw him a couple of times while working with Cora. I'll never forget the first time we were introduced." Vicky stared at the tabletop, as if she were reliving a traumatic experience. I watched as her chest started to rise and fall with anxiety. She wiggled in her seat and started to chew on her lip. I waited patiently to hear what she had to say.

"He was chained up. Blood covered his face. His torso was nothing but a mess of mangled skin and scars. He kept chewing on something like it was bubble gum, but it wasn't."

"Chained up? What do you mean?"

Vicky shuddered. "I can't get the image out of my brain. He was chewing on a severed ear. The crunch of cartilage was...unforgettable."

She let her words simmer between us for a moment. I drowned in the realization that Cora's brother was a complete psychopath. I ran through the news articles that Pest92—or Anthony—had sent me. Chunks of flesh had been missing from his victims. "He's a cannibal?" I asked. Saying it out loud felt ridiculous. Shit like that only happened in horror movies or with people snorting bath salts. I studied true crime and even this felt extreme.

She nodded. "He had scars all over his body and a split lip. Four men stood watch over him twenty-four seven. For some reason, I felt bad for him."

Vicky crossed her arms over her chest as I breathed in the smell of bacon. "You felt bad for him?" I asked.

"He was chained up by his powerful sibling. He was creepy, yeah, but what Cora was doing was wrong. I guess I could relate to him."

"Your brothers never chained you up, Vicky."

She fumed with anger at my words. "Just because you can't see the cage they built around me doesn't mean it didn't exist. You've been around long enough to see that there is no freedom for Civellas. Malice is a paranoid control freak."

She was right, but I didn't want to give her the satisfaction of agreeing with her. "Fine. So what does this guy have to do with anything?"

"I let him free," she whispered. "It was such a quick decision. I was walking out the door. He was alone for once. I just...it was easy, and I..."

"You let Cora's cannibal brother free?" I asked, seeking clarification. Maybe Vicky had impulse issues. I couldn't understand why on earth she thought to do that. I understood feeling bad for him, but...

She nodded. "And now he's on a killing spree. I know for a fact that he killed Cora. I'm next."

"Why would he kill the person who let him free?" I asked. That didn't make any sense. If anything, he would feel an obligation to protect her.

"I don't know why. He's not sane." She started rummaging through her purse and pulled out an envelope. "I found this in my car."

She slid it over to me, and I carefully opened it up and pulled out a worn looking piece of paper covered in what looked like red ink. The words "I love you" were written over and over and over.

I flipped the paper over and gasped at the sketch there. It was a man sinking his teeth into a woman's thigh, ripping out the tendons and exposing the meat of her body. It was bloody and erotic but also terrifying.

"I will consume you as you've consumed me," she whispered, quoting the words at the bottom of the page. I dropped the paper. "Be sure to wash your hands. That's not ink, it's blood," she said softly.

I quickly shoved the paper over to her, and she folded it up and shoved it back inside her purse, like it was nothing. "I need my brothers' help, Juliet. This guy is strong and smart and deadly. The police are calling him sloppy with his kills, but he's actually a genius. Anthony thinks he's staging fires in abandoned buildings to distract the police while he abducts his real victims. And he has to be working with people. No one ever has footage of him. No one ever sees his face."

My thoughts were wrapped around this problem. Even though it was grotesque, I couldn't help but want to track him down and bring him to justice. My humming mind was dissecting his note, his motives, and his habits already. This was truly a peculiar case.

"I'm not sure I can convince Malice and William to go to Miami," I admitted. They'd already made it clear that they were cutting ties with their estranged siblings. If they weren't going to go rescue Anthony, then they sure as hell weren't going to be there for Vicky. It was every man for himself these days.

"I'm not sure it'll take much convincing," Vicky replied before scooting out of the booth and standing up. "I've seen how they look at you. You have all of them wrapped around your pinky finger. I swear Anthony just plays your podcast on repeat."

My heart warmed at that. I wanted nothing more than to see him.

Vicky ran her hands down her side and started strutting toward the door. Confused, I quickly got up and started following after her.

A strange sense of déjà vu washed over me as I followed her out of the diner. I wasn't even sure she paid her tab. Once again, I was chasing after her under the blanket of night. The cool air welcomed me as my heels clicked on the concrete. "Vicky! So what do we do? I want to speak to Anthony."

She kept walking until she stopped at an inconspicuous Chevy four-door car. It was silver with Florida license plates. "You said it yourself," she began while digging through her purse. "You don't think you can convince

Nicholas and William to come help me. I can't run, because he'll just find me, and now Anthony is in this mess too."

"What do you mean Anthony is in this mess too? What aren't you telling me?" I asked. My voice was a pleading whine.

"Cora's brother knows Anthony is helping me," she said. "It is going to take all three of them to take this guy down." She straightened her spine and looked at me. I saw the determination in her gaze and briefly wondered what her plan was. I couldn't just drop everything and go to Miami. I needed more information. We had to at least try with Malice and William.

"What are you doing?" I asked.

"Leaving."

"You can't go just yet. Why even show up here if you're going to just give up like this?"

Vicky gave me a wicked grin, and suddenly I was struck with her intentions—quite literally. She pulled a rock from her purse, stared at it, then reared back and slammed it against my temple. Pain wreaked through my skull, and it felt like an earthquake was happening in my brain cells.

The last thing I heard was Vicky apologizing. "I'm sorry, Juliet. This was the only way."

chapter thirteen
william civella

I could be silent no more. I traded my sweats for a tailored suit. I shaved my face. I pulled myself together, got in my car, and drove across town to Juliet's house. I should've done this days ago, but my pride and ego were at war with my heart. Once again, I was the pathetic loser in our story. It took seeing her in the rearview mirror to realize that my vindictive bullshit was ruining us. I was disgusted with myself. It was time to man up and be what Miss Cross deserved. It was time to take down my brothers and claim what was mine.

It was time to fight. And if that meant I had to play dirty to get Juliet back, I would. And it started with now.

I knocked on the door. Grams was out of town on a bingo trip with her friends, but Juliet was supposed to be here. Not a light in the house was on. I pulled out my spare key and let myself in. The ghost of this house greeted me. Breathing in, there was an echo of her perfume that filled my senses, and the ticking clock made everything feel more ominous. Empty rooms, empty fridge, my empty heart beat loudly as I walked through the house. It was almost midnight, where was she?

I pulled out my cell phone and called one of my men. They had been reporting back to me over her whereabouts. They might work for my brother, but their loyalty was to me. I was the man who signed their checks. I was the one who promoted them to a better spot. And they knew that my brother was fickle, liable to murder or fire anyone on the spot. The only way up the ladder of our business was through me, and I planned to use that to my every advantage.

"Where is Miss Cross?" I asked the moment the line picked up.

"Working late," he gruffly replied. "Creepy as fuck outside the funeral home."

I waited for a moment and considered his words. It seemed odd that she would be working this late. "Go check inside the building and see if she's there and call me back."

I hung up the phone before he could reply and went to

her bedroom. Inhaling the scent of her perfume, I brushed my fingers over her desk. Hair ties, earrings, and a ten dollar bill littered the tabletop. A jacket I bought her two months ago was slung over the back of her desk chair, the desk displaying a photo of all of us sitting in a thin frame coated with dust.

A tiny twin mattress that creaked and groaned whenever someone sat on it was decorated with gray bedding and a memory foam pillow that I'd ordered for her. I moved to her dresser and slowly opened the drawer. It rattled as I did. The old wood was worn down and angry.

Layers of thin lace and taunting silk stared back at me. Smooth, soft fabric, small, dainty, and sensual. I ran my hand over it and inhaled deeply.

A particular pair of light blue panties caught my eye, and I picked it up to inspect. I couldn't help but think back on all the nights I'd followed her home in my car after her late shift at Dick's. It started out harmless enough. I convinced myself that making sure she was safe was protecting Vicky. I wasn't some fucking creeper lusting after a high school girl.

I befriended Grams at the bus stop so I could have another viewpoint into Juliet's world. I learned their routine so I could sneak into their house and fix things inconspicuously.

The refrigerator was acting up, so I replaced the dirty condenser coils.

One brutal winter, I caulked all the windows to make sure there wasn't a draft.

I mailed coupons to their house for food.

I paid other patrons at the restaurant to leave her a better tip.

And somehow, while doing all of this, I fell in love with her.

I grabbed the lace thong from the drawer and walked over to the twin mattress. While sitting down, I brought them to my nose and inhaled. It smelled like her detergent mixed with the sweet scent of her perfume. I closed my eyes and imagined her wearing them just for me.

Creamy thighs. Long, brown hair in waves around her shoulders. Smoky eyes daring me to taste her.

I lay back on the mattress and felt myself growing hard with that twitching need to touch her. Feel her. Love her. I needed to fix this—fix us.

I slowly unzipped my pants and pulled out my cock. I hadn't gotten off since my birthday. I guess in some ways, I was too ashamed to even jack off. It was really fucking with my mind to know that I shared her with Nick. I had to share *everything* with him.

I suppose it didn't really gross me out that we were brothers. Given my job at Eden's Place, I was a very open-minded asshole. No swords crossed, and my focus was entirely on Juliet. Aside from wanting to piss Nick off, I pretended he wasn't there.

What ruined the entire experience for me was seeing Juliet desperate to please us both instead of actually enjoying herself. She teetered between worrying about being in the middle, and letting go. And I hated that I'd put her through that.

What I really wanted was for her to come again, and again, and again.

I wanted her to look at me with her wide eyes full of lust.

I started stroking myself with her lace lingerie while imagining her on that bed in Eden's Place.

If I could do things all over again, I would have controlled the situation and made Nick please her. Kiss her. I would have fucked her so hard she couldn't choke out whatever bullshit words my ego was forcing her to say. Maybe Anthony would have been there too, kissing her curves. Making her smile—a feat I envied him for. He was always able to make her smile, and that was what our group was missing lately.

If I could start over, I would have made it about her.

And then I would have ripped her from their greedy hands and taken her home.

Maybe Nick had the right idea. Keeping her pleased, sated, and happy while keeping her soul all to himself.

I wanted that. I wanted to be the person she woke up staring at every morning. I wanted to be the person she ran to with every problem. I wanted to watch her live her best, most fulfilling and authentic life while knowing it was always me she'd run to at the end of the day.

I gripped my shaft harder, stroking and grunting in her bed. I came embarrassingly fast, the lusty promise of control heavy on my mind as I did. Ropes of cum soaked through the lace fabric of her underwear, and I let out a sigh of satisfaction once my pulse settled.

The sound of my phone vibrating mixed with my harsh breaths. I grabbed a tissue from the nightstand and wiped my palm off while feeling slightly disgusted with myself. I never thought I would be back here again, pining after a woman who felt out of reach.

At least when I was her silent stranger, I still had access to her mind. Now, I worried that we had fizzled into nothing. And I had no one to blame but myself. I reached for my phone to answer it. "Is she there?" I asked, deciding to skip over the pleasantry of greetings.

"She's not here," my man replied. "Doesn't look like anyone's been here for a couple of hours."

I felt my eye twitch with anger. What was wrong with these incompetent men and their inability to do a simple task? Nicholas was losing control of his army, and Juliet was suffering because of it. "Does Nick know?" I asked.

"Yes, sir," he replied stiffly. I could hear the terror in his tone.

I hung up the phone and quickly dialed Ruthie's number. Even though she was out of town on her bingo trip, she would answer for me. We had become friends over the years, and she would want to know where Juliet was.

It rang, and rang, and rang. Finally, she answered the phone, and her warm voice greeted me. "William?" she croaked. It was obvious that I'd woken her up. "Why are you calling? Is Juliet okay?"

Her question instantly alerted me that she had no idea where Juliet was. This was not good. Given Ruthie's history with Juliet's mother, I didn't want to scare her until we had more information. But if Ruth didn't know where her granddaughter was, then this was bad. "William?" she asked again. "Is Juliet with you?"

A lie quickly came to me. "Sorry to call you so late, Ruthie, but I wanted to let you know that there's been a minor gas leak at your house. Juliet and I are going back to my place, but I didn't want you to be alarmed if you hear that the fire department was here."

She let out a sigh. "I'm so glad everyone's okay. Thank you for letting me know. When do you think it'll be fixed? I'm supposed to go home tomorrow."

Another call started coming through, and I checked the ID before responding. Nicholas. "I should have everything fixed before you get home, Ruthie. But try to stay away until I can give you the all clear. I don't want you getting sick."

I could hear her smile through her tone. "Thank you, William. You always look out for us. Try to get some rest, dear. Good night."

The second she hung up, I answered my brother's call. "Did you find her?" I asked. There was no point in dancing around the semantics of how I knew she was gone. The one good thing about my brother being a crazy control freak was that there was a good chance Juliet had a tracker on her.

"She doesn't have her phone," Nick growled. "I was hoping she was with you."

Part of me wanted to record him saying that for later, but now was not the time. "I just got off the phone with

Ruth, and she doesn't know where Juliet is either."

Nicholas cursed. "Why would you involve her? Ruth does not need to be scared—you know how that makes her sick."

I rolled my eyes. Both of my brothers had a soft spot for that woman. "Of course I didn't needlessly worry her. I don't want to give her a panic attack. I made up a lie about a gas leak at the house and assured her everything was okay. No need to scare her until we have more information." Nicholas grunted, his agreement short and huffy. "Cora is dead," I added. It wasn't like the bitch could come back from the grave to haunt us. Every second that passed, my heart started to race more.

Cora wasn't necessarily our only enemy, but she seemed most likely to pull something like this. I still vividly remembered the last time Cora kidnapped Juliet. It was the worst day of my life. Even though we tracked her down fairly easily, it still made me sick to my stomach to think of the state we found her in, surrounded by dead bodies and a cackling Anthony. She didn't deserve this. She didn't deserve any of this.

"I still think that bitch faked her death," Nick replied roughly.

"Either way, Juliet is gone. We need to find her," I snapped. Every second that ticked by was another opportunity for something to happen to her.

"Do you think she deliberately got away from the security guards? She's really intent on being independent," Nick growled. I considered his words for a moment. But where would she go? Kelsey was working tonight, so I knew Juliet wasn't with her. It wasn't like she had many friends in the area. And she definitely didn't have any love interests. Unless she splurged on a hotel—which didn't make sense—she was gone.

I thought about our conversation earlier. She was very determined to find Anthony. But certainly she wouldn't go without a car, a plan, or even an idea of where he was.

"I think it's possible that she slipped away from them, but unless she fled the city, she should be back by now. It's the middle of the night, where could she be?"

I heard glass shattering, and I imagined Nick throwing something against the wall. He was always so prone to anger—it made him weak in times of crisis. He was more likely to run his fist through walls than find an actual solution to our problem. It was yet another reason why I knew I was a better leader than he was. "What are we going to do?" he asked me.

I couldn't even enjoy the helplessness in his tone, because I was just as worried as he was. It was shocking to me that he wanted to ask my opinion on the matter. Nick liked to pretend that he was in charge. He was the big bad boss, but I was the strategist.

"She said she was going to see Anthony. It's possible that she left and went to Miami."

I didn't like the idea of her traveling alone, and I wasn't exactly sure if going after our deranged brother was the best idea. It was the best guess. Juliet was passionate about getting Anthony back, and if she slipped away from the guards and disappeared, then that's where she was probably going.

"There's nothing on her bank statements. No car rental. No hotel. No gas, food, or anything. Plus, on her calendar, it says she has a test tomorrow. I know she's desperate to get to Anthony, but our girl is the type to plan. She wouldn't just disappear unless—" His voice cut off, as if sliced with the knife of thought. "She said she was talking to someone. Someone was giving her intel on the serial killer in Miami."

I almost dropped my phone. A rush of emotions flooded me, and I quickly got off the bed to look around for her laptop. As expected, it was sitting on her desk. "I'm checking her computer now," I replied before entering her password and opening her chat.

Page after page of theories from a Pest92 welcomed me. Some of the messages were flirty in nature, and it made my chest constrict. Was this the person she was talking to? While I was giving her the silent treatment, someone else was swooping in and feeding off her passions. This all felt too coincidental. It was a trap. Nick got impatient as I scanned the messages.

"She's been talking to someone about the Miami killer," I said. Nick cursed. I was reading through the last few messages when a chat bubble appeared. This Pest92 person was online, and I found myself wanting to reach through the screen and drag him through it so that I could cut up his face. I was naturally a jealous man, and if I thought it was bad to know that my brothers were with the woman I loved, then it was ten times worse to know a complete stranger was moving in on her. Especially since that stranger seemed to have ulterior motives.

Pest 92: is this William or Nick?

I cursed. "We have a problem," I said.

"What's going on?" Nick asked. I ignored him and typed out a response. I didn't negotiate with terrorists, nor did I have time to explain to my brother what was going on. I probably had five seconds to convince this person to tell me where Juliet was and what he wanted.

"Hold on," I growled.

Juliet: William.

Pest 92: I was hoping it would be you. Juliet is safe. See you in Miami.

He quickly ended the connection and blocked me. "FUCK!" I roared.

"Tell me what is going on right now, or I will end you," Nick demanded. I sat back in Juliet's office chair and tried to collect my thoughts. What the hell? Was this all a trap? What if this was a ruse to get us away from Kansas City—to isolate us so that we were weak and vulnerable?

Honestly, I didn't care. I'd go anywhere for Juliet. This was the only lead we had.

"Looks like we're going to Miami, brother," I said before hanging up.

chapter fourteen
juliet cross

Though I had woken up an hour ago, I kept my eyes pinned shut. As I rested my head against the rattling window of Vicky's car, the morning light threatened to break through the barrier of my stubbornness. I was curious where we were but wasn't willing to open my eyes to see. Once she knew I was awake, I'd have to confront her about this stupid plan, and I was too angry to deal with it.

In the driver's seat, Vicky was humming to some pop song, only pausing her boppy singalong to curse at slow eighteen wheelers driving in the fast lane. She seemed oddly...normal. I'd expected some sinister showdown or nefarious plot. Not a casual road trip with someone I used to consider a best friend.

I felt stuck in a limbo where I was angry...but also *not* angry at her for forcing me to go with her. Yes, my head hurt like a bitch, and she could have been a little less forceful about it. But driving toward Miami—toward Anthony—still felt like a win.

I was out of Kansas City. I was headed toward Anthony. It had been weeks since I'd seen him, and even though it made me sick to my stomach to sit beside Vicky in her car, I was looking forward to the destination—as foolish as it was. This could have all been a trap, but something in my gut told me that it wasn't.

I just couldn't imagine what Malice and William were going through right now. It was only a matter of time before they realized I was gone, and I feared the repercussions on Vicky's behalf.

"Are you going to stop pretending to be asleep? I have to stop at a gas station, and I need to make sure you're not going to run away," Vicky asked in a bored tone. "I already gave you one nasty bump on the head, and I really don't want to do that again." She paused, and I waited for her to continue, not quite willing to give up my napping ruse yet. "Or maybe I *do* want to give you another bump on the head." She started laughing, and I felt the car slow down.

The clicking blinker turned on as she exited whatever highway we were on.

"I don't need another bump on the head. I didn't really need the first one," I groaned before blinking the sleep away and sitting up. The bright light of day made my eyes burn.

"I didn't really have time to convince you," she argued.

We passed a sign that said Tennessee. "You know how determined my brothers can be. I had about thirty minutes to get us out of Kansas City before that entire place went on Civella lockdown. God knows I'd tried to run away plenty of times and never once made it out."

Vicky surprised me. For all our years of being best friends and talking about everything, this was a portion of her life I was completely blindsided by. It was on the tip of my tongue to ask her how many times she attempted to escape her family. I was scared of the answer. I also wanted to know why she felt like she had to run. But I guess I knew why. It was the same thing that motivated me to be independent and take a stand in my relationship. I loved them. Deeply. Irrevocably. But I loved myself, too.

She pulled into the parking lot of the truck stop. Once we were at the pump, she turned the car off and twisted in the driver's seat to look at me. "You going to run away?" she asked.

I shook my head. It was too late to run away. Besides, I wanted to see Anthony more than anything. It was probably foolish of me, but being here felt right. "Eventually, I'll need to call my Grams," I replied. "I don't want her to worry."

Vicky squinted at me, her assessing eyes taking in every

bit of my expression. "Fair enough. Are you going to call my brothers?"

I chewed on my tongue for a moment. Vicky took my silence as an answer.

"You really are on the outs with them. Anthony wasn't clear on the details. Did you finally realize that Nick is a controlling asshole and that William is a jealous pussy? You already know about Anthony, I assume." I did not want to give her the privilege of being right. Just because we were struggling didn't mean the love wasn't there.

"We're working through some things right now," I gritted back. "Dating all of them is—"

Vicky cut me off. "Weird? Hard? Impossible? They're all insane and have the emotional range of a thimble."

"Every relationship has road bumps," I argued back.

"True, but I *know* you, Juliet. You're better than this. Seeing you with them feels like…" Vicky paused, seemingly trying to come up with how to describe it. "Feels like a lie," she finally decided on.

"What makes you say that?" I replied roughly before crossing my arms over my chest.

Vicky shrugged. "I don't know. You were this badass, independent chick that took care of her shit. I think the hardest part of you falling in love with my brothers was losing her." She reached into her tote and pulled out a twenty-dollar bill, abruptly ending our conversation. "Go get us some food, I'm starving."

Snatching the twenty-dollar bill out of her fingers, I quickly unbuckled and reached for the door, pausing for a moment to have the last word. "I'm still her."

Without waiting for her response, I went inside the gas station, not bothering to look over my shoulder at her as I left.

After using the bathroom and washing my bruised face, I went to stretch my legs, perusing the aisles in a leisurely way. I kind of hated myself for remembering all of Vicky's favorite snacks. Reese's. Pork rinds. Teriyaki-flavored beef jerky. I also grabbed some pickle-flavored sunflower seeds and two doughnuts as well as coffee and Diet Coke.

The total came to $23.47. I handed over the cash that Vicky had given me, then reached into my pocket and pulled out my small wallet with my debit card. I stared at it for a lingering moment. Someone cleared their throat behind me. "Ma'am? You still owe three forty-seven," the gas station clerk said. He had long curly hair and a tired look on his face.

I knew that the moment I swiped my card, Nick and William would know where I was. They had to be monitoring my bank for any transactions by now. I was surprised Vicky hadn't taken my wallet from me while I was knocked out.

I briefly looked out the front window at Vicky, who was pumping gas and smiling at a guy who stood at the pump opposite of her. Maybe she wanted me to alert them. She wanted them to come to Miami, after all. I knew in my gut that I couldn't trust her. But there was a small part of me that wanted to get a little closer to Anthony before alerting them. I felt like I was betraying my men, but we needed a bit more time.

So after a shaky breath, I danced between my desires of wanting to see Anthony but also wanting the men I loved to know that I was safe, and told the attendant to take off the beef jerky and paid with cash.

With an extra sway to my steps, I marched back to Vicky's rental car while carrying the sack of food. She was applying lipstick in the front seat when I sat down beside her. "I got all your favorites," I replied, surprising myself with the relief in my tone. Eventually, I would have to let my men know where I was. I couldn't just let them worry about me. But they made their decision when they refused to let me see Anthony. I was committed to finding him, and that meant I had to put my trust in Vicky.

"It's cute that you still remember my favorite snacks. Remember how we used to always talk about going on road trips?" she asked before digging through the bag and pulling out a doughnut.

"It was all talk, though," I said quietly. "We were never going on a road trip. You were never going to tell me about your life. I was just the friend that you lived half-truths with."

Vicky tore at her glazed doughnut with her teeth and slowly chewed the sickly sweet breakfast while staring at her thighs. "I wanted to go," she replied softly. "I wanted it all so badly that it drove me crazy."

She turned on the car and silently got back on the highway.

—

"Are we stopping for the night? We still have five hours until we get to Miami," I groaned. My back was killing me, and every muscle in my body was stiff from sitting all day. Vicky looked about two seconds from passing out and driving into oncoming traffic. I'd offered to drive multiple times, but she refused.

"We can't," she said with a yawn. "We don't have much time. If I had to guess, my brothers have already pulled security footage from the gas station we stopped at."

I snapped my attention to her. "What?"

"They can be resourceful assholes when they want to be. It'll come in handy when taking down Cora's brother, I suppose. But right now it's a pain in the ass. The whole goal is to get my brothers all to Miami, but we have to actually make it there first." I watched opposite traffic drive by, the headlights bouncing across my vision as I absorbed her words. "You look worried," she observed.

There was no point lying to her. There was a time I told Vicky everything about my life. "I'm worried we won't get to Anthony in time. And I'm also worried they're going to kill you before we have a chance to explain. I think that once again, you just impulsively made a rash decision and—"

"Is this about hitting you with the rock?" she interrupted.

I shook my head in frustration. "It's about knocking me out, keeping me in the dark all those years, and trying to get us killed with Cora."

165

Vicky had the decency to look ashamed. "It's okay," she replied while checking the rearview mirror. "Everything is going exactly to plan."

"And what plan is that?"

Vicky passed a slow-driving truck and accelerated. "Get you to Anthony. He's impossible to work with while he's mopey. It's like watching a puppy that's been kicked and abandoned. Breaks my heart."

I rolled my eyes. "I'm surprised you care."

Vicky lost some of her sleepy bravado at my tone. "Of course I care."

"You have a terrible way of showing it. Should I list every shitty thing you've done again?"

Vicky tapped the brakes and pulled over to the shoulder of the road. We were somewhere in Florida, the abandoned road was dark and the air muggy. My morbid sense of humor made me think that this was a great spot to dump a body.

Anthony would love it.

"Why did we stop?" I asked.

"I'm sorry I tried killing you," she blurted out. It was such a strange apology and seemingly lacked sincerity.

"Thanks. I feel so much better now," I replied sarcastically. Thankfully, the car was dark enough that Vicky couldn't see me rolling my eyes.

Vicky leaned over the center console and grabbed my arm. "You don't have to forgive me. I'm just asking for some of the grace you give my brothers, okay? We're all cut from the same cloth. I know why Anthony is here. I know

Nick fucking brought you to a shootout and almost got you killed. William betrayed you. No one is innocent here. And as much as I love you, the only difference between my brothers and me, is that I can't distract you with hot sex, though I'm willing if that's what it takes."

I snorted at that. The guys were good at sexing me into forgiveness. It was pathetic and fucked up, but I could be honest with myself. Despite their superior dicks, the constant flow of orgasms wasn't why I kept coming back. "The guys never pretend to be something they aren't, Vicky. You let me be blindsided by your world. And I thought we were best friends. Through thick and thin. I didn't think it was possible for anything to get between us."

"I was trying to protect you," she immediately insisted.

"I get that," I pressed. "I really do. But your betrayal cut deeper than anything they've ever done because I never expected you to hurt me like that."

Vicky wiped at her cheeks. I'd been so wrapped up in my own pain that I hadn't noticed the tears falling steadily down her face. "You were mine first." I watched as she picked at a piece of lint on her black pants. "I had nothing. No identity outside of the Civella name. No freedom. Every guy I dated was with me to get closer to my brothers. Every grade I earned at school was because the school administration feared Nicholas. Hell, even my parents weren't mine. They wanted sons to pass on the family name and run their empire. You know Nick was already looking at potentially marrying me off?"

I felt sorry for Vicky. I really did. I'd only been in this

life for six months, and the suffocating nature of it was killing me. I couldn't imagine what she was going through.

But still...

"We could have talked about it. You didn't have to go to Cora."

Vicky grabbed a napkin from our fast food lunch bag and loudly blew her nose. "I was sad and in this twisted state of fight-or-flight. I regret it."

Understanding where she was coming from helped me navigate the anger I felt toward her, but there was still something bothering me. "What about Anthony?" I asked.

"What about him?"

I let out a harsh breath. "You said a lot of hurtful things about him, Vicky. He loves you so much, and your betrayal made him spiral. You were close. Like twins."

She nodded. "I guess I wanted to push you away from him because I was jealous. It was an ego boost to know I could get through to him. I loved knowing Nick needed me to calm him down. It was the one thing I was good at. They didn't respect me otherwise. And I do care about him. It was a slap in the face to see how excited he was to see me. After everything I did, you know how he greeted me?"

"How?" I asked.

She choked out her answer on a sob. "He hugged me, Juliet. After everything. I told him I was sorry, and he said..." I could hear the emotions in her voice. Raw grief wrecked her throat. "He said he understood. He was just happy to have me in his life again. It was forgiveness I didn't deserve. I suppose if anyone is going to understand my temporary moment of insanity, it would be him."

My heart warmed for the man I loved, the friend I lost, and the future that felt both hopeful and uncertain all at once. Vicky's motives still felt uncertain to me. I couldn't tell if she was being genuine or if this was just another setup. It bothered me that I couldn't just read anyone at face value anymore. But I had to see where this was going. I had to get to Anthony.

I knew that if I wanted to move forward—if I wanted to work at getting our family to be whole again, we'd have to take a step toward grace to get there. "I will work on forgiving you, but I'll never forget what you tried to do," I promised. "And you need to work on accepting my relationships with your brothers."

Vicky nodded enthusiastically. "Yeah, I think I can do that. Is there a relationship, though? You haven't even tried calling them once."

She was probing for information, but I didn't know how to answer her. Anthony was gone. I'd drawn a line in the sand with Nick. William was giving me the silent treatment. It was heartbreaking and toxic, but I had a feeling we'd all find our way back to one another eventually.

"It's simple really," I mumbled, even though it was far from the truth. "I love them all. I just need them to love me back the way I deserve."

Vicky put the car in drive and merged back onto the highway. "Damn right you do. Give them hell, bestie."

chapter fifteen
anthony civella

Yellow curtains.

Bright. Warm. Tacky.

I wasn't sure how Vicky paid for this 1980s time capsule of a condo. But it overlooked the ocean, and if you didn't have a soul like mine, you probably would've enjoyed how vibrant and full of life the space was.

It made me itch. Fucking yellow curtains.

I stared at the clock. Be gentle, gentle, gentle, I reminded myself while tugging at my beanie. My rotting nerves were shot to hell. Juliet was near. I felt it in my bones. Nick and

William would storm this castle, slay the dragon, and take her back to their sharp tower.

Soon I'd be nothing but teeth and ash. A delicate crime scene, swept under the rug. Worm food. Dead man's company. Hell would be an eternity of hovering my soul over hers and knowing I caused this—I ruined us.

"Gentle, gentle, gentle," I whispered again.

I had rules now.

Don't be alone with Juliet.

Don't touch her.

Don't hurt her.

I found therapy at the bottom of harsh regret. I healed my mind because I had to. Weakness was no longer an option. My obsession with death was locked away in that tiny box again. I had to let out my abandonment issues so there was enough room, but luckily I found my sister in all of this, so my fear of being left alone again had a couch to sleep on and yellow curtains to stare at.

Soon. Juliet would be here soon.

Tired. Hurting.

Nick and William were about an hour outside of Miami. I gave it two hours before a convoy was parked outside Vicky's building.

Three hours before I was dead.

But we had no choice. We needed help.

The front doorknob twisted, and the tendons in my body went tight from anticipation. I inhaled and stared at the door until it slowly drifted open, creaking as it did.

"Anthony?" Juliet said, her sweet tone full of relief. I

braced myself for her brown eyes and—

"What the fuck happened to your face?" I growled while walking toward her. She reached up to stroke the leftover dried blood on her temple and flinched when I reached her.

"I could ask you the same question. You've got a ton of faded bruises, Anthony. Vicky knocked me out. I cleaned it, but…" I wrapped my hand around her wrist and tugged her toward the bathroom.

I had to get the blood off of her.

Heal her.

Help her.

Protect her from fucking everything.

Including me.

"Anthony, I'm fine," she cried out as I picked her up and placed her on the bathroom sink. The shudder that escaped her lips the moment she was in my arms made me hard as a rock, but I ignored the pounding need. I grabbed a washcloth, got it wet, and lightly dabbed at her wound, fixating on the things in my control while ignoring the tension between us.

"It's bruised," I said in a monotone voice. "Where is Vicky?" Hurting Juliet was not a part of the plan.

"She is parking the car at a public beach to lead Nick and William away for a bit and buy us some time," she replied.

I dropped the rag and took a step back. Then another step. Then my back hit the bathroom wall. "We can't be alone together." My shaky voice made the room feel smaller.

Juliet cocked her brow at me. "What do you mean?

Why can't we be alone together, Anthony?" I hated how she spoke to me like a wild animal. Shouldn't she be demanding answers? Shouldn't she be hating me for what I'd done?

Keeping my back against the wall, I inched as far away from her as possible, slinking down the hallway and into the living room. She followed after me, pressing, pressing, pressing. "What's wrong, Anthony?"

A bitter laugh escaped my lips. "Everything. Stay over there. You can't—"

"Can't what?"

"Can't be alone with you," I forced out before clenching my jaw so tightly that I was certain I'd crack all my teeth.

"Do you not trust yourself with me, Anthony?" Juliet asked while sauntering closer. "Or are you done with me?"

I held my hands up like a shield. I wanted to close my eyes so that I couldn't see the tears welling up in her big, beautiful eyes. "I can't hurt you anymore, Juliet."

She wrapped her arms around herself and nearly crumbled on the floor. "But you're hurting me, Anthony. I'm not okay when you're gone. You left without saying a word."

"I also choked you out. I...I fucked you. I'm not even sure if you wanted it or not." I was so disgusted with myself that I could barely breathe. I'd become what I hated. "And here you are. Looking at me with so much pity."

"So what if I pity you?" Juliet countered. "I've missed you so much. I had no idea where you were or if you were safe. You just left, and now you won't even..."

I stalked over to her, clenching my fists so tight that

174

my nails dug into my palm. "I need you to hate me," I whispered. "I need you to yell at me. Fear me. Hit me—"

She cut off my words by marching over and slapping me across the cheek. The echoing smack bit at my ears, and the stinging pain in my skin made me hiss. She shoved my chest. She clawed my neck. "Is this what you want, Anthony?"

She leaned forward to drag her sharp teeth against my neck before sucking hard on the skin there. "Fuck," I cursed, because this didn't feel like punishment. This felt like the hottest damn thing to ever happen to me. She cupped my cock and squeezed me over the sweats I was wearing.

"I'll punish you, if that's what you really want. But I'd much rather love you instead."

She was so warm. I could feel her vibrant pulse under her skin, thudding in time with her wild heart. She was alive and sizzling with energy. There wasn't a single bit of her that felt dead.

And I kind of hated it. That was the problem with me. Breathing was supposed to be the most natural thing in the world, but I couldn't do it without thinking of suffocating. Juliet was trying to resuscitate me with her blunt life.

"Wait," I begged. Jerking out of her grip, I took a moment and steadied my breathing. I couldn't fucking lose control like this. Losing control was what got me into this mess in the first place. "I ruined us," I choked out.

Juliet looked me up and down, her eyes soft. "Do you want to stay ruined, Anthony?"

She didn't deny that we were broken beyond repair.

But she offered a chance to rebuild.

"I can't," I whispered.

"No," Juliet said. "I've let you fuck me with a chill on my skin. I've buried bodies. I've waited. I've danced around your needs and never once complained. And it's not working, Anthony. So either you're going to feel alive with me or this relationship will die."

She surged forward like a fucking tidal wave, not giving me a moment to process her words—her ultimatum. She knew if given half the chance, I would run the fuck away. I was messed up in the head. I couldn't do this. I couldn't be what she—

She kissed me. Hot. Wet. I flattened my arms to my sides and pressed as hard as I could. She pulled at the waistband of my sweats and wrapped her hot hands around my cock while lavishing me with her dancing tongue. I tried to stay still. I really did. But she stroked me good, and I jerked in her palm. The moment a gasp escaped my lips, she deepened the kiss. Our open-mouthed fight for dominance slowly, slowly, slowly loosened every joint in my body.

I relaxed my hands and reached up to grab her hips. She pulled her hand out of my pants, and I moaned at the loss of contact. Locking her eyes on me, she lifted her palm and delicately licked it from wrist to the tip of her middle finger before continuing her work of stroking me.

My mind was a chaotic stream of consciousness I couldn't get a hold of.

And we were kissing and sucking and fucking with our tongues I couldn't fucking breathe it was so good and then she inched me to the yellow fucking wall I hated with its sunshine and brightness and then she shoved me into it and pressed her pulsing hot skin against mine as she ripped my clothes off ripped my mind open ripped my soul to shreds and hands on my neck and teeth in my lips breathe—she was breathing, breathing, breathing harsh little proofs of life against my ear moaning when I cupped her breast sighing when I tore the clothes from her body crying when I kissed her eyelids with tender apologies no no no it was a lot it was too much no no no I could feel my heart beating no no no she turned around and arched her back yes she did she pressed her ass against my bobbing cock she looked over her shoulder daring me to live.

I breathed.

In and out.

I calmed my mind.

Wait for it.

Wait for it.

Every muscle in my body released, like poison seeping from my pores.

"Fuck," I cursed before walking her over to the couch. "I love you, Juliet." I gently laid her down and got on top of her. I kissed her deeply. I slid inside of her slick pussy. In and out, in and out. Sex was a metaphor for life. I just wasn't smart enough or calm enough to make that connection right now.

"I'm so sorry," I sobbed while making love to her.

"I love you, Anthony. We can get through this. Please don't ever leave me again."

"I'm so sorry," I repeated as she ran her fingers through

my hair and stared into my eyes with such divine devotion.

Gentle, gentle, gentle. In and out. In and out.

I was going to do better. I was going to be better.

I was going to be worthy of this beautiful woman I didn't deserve.

chapter sixteen
juliet cross

"Soooo, we're just going to wait here for them to show up?" I asked while perched on Anthony's lap. Vicky was eating a cup of yogurt on the yellow couch opposite of me. I waited patiently for her answer as she licked the spoon. This felt strangely anticlimactic for the situation. After road-tripping for almost two days nonstop across the country from Kansas City to Miami, I'd expected the reunion to have a bit more drama. Anthony was rubbing little circles on my back with his thumb. He hadn't even bothered to put a shirt on. It was on the tip of my tongue to ask him to wear a bulletproof vest.

"I mean, at this point, it would be embarrassing if they didn't figure it out," Vicky said, her mouth full of yogurt. "Have you all lost your touch since I left?"

Anthony leaned forward and kissed my neck. "They'll be here soon," he murmured. "Nick can't go more than five minutes without seeing Juliet."

I chewed on my bottom lip. The truth was, Nick and William hadn't seen me much at all these last few weeks. There was a nagging insecurity in the back of my mind that worried they'd given up on me. Not that I would blame them. I gave them an ultimatum, and I had to stand by it.

"William probably wanted to shower and get his hair trimmed for their grand reunion," Vicky snorted. "Every week before meeting up at Dick's Diner, he would stop by the barber."

I smiled at her sisterly insults. "Do you remember his cologne phase?" Anthony asked while wrinkling his nose.

Vicky gagged. "The worst! We had to beg him not to bathe in that shit. But you have no room to talk, Anthony. When you were eleven, Nick had to hold you down and put deodorant on you. Why are teenage boys so disgusting?"

Anthony laughed while shaking his head. "I read online that women love the natural musk of a man."

Vicky pointed her spoon at him. "Hasn't anyone told you not to trust what you read on the internet? Thank fuck you grew out of that stage. Juliet might overlook a lot of shit with your crazy ass, but there's no way in hell she would have ignored that stench."

I smiled hard. Anthony laughed so much that his body shook. I'd never gotten to see how the siblings interacted with one another. Our friendship crashed and burned so fast that I missed an inside look at how they were before Vicky betrayed us all. It was nice to see that they had the potential to be normal. I wondered how they would be if the pressure of running their organization didn't sit heavily on their shoulders.

A buzzing sound drew my attention, and Vicky grinned gleefully while answering her cell. "Unknown number," she mouthed to us before speaking to whoever was on the other end of the line. "Hey there, big bro, thanks for playing the most epic scavenger hunt ever with me. Did you like the note I left in the rental car? I thought the code was a nice touch."

I pointed at the phone, wordlessly urging her to put it on speaker. She nodded and happily obliged.

"Vicky. If you hurt a single hair on her—"

"Yeah, I'm not really in the mood for threats," she boasted, interrupting Nick with ease. The nonchalant way she spoke to her brother reminded me of Anthony. "We haven't spoken in six whole months. What happened to 'Hello? How are you?'"

"I have a sniper with his eyes locked on you, Vicky. That's a nice shirt, by the way. It's a breath of fresh air to see you incorporating some color into your wardrobe."

I tried hopping off of Anthony's lap to duck on the ground, but he held me in place, his steady hands gripping my hips with ease. I looked at him as he whispered, "He's bluffing."

Vicky looked down at her yellow camisole and smirked. "Glad you're liking my new vibe, bro. I figured since I'm in Miami now, a little brightness in my life was needed. Why don't you come up here and we can chat. Since you have eyes on us, you know that Juliet is safe and sound. We just want to talk."

"We could have talked in Kansas City, Vicky. You're not exactly the most trustworthy member of our little family." His growl made me shiver.

She snorted. "That's rich coming from you." Vicky pulled out a vape pen and took a long drag, her eyes practically rolling in the back of her head as she did. "I wanted to meet you on my turf, big brother. I think it's good for you to be thrown off your game from time to time. You would have never let Anthony or me see Juliet otherwise."

Nick cursed. I couldn't tell which persona he was today. The murderous Mafia boss that killed first and asked questions later or the caring man that would go to the ends of the earth for me.

There was a long pause on the other end of the phone. Nick had weaponized silence. He knew just how long to let the quiet stretch to make his opponent uncomfortable. I had seen him do it during many interrogations over the last six months. He waited. And waited. As more seconds ticked by, Vicky grew more and more excited. The plump grin on her face grew, and she relaxed in her seat. It seemed that Nick had met his match.

"What do you want?" Nick asked. I found it strange that he broke first. "And don't you give me some bullshit that this is about a conversation. I know for a fact that you don't want a family reunion. So just blurt it out, and let's get this over with. I have dinner plans."

Vicky looked at her nails. Anthony ran his index finger down my arm, creating a chasm of goose bumps to erupt on my skin. I could feel his hot breath on my neck as we waited for Vicky to respond. It was strange to see her this way. She was completely in her element. I was used to Nick and William and Anthony taking charge in their own respective ways. However, Vicky was a storm of her own. She was raised in the same brutal way as her brothers and was more than capable of handling herself in this situation.

"I want a conversation. No guns. I'm sure you're hungry from all that traveling. I can make you a sandwich? Let's just have a little chat, and you can leave all your anger and bodyguards downstairs." She stood up and sauntered over to the refrigerator. "Do you like salami, brother? Of course you do."

Another voice cut through the line. I recognized it immediately as William. "Let's just talk to them," he said softly. I imagined Nick and William bickering like they always did over how to handle the situation. After squeezing Anthony's hand on my hip, I stood up and walked over to Vicky. She held out her cell phone to me, and I took it from her grip.

"Nick?" I called out, using his real name to appeal to his softer side. I didn't want a boss right now.

"Are you okay? I saw that you are bruised on the security camera footage at the gas station," he rushed out. "Do you need medical attention?"

I gave Vicky a stern look. Her eagerness to get me here was making negotiations a little more difficult to navigate. "I'm perfectly fine. Anthony is here. I'm safe. He wouldn't let anything happen to me." I locked eyes with him from across the room. It was important to me that Anthony heard me say this to his brothers. He needed to know that I trusted him with my safety, and I needed Nick and William to trust him, too. I was tired of this family breaking apart because of me. It was time for all of us to come back together.

"Juliet, I don't like this," Nick said in a deep, gravelly voice. There was a vulnerability in his tone that made me break.

"Do you trust me?" I asked. "Do you trust me to be in control of the situation, Nick?"

Trust and control. Those two concepts were draining our relationship dry. He struggled with it, but if we were ever going to be in a safe and happy relationship, he would have to take my lead sometimes.

"I trust you," he said softly. "It's the rest of the world I can't trust."

I understood that. For a long time, after my mother's disappearance, I struggled to trust, too. The whole world was my enemy. Everyone was a suspect. And the people I cared about became even more precious to me. Fear had me clutching those who I loved close to my chest. But it wasn't a way to live.

"Trust me. Come on, let's have dinner together. No men. No guns. No threats. You can be mad at Vicky for the way she handled this little meetup—"

Vicky snorted, interrupting my little speech. "So I have a flair for the dramatic," she said with the roll of her eyes.

I continued. "But we really do need to talk. All of us."

Nick bathed in the silence of my declaration. I could feel my heart racing. Unlike Vicky, I struggled with the empty space settling, simmering, boiling, burning between us. I ached for resolution and peace.

"Nick?" I was weak. He didn't answer. The line went dead, and I looked up at Vicky and was concerned. What did this mean?

It was Anthony who spoke, though. "Come sit with me," he asked in a loving tone. "You did great."

With slumped shoulders, I marched over to Anthony and crawled into his lap once more. Cradling my head against his chest, Anthony stroked my jaw and hummed for a brief moment.

"You did perfect," Vicky said with a smile. "They'll be here any minute now."

I resisted the urge to scoff. Nick couldn't even respond to me. Trust and control was the catalyst for our demise. When put on the spot, Nick refused to unclench his fist. "He's not coming. Should we hide? Where would we even go?"

Vicky put the finishing touches on her sandwich and took a big bite. "Anthony is pretty smart," she began before nodding in our direction. "Using you as a human shield? Brilliant."

Anthony's chest rumbled from the laughter caught in his throat. "I'm not using her as a shield."

"Right. Maybe she could sit in my lap next. I think between the two of us, Nick is more likely to kill me. Want to cuddle, Juliet?" I was not amused by Vicky's morbid joke. In fact, I was about to tell her how tasteless it was, but a gentle knock on the front door stopped me in my tracks.

Vicky straightened her spine and stared at the door. Despite her casual approach to this entire ordeal, she suddenly seemed nervous. With my ear pressed to Anthony's chest, I could hear how his pulse started to race. Vicky cleared her throat. "The door's open," she called out. Her unlocked apartment felt like a metaphor somehow. Vicky might've brought me here, but she was inviting healing into her life. Even if it was motivated by the desire of self-preservation, there was opportunity here to be better than what we were. There was opportunity to heal.

Slowly, the knob twisted, and I held my breath as William walked through the threshold.

I was surprised to see him here, even though I knew he was downstairs from what I heard over the phone. The last time I saw him, he drove off in a cloud of smoke, leaving me to obsess over what his silence meant. I thought we were over. And I hated that I couldn't figure out what his motivations were for being here. Was he following orders? Or did he—

William nearly crumbled onto the floor. His shaky legs

carried him over to me. Anthony, my intuitive man, eased me off his lap and gently nudged me closer to William. Strong arms wrapped around my body, and I felt safe and warm all at once. William kissed the soft skin on my neck.

The tenderness with which he held me close and peppered kisses along my exposed skin felt immaculate. He was so gentle with me, treating me like a treasure instead of like turmoil. And when he pulled away to lock his gaze on mine, I saw love in his eyes. It was powerful. "I was so worried," he choked out. It was as if the emotions were strangling him. I felt guilty for worrying him, but somehow, a darker part of me felt like we needed this. William was never going to appreciate the parts of me he had unless he feared losing me.

"I'm okay," I replied. "I promise."

William cupped my cheeks, leaned forward, and gently pressed his lips to mine. The scruff of his jaw raked against my soft skin. He tasted like cheap gas station coffee. I wrapped my arms around his neck and stroked the disheveled hairs on the back of his head. He lifted me up slightly. Our bodies were flush against one another, and I forgot where we were, what we were doing, and why this meeting was so important. It was only William. It was only me. It was every move of his mouth that I felt our relationship mending.

"Where is Nick?" Vicky interrupted. We separated, his kiss leaving me to feel dizzy and dazed as William tucked me into his side and wrapped his arm around my shoulders. We both turned to look at Vicky, who had her slender arms crossed over her chest and a look of impatience on her face. "Sorry to ruin the little reunion, but I really didn't want to puke in my kitchen. Seeing you kiss is like watching a dog walk on its hind legs." She shuddered like sisters do. "Wrong. So wrong. Where is Nick?" she asked again.

William looked around the room, pausing when his eyes landed on Anthony. I watched their silent standoff for a brief moment. What would they say? Nick was the one who sent Anthony away, but William didn't necessarily try to stop him. Anthony was a forgiving person by nature, but I still didn't know how to mend the bridge that was between them. Nick might've burned it to the ground, but William held the match. Anthony fanned the flames.

"Good to see you," Anthony said. He wasn't afraid to take a hit to his pride and speak first. It was one of the many things I loved about him.

Vicky huffed in annoyance.

William pulled me closer before responding. "Nick is downstairs. We had a bit of an argument. I decided to come up here, he decided he wants to kill us all—except Juliet, of course."

"Why is he such a drama queen?" Vicky asked in an exasperated tone. She slumped her shoulders and tore another bite out of her sandwich, chomping on it angrily while staring at us.

William twisted his neck to look at the bruise on my face. "You're the last person that should be calling anyone a drama queen, Vicky," William growled. "What is this?" he asked while pointing at the bruise. I blushed.

"We were outside Dick's Diner. I wasn't sure if there were any video cameras, so I had to make it look convincing, or you wouldn't have come."

"We want to be wherever Juliet is," William argued. "You could have flown her first class, and we would have walked to Miami if necessary."

His declaration was jarring, considering our last meeting.

"I didn't really have the means for that. Besides, you remember how much Juliet and I talked about taking a road trip after graduation. I wanted that time with her. And I have to be a bit secretive with my travels these days."

I chewed on the inside of my cheek.

"Why?" a chilling voice asked. Every muscle in my body tensed, and slowly, I turned to look at the front door. Nick was standing there, a gun in one hand and a balled up fist in the other. He was glaring around the brightly decorated room. "Juliet," he said in a commanding tone. "Come here right now."

Vicky rolled her eyes. "You get more flies with honey than vinegar," she said. I heard a slight shake to her words, though. She wasn't as icy as she tried to portray.

I pulled away from William slightly, and Nick must've thought I was moving to walk over to his side. His face broke out in a dark grin that made the severity of his expression take on a sinister tone. He looked like a villain who had won. "Why don't you put that gun away," I said.

The smile on his face was gone almost immediately. He lifted his arm and aimed the gun at Vicky. Time seemed to stop. My heart raced, and I quickly moved to stand in front of her. The betrayal on Nick's face crushed my spirit. "What are you doing?" he asked.

"Please," I begged. "Put the gun down."

Nick looked around the room with manic, jerky movements. I watched as he licked his bottom lip. "This is ridiculous," he said. I twitched, and he held out his free hand to me once more. "Come here and I won't hurt anyone."

I knew that he was lying. "Nick. We just need to talk. All of us. Vicky is in danger," I said. It wasn't exactly how I wanted to explain things to him, but I was currently staring down the barrel of a gun aimed at someone who just six months ago tried to have me killed.

"No shit she's in danger," he snapped. "She came back to Kansas City, she hurt you, brought you here, and now she wants to call the shots? We can't trust her, Juliet. The only person in this world you can trust is me."

I shook my head. "I trust you. But I also trust William. And Anthony." I looked around the room, sharing a tender look with both of them before turning back to Nick. "And I might not fully trust Vicky yet, but I believe her. Please just let us explain."

Nick scanned the room, as if assessing the odds in his mind. I knew that Anthony was unarmed. Vicky had a switchblade in her pocket, but no gun. William was probably packing, but I wasn't sure whose side he was on.

"You have five minutes."

My eyes widened. "Five minutes is all I need," Vicky replied smugly.

chapter seventeen
nick civella

Vicky was a motherfucking liar. Anthony was a dead man. William was about as useful as wet tissue paper, and my ass? My pathetic ass was pussy-whipped.

Cora's cannibalistic brother was supposedly hunting Vicky down. Boo-hoo. Maybe she shouldn't have been working with the psychopath in the first place. The way I saw it, this was karma working in my favor.

"So what are we going to do?" William asked.

They all looked at me. This was the fucking problem with our family. No one wanted to listen unless it was on their terms. They only submitted to me if it was to save their own ass. No one wanted to be the bad guy. No one wanted to get their hands dirty.

I looked at Juliet, who was sitting quietly on the couch beside William. This entire situation pissed me right the fuck off. She should be sitting beside me. As we drove to the airport. While this entire building burned to the ground.

"I'm not doing anything," I replied, albeit a bit smugly.

Maybe they'd start appreciating me more if I stopped dropping every goddamn thing to help. I was tired. I just spent the last twenty-five hours driving to fucking Miami of all places in search of a girl that wasn't even in trouble. I wanted to take the jet, but William said we'd have a better chance of spotting them on the road if we caravanned. If I never saw another eighteen wheeler, that would be fine with me.

Granted, I was thankful that Juliet was safe, aside from the nasty bruise on the side of her face—Vicky would be paying for that—but this was ridiculous. The only reason I wasn't madder at Juliet was because I practically pushed her into this little stunt. She was here because of Anthony. She told us she'd do anything to get him back, and I should have believed her. I challenged her to get out of Kansas City and find him, and she used the first scapegoat she could find to get here. But she didn't honestly expect me to stay, did she? Vicky was using Anthony to get to Juliet and by extension, me. I didn't trust my sister one bit.

"What do you mean you're not doing anything?" Juliet asked. She overestimated my protective instincts. When I kicked Vicky out of our family, I was done. My family tree was poisoned. Vicky burned her bridges, and now she had to paddle her own damn boat.

"Are you not listening? Cora's brother is insane," Juliet pressed.

I arched a brow at her. "You say he likes blood? I'll send him a bottle of perfectly aged O-negative for saving me the trouble of killing Cora. The enemy of my enemy is not someone I really want to piss off. Maybe Vicky should've thought of that before she started working with them."

"You don't remember, do you?" Vicky asked while squinting at me.

"Remember what?"

"You shot him. Five times, to be exact."

"I shoot a lot of people."

Vicky's leg started to bounce up and down, a signature move that let me know she was freaking the fuck out. "He sent me letters. Flowers. I got a box with a severed pinky finger before coming here."

I frowned. "You always said you wanted a man that would lavish you with gifts. Just because they're handmade doesn't mean they aren't just as special," I snapped back sarcastically.

"You're an asshole," Vicky gritted.

There was a tiny part of me—a very minuscule speck in my soul—that felt sorry for Vicky. It was like muscle memory. After vowing to take care of her, it was hard to separate that lingering responsibility in my soul. Luckily, I was good at ignoring guilt. You couldn't get to the top of this food chain otherwise.

"It's not just Vicky. He's killing others," Anthony said.

I looked over at Anthony and had to force myself not to lunge for his neck and squeeze until his head popped off and rolled across the living room floor. "Are you seriously trying to tell me that you suddenly care about the value of human life?" I asked incredulously before throwing my hands up into the air. "You? You of all people are sitting here telling me that he is a threat to society? Have you looked in a mirror lately?"

"We have to stop him." Juliet had a beautiful scowl on her kissable mouth. I wanted nothing more than to angry fuck some sense into her.

"We're not the police. Last I checked, we're the bad guys. I don't care about random victims in Miami of all places. He's not on our turf, so he's not our problem. Let the cartel deal with him."

Juliet shook her head, and I saw a tear well up in her eyes. Fuck. That single, bleeding emotion was my one weakness in this world. I could handle pretty much anything except seeing my girl cry. I softened my tone some, even though I was still pretty pissed off. "Juliet, let's go home. I will even grant Anthony and Vicky temporary asylum in Kansas City if it means we can get out of this humid shithole."

Anthony rolled his eyes. At least he was acting normal these days. Vicky did always have that effect on him. If Juliet was fucking determined to keep the psycho around, then I probably needed to keep Vicky too, just so I had someone else to make sure he didn't go off the fucking deep end again. "I don't want to go back to Kansas City," Vicky interrupted. "I actually like it here."

She was always looking for an argument. She never wanted to take the easy solution, even when I was being generous and helpful. "You either stay here and die or come home and live. I'm not arguing with you, I'm not helping you. This is not my problem. You're lucky you are alive. In fact, both you and Anthony should be looking at Juliet and kissing her goddamn feet. Because if she didn't care about either of you, you would both be six feet underground."

It wasn't like me to admit my weaknesses to everyone, but I let the truth spill from me in a moment of anger. Alongside Juliet, William looked smug. Of course he got off on knowing that I was a weak bastard.

"I care about the victims here, Nick," she said quietly. Hearing my true name on Juliet's lips made me want to shove her against the wall and taste those syllables on her tongue. "We need to do something."

I sensed that there was a hidden struggle at war in her soul. Juliet had empathy for the victims of criminals. Which made our relationship morbidly ironic. When she heard about someone dying, she didn't see a stranger, she saw her mother. No matter how much she healed from that, it was impossible for her to move on. She had no closure. No body. No answers. Just a missing person. It was devastating, and in moments like this, I wish I could go back in time and kill whoever twisted her thoughts up like this.

"It's not our place," I said softly.

Juliet, who seemed to want to pick her battles, pinned

her mouth shut and crossed her arms over her chest. She had already won. I was going to let Anthony come back home with us, and the door was open for Vicky. She knew that if she pressed me any further, I would lash out at the two things she wanted most right now.

"Well, I'm just so happy that I drove all the fucking way here to have this meaningless discussion," I said before clapping my hands together. I didn't like being far away from my kingdom. I had too many enemies eager to take over, and having everyone here was an opportunity I never wanted to create. Maybe that was Vicky's plan all along.

"I'm going to talk to my men and get a private plane out of here within the next couple of hours. If everyone could refrain from doing anything stupid for that short amount of time, that would be greatly appreciated."

Juliet sighed deeply and rubbed at her brow with the tips of her fingers. This was far from over. I had plans to take her back to my house—where she belonged—and spank her. Then, make her come so hard she passed out. And then wake her up just so she could swallow my anger once more.

I nodded at William, mostly because he was the only person in this room that I at least had a fraction of trust in. He wouldn't let Juliet out of his sight for even a moment.

Vicky's condo building was old and a health hazard. Mold was growing in the stairway, and there were some pretty shady characters living next door to her. It wasn't exactly what I envisioned for my sister, and I had to resist the urge to ignore her wishes and pluck her from this place and put her somewhere safer. Which was a strange compulsion, considering we were both threatening to murder one another just a few months ago. Blood was thicker than water and stronger than resentment, I suppose.

I headed out to the parking lot to see Luca but stopped in my tracks when I noticed a man standing under a streetlamp, clutching a box with a bright red bow. He had this shady way about him that made me cock my brow. I was a couple of yards away from my guards, but I turned my attention fully to this strange man. He had dark hair, wore dark clothes, and had this shifty look about him. He kept twisting his neck from side to side, looking around the parking lot for something.

My instincts were screaming at me. Something was wrong with this man. He was shaking hard and clutching the box in his hand like it was a lifeline.

His cheeks were wet with tears, and at first glance, I thought he was a tweaker.

But no, he was distressed.

He hadn't noticed me staring yet, but he pulled his phone out and frantically dialed a number. "Sir, her car isn't here." The weak fucker had a trembling voice and nearly dropped the box in his arms as he spoke. I knew fear when I saw it. Hell, I caused fear. I was the product of many nightmares. "There's people watching. I don't feel comfortable—"

The guy sobbed harder. Whoever was on the other line was scaring the fuck out of him. "Please don't hurt her," he begged.

I couldn't help but be curious. Knowing everything was another lesson my father taught me. He said I should never be ashamed of seeking answers, because the more I knew, the more powerful I was. Miami and all its bullshit was really none of my business, but my gut was telling me to go talk to the guy.

I pulled my gun from my holster and slowly made my way over to him. The night sky veiled me in darkness, but my men were attuned to me. They went from leaning against the car to straightening their spine and following my move. I held up a hand, silently warning them to stay back. My victim was so consumed with his phone call that he hadn't even noticed that I was approaching.

"Please. Let her go."

The pleading made me smile. A wise man would never beg. The more you show your hand, the easier it is for your enemies to destroy you. He dropped his cell phone and fell to his knees in a fit of sobbing. The box landed beside him on the concrete as I walked up. "Is there a problem?" I asked while looking down at him. He smelled like he hadn't showered in a couple of days, and despite living close to the beach, he was pale as a ghost, as if all the blood had drained from his body.

"We have to save her. We have to save her." The man was rambling on about something, but this box was what had my attention. A certain stench in the air—a smell I was familiar with but couldn't quite place at the moment.

Slowly, I crouched down while the man completely

broke into shattering sobs. He was so distraught he didn't even look at me—didn't even acknowledge my presence. It was strange to be ignored so. I was the sort of man to strike terror in others, but whatever had him by the balls was far scarier than me.

I slowly removed the blood red ribbon from the box before lifting the lid. I was suddenly slapped in the face by the smell of rotting meat and fermented fruit. It was a sweet, decomposing, sour stench. I wanted to gag. The man stopped crying and stared at me. "You don't want to know what's in there," he cried out.

I continued to lift the lid, and what I saw made my stomach curdle. In the box were strips of skin pinned to an elegant square of card stock and cloth. The skin was varying shades, and had been carved into a script font.

Vicky, it read.

A fly swarmed the elegant but gruesome gift and started crawling along the cursive letters. The skin was hard, like it had been preserved somehow, but it was painfully identifiable.

I dropped the lid and shot up. The man had resumed crying and rocking. "Who gave this to you?" I growled. Was this some sort of trick? My first instinct was to think that this was Vicky trying to convince me to go on whatever wild chase this was. But not even she would do something this disgusting.

Despite my angry tone, the man didn't even flinch. I reached for the collar of his shirt and jerked him into a standing position. "Tell me who sent you," I demanded.

His body went slack in defeat as he looked up at me with bloodshot eyes. His lips were chapped, and he had this hopeless expression on his face that I knew well. It was the look of a man who had completely given up.

"The devil," he mumbled incoherently. I shook him with all my might.

"Tell me," I demanded again.

More tears streamed down his face, and snot dripped from his nose, landing on his upper lip. Up close, I could see the dark circles under his eyes. He had dirt on his skin, and his shirt was wrinkled. There was enough grease in his hair to fry chicken. "He's gonna eat her," he said. "He already took her hand."

I felt my guards stand behind me. They were on alert, ready to take this guy down—even though they weren't sure what was going on. "Who is he going to eat?" I asked. It felt like a foolish question, something I never imagined would come out of my mouth.

"My wife," he sobbed. The crack in his voice was full of gutted emotion. "He has my wife. I was supposed to follow this lady named Vicky. I was supposed to deliver this present. But I couldn't find her car," he rambled. "I'm just an English teacher. I'm not a private investigator."

Shit. "Tell me where he is," I demanded.

"I-I don't know. I only see him on that phone."

I dropped the idiot and didn't flinch when he crumbled once more to the concrete. One of my men picked up the cell phone and handed it to me. Naturally, the screen was cracked. Fucking useless. If anyone had Juliet, you wouldn't catch me dead sobbing on the concrete. How could this man say he loved his wife but still give up so easily?

A new message came through, and I opened it. There was a single image. The composition was meant to shock someone, but my heart rate didn't even increase. I was numb to destruction and death. "Your wife is dead," I said in a bored tone. In the photo, her lifeless body was on a table, and her left breast had been severed, leaving a meaty hole in its wake. Her smooth skin was butchered and raw. Fresh warm blood covered every inch of her body. Whoever this person was, they were sloppy and cocky. I wouldn't be caught dead with photographic evidence of my kill.

The man let out another defeated cry as he looked up at the dark night sky, crying to the heavens with both his hands balled into angry fists. I couldn't even force myself to feel sympathy for him. There was no pity in my gaze. He was weak. He wasn't strong enough to protect those that he loved. It was survival of the ruthless.

"Let me see," he begged. I shrugged. A kinder man probably would've hid the graphic image from him, but hiding from reality never did anyone any good.

I held up the phone, and he looked at it through bleary eyes. "Baby," he croaked. If it was possible to die from grief, he would've left this world right then and there. He was horrified. Stunned. I'm sure it was something that would haunt him until the end of his days. Good.

I quickly pocketed the phone and turned to look at Luca. "Bring him to a secure location. I would like to ask him a few questions."

Luca looked conflicted but obediently nodded. "Are we staying in Miami for a while, boss?" he asked.

I pulled a joint from my pocket and a lighter. He waited on my answer as I lit up and took a slow drag. Letting the smoke and high fill my lungs, I debated on my answer for a good minute.

"We'll be staying here for a couple of days."

chapter eighteen
william civella

It was shocking to me how efficient and organized my brother could be when it suited him. He'd let bills and bank statements pile up in a stack on his desk, but when it came to torturing a man, he had secured a warehouse within the hour and had already pulled every single nail from his fingers.

I didn't want to be standing in this humid warehouse, listening to blood-curdling screams while watching my brother get off on ripping an innocent man to shreds. I wasn't sure he was doing this to help Vicky. I think he just had a lot of pent up anger saved in his soul, and this man was the perfect victim to unleash it on.

"Please. I don't know where he is," the man cried out. Nick was truly in his element, slapping his palm with the head of a hammer as he looked down his nose at the man.

"You loved this woman, and you let her get hurt," Nick sneered. It didn't take a therapist to recognize that my brother was projecting. "If you were a man, you'd tell me where he is so you can at least die knowing you avenged her death."

"I don't know," he sobbed. Nick reared back and slammed the hammer against the sobbing man's kneecaps. A shattering sort of cracking sound made bile travel up my throat. His screams filled the empty warehouse, and one of our men flinched from the brutality of it. This was only the beginning. Nick knew how to draw out the torture. He'd make him suffer but keep him alive until every bit of hope was drained from his body.

The man screamed until his throat was raw. Gnats kissed my skin, and I swatted at them while watching the spectacle.

"Coward," Nick growled. "Nothing but a fucking coward."

I checked my watch. We weren't getting anywhere with this. It was obvious this man had already given us whatever information he had. Nick just needed someone to beat the shit out of.

"I'm heading out," I replied in a bored tone.

Nick, with his sleeves rolled up and his wild eyes practically glowing in the dim night, spun on his heels to stare at me. "We are not done here," he growled. "I still have information I need to get."

I looked at the pathetic mess of a man in a crumpled heap on the floor and arched my brow. "He doesn't know shit. His wife was taken from a nightclub called Space. My time would be better spent looking at their security footage."

"Your time is best spent wherever I tell you to be," Nick growled. He didn't like when I had better ideas. And right now, he was knee-deep in his bullshit.

I was over this. I wanted to figure this out so I could go back to Juliet. I didn't like that she was at Vicky's place with Anthony. Even though Nick had set up a few guards at her place, it wasn't ideal. "So you want me to just stand here and watch you kill this man instead of actually being productive? I just want to make sure I understand correctly."

My reasoning made his lip twitch in anger. The glow of the single overhead light gave him a menacing look.

"Do you remember the first time our father brought us into an interrogation room?" Nick asked. I had a visceral reaction to his question. My stomach dropped and a wave of sweat broke through my pores. I had to swallow my nerves as Nick continued. "Of course you remember. How could you forget?"

Nick slowly walked over to me. "What's your point?" I asked gruffly.

"You were so weak. Dad wanted you to break his finger, but you couldn't do it." He stood toe to toe with me, a splatter of blood on his face and the soundtrack of his moaning victim in the background. "Didn't you cry?"

I tilted my chin up. I was fucking seven years old. Unlike Nick, evil wasn't this innate thing in my psyche. I was just a normal kid who wanted to play video games. When Dad handed me the hammer, I wanted to puke. It felt wrong.

Looking back, I realize it was a defining moment in my childhood. It was then that my father realized I wasn't cut out for this job. It was then that I officially became the weakest link—the disappointment. That same night, Nick killed his first traitor, and he'd had a permanent stain of blood on his hands ever since.

"I think this could be a redeeming moment for you, William," Nick said with a smirk. "Why don't you finish him off for me?"

I rolled my eyes as Nick held out the hammer for me to take. "I've killed and tortured plenty of men over the years. I have nothing to prove to you."

Nick pressed the metal edge of the hammer against my cheek while leaning closer. "You need to prove your worth with every breath you take, brother."

Rage like a tidal wave built up in my chest. Hadn't I already proven myself? I'd been silently running things behind the scenes without recognition. I'd built up our club. I'd even shared the woman I loved. Killing this man meant nothing.

For a moment, I fantasized over the idea of grabbing the hammer and bashing Nick's skull in. He was the source of all my problems. Life would be significantly easier if he were gone. I was no longer the seven-year-old disappointment. Even though I couldn't shake my father's scowl from my mind, I could erase my brother's smugness.

I took the hammer and kept my face void of all emotion. It was just another kill. Just another scream. Another broken bone. Another body for Anthony to bury.

I couldn't help but feel small in that moment. All eyes were on me, and my wandering mind felt the presence of my father in that warehouse. I could almost imagine him standing in the corner, frowning in disapproval at me.

"Come on, William. I had my first kill at your age."

"He's a traitor. Civella men don't let traitors live."

"Don't you fucking cry, William."

As I dragged my feet across the concrete ground, my suit started to feel too big. My shoulders slumped. I breathed in, the smell of piss like a slap to the face.

The victim was rocking on the ground, holding his thigh and sobbing from the pain. Pretty soon he'd pass out. I kind of wished he would. This sort of pain was unnecessary.

"Please don't hurt me," he cried out.

I glanced over my shoulder at my brother, who was rubbing his hands together with glee. He was so fucked up in the head. For so long, I wanted his life—his privilege and approval. But I learned the hard way that there wasn't just one bloody road to the top. I was smarter. Worked harder.

I crouched down to look him in the eye. There was a cut along his eyebrow. The open wound sent a steady flow of blood down his face. He wiped at it with the back of his grimy hand and whimpered.

"Why your wife?" I asked. "He could have taken anyone, why did he take your wife?"

Another sob broke through his cracked lips. "I-I don't know. Coraline did nothing wrong. She was innocent."

Coraline? That name was too much of a coincidence. "Coraline was her name?" I asked while tilting my head to the side. Maybe I could relate to this brother. Maybe he hated his sibling as much as I did.

"He kept calling her Cora," the man cried out. "I don't get it. Why would he hurt her? She was so kind and generous. Was going to college for social work." He sniffled. The poor woman's only crime was to share a name with a criminal. This psychopath didn't see her—he was triggered by her name.

The right thing to do would be to put him out of his misery. A swift death. I wasn't like my brother. I was just a man with a grudge. I dropped the hammer to the floor, and it echoed around me. Nick immediately shouted, "You coward! You can't even—"

The sound of my gun going off stopped him in his tracks. I aimed. Shot. And fired. The bullet hit him right between the eyes, and the man died efficiently. Time was money—a luxury. I didn't need to torture this poor idiot to prove myself. I needed to figure out who was after Vicky and prove myself to Juliet.

I looked at one of the men. "Clean it up. See if Anthony wants to do the pleasure of burying him." I wanted to test our younger brother with the temptation of a dead body to see how he handled it. It would help me decide the level of caution required moving forward.

"Yes, boss," Gerald, one of my men, said.

"I call the shots around here," Nick interrupted while holding his arm up. "Stay right where you are."

Gerald looked at me, as if waiting for me to give him permission to follow my directions anyway. I was tired of leading in the shadows. "Get it done," I told him before walking over to my brother and wrapping the murder weapon in a handkerchief.

"I wasn't finished with him," Nick seethed.

"But I was. Unlike you, I actually want to find this guy and move on. I'm not here to play games, Nick. Dad picked you to lead our organization. But if he were still alive today, he'd see that it's me that gets shit done."

I thrust the murder weapon into his hands before shoulder-checking him on my way out of the door.

—

Vicky's apartment was small. Her bathroom was tiny and decorated with neon pink accents everywhere. I had to use her apple crisp shower gel but was happy to clean the blood off of my skin. When I exited the bathroom, clutching a towel around my waist, I was greeted by Juliet in the hallway.

"Can we talk?" she asked in a shaky voice before looking up and down the hall. I nodded, and she pushed me back into the steamy bathroom before shoving the door shut behind us.

"What happened out there?" she asked. Stupid me for thinking she wanted to talk about our relationship. She was just curious what I did with Nick. "Are you okay? You came home covered in blood, and your eyes..."

She reached up to run her knuckles along my cheek bones. Even though we'd spent the last two weeks distant and fighting, she saw the pain in my expression and reached out to soothe it. This woman. This fucking salt of the earth.

"I'm fine. Nick is out looking for answers. We're going to stay here a couple of days until we can get this sorted out. After I've gotten some rest, we can look for a hotel with more room for all of us, but right now I just want to crash on the couch."

Juliet grinned. "I knew Nick would stick around."

Her faith in him seriously pissed me off. "Nick isn't staying because he gives a shit about Vicky or Anthony."

She looked up at me with gentle eyes. "I think he cares more than he lets on. I think you care, too."

I looked down at where her nimble fingers rested on my chest. "Of course I care. Unlike my brother, I don't pretend otherwise. I send Vicky money—it's not much, but every month she gets an anonymous check deposited into her account. Before Anthony lost his fucking mind and hurt you, I brought him bodies. And if you would have loved me back, I would have given you the world."

Juliet reached up and grabbed me by the chin, forcing me to look her in the eye. And fuck, what a determined, beautiful stare she had. "I loved you back. I still do, you know."

"You also loved them," I countered, once more feeling like that little kid who was never good enough—was never chosen.

"It doesn't change the fact that I love you, William. You've been my silent stranger. I feel safe with you. I feel like I can be my most authentic self when I'm in your presence. I know that what I'm asking you is selfish," she said, her voice starting to crack. "You've had to share everything you've been given with your family. And I'm not sure I'm enough."

She was enough for me. She was more than enough.

Being without her sure as fuck made me think I'd go to hell and back for her. I'd put up with my idiot brothers for her, too. But I couldn't be second string. I couldn't let this relationship be one more thing that my brother controlled. I was done letting him run my life. In fact, more and more, I was feeling like maybe it was my turn to be in charge.

"I love you," I whispered. The declaration was painful to say, but still glaringly true.

"I love you too," she said back before lifting up on her toes and kissing me deeply. Her tight little pajamas left most of her skin exposed, and when she crushed her skin to mine, I gasped at the soft contact.

This didn't feel like a makeup moment. When we kissed, I wasn't overwhelmed with clarity. It didn't feel right, but it didn't feel wrong either. I just knew that I loved her, and she loved me. And Anthony. And Nick.

Maybe I was never meant to wrap my head around it. Maybe I was supposed to keep fighting—keep working to steal her for myself.

My towel dropped to the floor, and she hooked her fingers behind her silky shorts and jerked them down. I pulled at the hem of her shirt and yanked it over her shoulders. Frantic. Far from romantic. Every move she made was like trying to prove something. She was too eager. Too responsive. She was desperate to get me back.

But I was too tired to call her out on her shit. If she had something to prove, I'd let her work my body with hers. I'd selfishly eat up her guilt and determination, because at the end of the day, I couldn't resist.

She switched positions.

She hopped up on the bathroom counter.

She parted her thighs, lined me up at her entrance and tossed her head back when I slammed inside her tight, wet pussy.

"Yes," she hissed. I couldn't help but wonder if she was really here with me or imagining someone else.

I gave her a raunchy, open-mouthed kiss. Our tongues danced. "Open your eyes," I demanded.

She pried open her hooded lids.

"Take it all, Miss Cross."

This wasn't a romantic fuck. She was used to pearls, satin sheets, four-poster beds. Champagne. Chocolate-covered strawberries.

I slammed in and out. My calculated movements were as efficient as the murder I'd committed earlier. I knew where to hit to make her come hard on my cock. I knew how to touch her. I knew that when I grunted, gasped, and moaned, it made her pulse race. She loved the sounds I made.

Thankfully, she didn't declare her undying love for me again. I didn't want to cheapen the moment with the reality that I only got a third of her heart. She left me. She wanted them.

Just break his finger, William.

It's not that hard.

If you want to be a Civella, you need to suck it up.

Why can't you be more like your brother?

She gripped my back, digging her long nails into my heated skin. She clawed at me, like I was the only thing holding her in place. "Yes, yes, yes," she cried out as she creamed my cock. She tossed her head back, rode the wave of bliss, and I felt myself finally growing soft. There was no pleasure in this. My mind couldn't fucking do it.

I pulled out and bent over to pick up my towel, wrapping it around my waist as she straightened to look at me. "Are you..." She didn't bother finishing the embarrassing question. I didn't come. I didn't get off.

"I'm tired," I said. "Going to go sleep on the couch. Try to get some rest."

She reached for my arm as I tried to turn away. "I'll sleep with you. We can cuddle?"

"I need to sleep if I'm going to find this guy. I've been driving all day..." Chasing after you, I wanted to add. I was always chasing after her.

"Oh," she replied, deflated. "Okay. Get some rest."

I nodded and almost left, but because I felt like an

asshole, I paused to kiss her on the cheek. I really did love this woman. I just needed to figure my brain out and take control of my life. I needed to get rid of the competition.

"Good night, Miss Cross," I whispered.

"Good night," she replied.

And as I left, I pretended not to see the tears in her eyes.

chapter nineteen
nick civella

I found the nightclub to be loud and classless. I bet they let *anyone* into this little hellhole. These idiots didn't even charge a cover, not that their clientele could afford it.

Usually, it was William who stuck his nose up at the lower classes, but as some of the greasy college kids tripped over themselves to do coke in the bathroom, I realized that I had become a snob. People were disgusting. I would much rather be at Eden's Place, watching the talent fuck while caressing Juliet's upper thigh as she sat on my lap.

"What can I get you to drink?" the bartender screamed at me. Yes, screamed. Because this music was so fucking loud that the only way I could hear him was if he tore at his vocal chords.

"Tequila and lime," I replied. Not my usual drink of choice, but I was doing things differently tonight. The party was in full swing, I had blood on my hands, and I told my guards to stay in the parking lot. I needed time to myself, time to think, time to process. Time to drink and curse my family for being so fucking pathetic. William was like the hard punch of sobriety after a long night out. He had real solutions, and I just had this fucking anger.

So I came here, asked for the footage, and tried not to puke from the smell of cheap perfume, vomit, and alcohol. Sex was in the air. Clingy, disgusting, desperate sex.

Did I mention how much I hated this club?

At least I had a couple of drinks flowing through my veins to make it bearable. I was buzzed and didn't give a fuck today.

I just needed the manager—who accepted a wad of cash—to bring me the footage so I could get the fuck out of here and find Cora's cannibal brother. We didn't even have a fucking name for the asshole. How scary could he be if he was nameless? I'd been racking my brain, trying to remember the guy I shot five times a few years ago. I was surprised he survived. Must be a determined asshole to pull himself up and out of hell like that. No wonder he was a fucking psycho.

A towering man walked up to the bar and stood beside

me, brushing his arm against mine. I sneered and pulled away from him. Everyone in this fucking club wanted to invade my space. I hated it. If I were smart, I'd go home and fuck my girl and try to figure out how the hell to be worthy of her.

The man beside me didn't have to order. The bartender took one look at him, then poured him a glass of fucking milk. Yeah. That was weird. My psycho senses were tingling. Didn't even have to really observe him to know something was off. I turned to stare at him just as he took a gulp of his drink. He had tan skin, bloodshot eyes, and two thick eyebrows like seventies pubes on his face. He looked familiar, in a strange way. His beady eyes swept across the bar, and I wasn't sure if it was the club or his clothes clinging to a sickly rotten smell.

He then faced me head-on, a challenge in his brown eyes as he reached into the inner pocket of his leather jacket. I resisted the urge to grab him by the back of the neck and knee him in the chin. I wanted to ask this asshole what the fuck he was looking at, but the music was so loud that I'd have to scream and probably repeat myself. Silence was the better option.

The mood was tense all around us even though some bubbly pop song roared through the club speakers. Half-dressed women danced all over each other, but he sipped his milk like a psycho. And when he lowered his glass, a white mustache was left behind that he wiped with the back of his hand. I wanted to ask who he was. Why he was staring at me. If we were on my turf, I would have already had him dragged out of here and beaten within an inch of his life for looking at me in that lingering way. But the music was loud. The room was crowded. I didn't have the cops in my pocket.

He pulled a plastic bag from the inside of his jacket while smiling at me. So he was a druggie. Typical. I stared at it, wondering what his drug of choice was. He seemed like the type to snort bath salts. It wasn't until I saw a green finger with a perfectly painted nail in the shade of ruby red, that I realized what was happening.

He smiled and smiled, slowly revealing sharp teeth and chapped lips as he pulled the finger from its plastic grave and dipped it into the milk. The white milk became cloudy from the rancid invasion.

I felt the sudden urge to puke.

This man was Cora's brother. This man was the cannibal. He was right in front of me, balls to the wall dipping a finger in his milk like it was a delicate bag of tea.

Strobe lights illuminated his face. A million words were stuck on my tongue. With him standing right here, I felt a wave of familiarity wash over me. It was obvious that he was related to Cora. He had the same determined look in his eye that I loathed. A memory flashed across my mind, and I thought back to the night I shot him. It was one of those impulsive kills. I wanted Cora to pay. I wanted her to suffer like I was.

It pissed me off that he survived and had become this disgusting *thing* that killed and consumed people.

But this was good. I could kill him. I could end this and

go back to my life. I just needed to get him out of this club and somewhere I could shove a knife through his eyeball.

He sucked on the finger, removing every single drop of milk from the rotten skin with his nasty mouth. It felt like a cocky invitation of sorts. He wanted me to know who he was. It was fucked up, but he probed his mouth with that thing like it was a dick and he was trying to make the severed finger come. His tongue swirled around the pad of it, and even though I couldn't hear him over the music, I was almost certain that he was moaning. The sight was grotesque and erotic. I wasn't disturbed by much, but this man had my stomach rolling. I regretted the drinks I'd had.

He then leaned closer to me, his rancid breath washing over my skin like pollution. One second. Two seconds. It took all the restraint I possessed not to shoot him right here and now. He stared at my mouth. My neck. My whiskey glass.

He then plopped the finger in my drink before straightening. I refused to be disgusted. I wasn't afraid of sickos. My brother loved the dead. But there was something unhinged about this guy. I wasn't sure if it was his complete disregard for my power that confirmed his insanity, or the bodies he liked to munch on.

Either way, he needed to learn a lesson.

Everyone needed to learn a lesson.

I was not someone you could fuck with.

Maybe I was projecting my issues, as William claimed, but this motherfucker challenging me was the last straw.

He spun on his New Balance sneakers and started

walking through the crowd toward the back exit. Naturally, I followed after him. That's what he wanted, after all. I was more than happy to show him who the fuck he was messing with. I never got the chance to kill Cora, but I'd end her bloodline like she tried to end mine.

We cut through a back hallway, him keeping a steady pace as he walked, and me shoving through the crowd to keep up with him. It wasn't until we got outside, where the humid Miami air was huffing down my neck, that I spoke.

"So you're Cora's brother, hmm? Does her killer have a name? I'd like to know who to thank for getting rid of her."

The light overhead flickered, a rat scurried across the pavement toward a pile of rotten trash. The man turned to face me.

His leather jacket was tight on his body. He wore white-wash jeans and had a tattoo on his hand that looked like an anatomical heart. His voice was smooth, clear, and of a slightly higher pitch than mine. "My friends call me Norman."

I frowned. "We're not friends."

His long fingers twitched at his side. "No, I suppose not. I guess if anything, we're enemies. You almost killed me."

I wasn't fazed. "You deserved it," I countered.

Norman slowly tilted his head to the side. "Death is a freeing experience. Believe it or not, I'm thankful for you, Nick. My idiot sister saw the Civella family as competition, but I think you could be my savior."

I rolled my shoulders back, trying to get information while looking equally calm and intimidating. He might have been completely off his rocker and talking in circles, but this motherfucker would be easy to take down. "So you think Cora's a cunt, too? Glad we're on the same page." I swayed a bit on the concrete. Fuck, I needed a nap.

His lips curled. Ah. His sister was a sore subject. I made a mental note of that. "My sister locked me up," he growled. "She wanted so badly to have power, but she was really an amateur. I'm surprised she almost pulled one over on you."

So maybe the guy wasn't all bad. At least he recognized that his sister was a fraud. "She had help," I replied.

"Vicky," he hissed while rolling his eyes back. I was worried he'd pop a boner right then and there from just saying my sister's name. Disgusting. "Did she like my gift?"

I clenched my jaw, forcing my mind to calm down before responding. "I'll be honest, Norman. Your gift-giving needs some work. Didn't Cora teach you how to woo a woman?"

Once again, at the mention of his sister, Norman's face twisted into rage. I catalogued his weakness in my mind. "She didn't really teach me anything. Just locked me up when I started developing a certain palate for death. I was all alone. Chained like an animal. Starving."

I couldn't even blame Cora for her actions. There were plenty of times where I saw Anthony inching toward the deep end, and I debated on locking him in his little dungeon of doom. "She hired people to kill my parents," I replied. "I agree that she was a total cunt." His fingers twitched more at his side. I wondered what that meant. "So you killed her. You're free. Now you're frequenting this shit hole and taking girls back to your place to fuck them? Eat them? I'm not judging, Norman, just trying to figure you out. Everyone has their vices. Some are just more disgusting than others." My vision blurred slightly.

Norman smiled. His lips pulled so tight I thought they'd crack and bleed. He had laugh lines on his face that felt out of place. "My sister wanted to figure me out. She also wanted to control me."

I could relate to that. My own siblings were a pain in the ass. They needed constant direction and supervision. "I guess you and Vicky have a lot in common," I prodded. "I controlled her and she retaliated, too. She obviously wasn't as successful as you. Is that why you're following her? Sending love notes carved into skin?" I licked my dry lips. My tongue felt heavy.

Norman didn't flinch at my accusation. This conversation was getting boring. I didn't know why I bothered to entertain him. We both knew he wouldn't be leaving this alley alive. Call me cocky, but I was the deadlier of the two of us.

"Vicky is mine," he replied, tilting his head. "She freed me, so I'm going to free her soul from her body."

That was a chilling statement. This guy needed a psychiatrist. "It's a shame you're batshit crazy, Norman. We probably could have been friends. But you wanting to kill my sister is really an inconvenience right now. I'm trying to win my girl back, and I can't do that with you running around, drinking milk, and gnawing on fingers at bars."

I sounded like Anthony, taunting the danger with humor. He replied with cold strength. "I do what I want. No one controls me anymore. Not Cora, not you. No one."

I casually reached for my gun so I could shoot the sorry son of a bitch and get this over with. Time to go back to Kansas City. Time to—

Norman surged forward with impossible speed. Maybe it was the drinks in my system, but there was a sluggish nature to how I processed his movements. My own hand felt like it was detached from my body as it hovered over my weapon. "How are you feeling?" Norman asked. "You know the people at this nightclub love me. Since I inherited all of Cora's money, I've been making lots of friends. The bartenders are just really great at making drinks at my request."

Rage was the only thing spurring me forward. I went to shove at his chest, and he merely stepped out of my reach. "Did you fucking drug me?" Coward.

"People are easier to deal with when they're tired, don't you think?" Norman replied before pulling...something out of his inner pocket. I couldn't quite figure out what it was. It was stark white, sharp, and smooth. Like...

"A bone?" I stammered.

The alley seemed to tip on its side, and I slanted my body to straighten it. "Do you like it?" Norman asked. "Cora never liked it when I played with my food."

I blinked twice at it as he took what looked like a carved, pointed part of the bone and licked it. "You're really fucked up, you know that?" Drool dripped out of my mouth as I spoke.

Norman frowned.

"I was made this way. Shot five times. But I got better. Got stronger. You know what made me stronger, Nick?"

I collapsed to the pavement on my knees. I could feel my body slipping in and out of consciousness. "Nothing builds strong bones like milk." He reared back his weapon and stabbed me in the gut.

The pain was instant. Whatever he'd given me wasn't enough to dull that spike of stabbing agony that rocked through me. I cried out and he stabbed me again, this time in the arm. "I'm going to do you a favor, Nick," he said before licking his weapon. I tried to roll out from under him, but he easily pinned me down. "I'm going to bring you to the brink of death. It's a gift, really. I'll give you what you've given me." He stabbed me again, this time in the thigh. I cried out in pain, but I was losing consciousness. "I'm going to give you some fresh perspective. A new lease on life."

The last thing I heard as he stabbed me again, and then again, was, "You're welcome, Nick."

chapter twenty
juliet cross

Mercy Medical in downtown Miami was packed with people with varying injuries and illnesses. It was like marinating in a pot of germs and sick. I sat in the uncomfortable waiting room of the emergency department as coughing individuals curled up in their chairs beside me. Someone drunk off their ass had puked in the main lobby, and a disgruntled janitor was currently trying to clean it up.

I hated hospitals.

When Mom went missing, Grams and I went to every single hospital within a fifty mile radius to see if she was there. I'd never forget the hopeless feeling of walking through the doors and not finding her.

In the corner of the waiting room, Anthony was pacing back and forth. Back and forth. Back and forth. It made me dizzy to watch him. William wasn't here. He had left about an hour ago with a team of men to look at the crime scene. I could tell that he didn't want to leave me, but we all wanted answers. We all wanted someone to blame.

I couldn't bring myself to cry. Crying would mean that Malice—Nick—was really in bad shape. I was determined to convince myself that he was okay. Nick was a god among men. In my mind, he was indestructible. Although the multiple stab wounds in his battered body required emergency surgery, I knew that he would get through this. He had to get through this. The alternative simply wasn't an option.

It was Vicky's reaction that stumped me. For someone who wanted us all dead just six months ago, she was not handling the news well. She was rocking in her seat with hot tears streaming down her flushed cheeks. Up until this moment, I didn't think she particularly cared about her brothers. I thought they were just a means to an end. She wanted us dead, after all. But maybe it took almost losing someone to realize what you had.

"Do you think he's okay?" she asked for the fifteenth time. Whenever that repeated question escaped her raspy throat, a bit of my resolve to be strong was chiseled away.

"He has to be," I answered. Because the alternative would mean that Nick died before he and I got a chance to get better—before we healed and grew. We had so much life ahead of us. I loved him. Deeply. He couldn't be gone. I absolutely refused that outcome.

Anthony marched over to me. He had been strangely quiet since we got the news and drove here. The only sign of fear you could sense in his body was the way his legs twitched on the car ride over here. He couldn't keep still, and occasionally I heard him mumbling under his breath.

"He's going to be fine," Anthony assured us both. "Fine, fine, fine, fine, fine, fine, fine, fine."

I reached for Anthony's hand, and he pulled me up from my seat to wrap me in a hug. A man mumbling to himself and hacking up phlegm whistled at us. "I'm going to be strong for you, Juliet."

The promise that escaped Anthony's lips surprised me. "Okay," I replied, my voice cracking. I didn't know how to respond to that. Anthony was always the one forcing me to be strong. I'd never allowed myself to give him control of my safety like the others. It was jarring to relax in his strong arms and trust him.

Anthony ended our hug to hold me at arm's length, his hands gripping my shoulders as he looked intently into my eyes. "I'm here for you. I'm going to be strong for you." His index finger lightly tapped at my shoulder, the one crack in his strong façade.

From the corner of my eye, I saw Vicky's brows lift in surprise. Anthony eased me back into my seat and crouched until he was eye level with me. "You haven't eaten. I'm going to get you a snack. And coffee. Are you cold?" he asked. "Yeah. You need to eat." Before I could answer, he was spinning away and walking over to a vending machine that had a line three people deep.

"Shit," Vicky choked out. More tears had spilled from her eyes. "I expected him to be losing his shit right about now. He hasn't even *tried* to break into the hospital's morgue. I'm impressed."

I reached into my purse and grabbed a tissue. While handing it to her, I spoke. "I'm glad you found him when he ran away. He wasn't in a good place. I think we both help him."

Vicky blew her nose. "If Nick dies," she began, her words lifted like a question—we weren't sure how he was doing in surgery. "It's going to take an army to bring Anthony back to sanity."

We might've been a little broken, but the Civella family *was* an army—an impenetrable force that could survive anything.

Or at least, I hoped so.

Feeling a bit helpless, I reached over to grab Vicky's hand. I wanted us to be better, even if I couldn't quite bring myself to get there just yet. We had been going back and forth in our friendship, teetering between resentment and trust, but at the core of things, there was a glimmer of forgiveness...and hope...and love. "He's going to be okay. We are all in this together."

She squeezed my hand just as William walked through the electric revolving door at the emergency room's entrance. As William approached, Anthony brought over a handful of snacks and set them down in our laps.

"Did you find anything?" I asked William as he approached. The solemn look on his face was not encouraging. "Luca collected the owner of the nightclub and is interrogating him now. I spoke with someone with Miami PD, and it looks like some of the girls that were taken frequented this club regularly. The tracks have been hard to follow because the owner of the club has been deleting footage and records of them being there."

I curled my hand into a fist, and my legs started shaking, sending all the snacks Anthony had just gotten me to the nasty hospital floor. Luckily, most of them were in plastic bags. Ignoring William, Anthony knelt on the ground and started picking them up again while whispering to himself, "Fine, fine, fine, fine, fine, fine, fine, fine."

William looked down at him but didn't say anything. And when Anthony stood back up, his expression was void of all emotion—as if he had forced all the dark thoughts in his mind at bay. "Before you all got here, I was doing some investigating. All the victims, or at least what was left of them, were found in alleyways where there were no cameras. He obviously has either connections or extensive knowledge of the Miami scene. I don't think he does any of his killings in the city, though."

William crossed his arms over his chest. "Why not?"

Anthony tapped his foot on the tile floor, responding, "According to the medical examiner, three of the bodies had a very specific residue on their skin."

Vicky rested her chin on her fist. "What kind of

residue?" she asked.

"Algae," Anthony replied, his voice a stutter. "Like from a swamp."

William nodded and pulled out his cell phone to type a message to someone. "I'll have my men investigate. Any word from the doctor? He's been in surgery for six hours now." Had it already been that long? Time moved slowly, like molasses. My stomach grumbled, and Anthony gave me a pointed look. "Eat, or I will feed you like a baby bird."

I grabbed a package of Chex mix from his arm and forcefully opened it. I could barely taste the salty food on my tongue, but I knew I would need my energy if I was going to be one hundred percent for Nick.

Vicky also grabbed a sleeve of cookies from the pile and started munching on it nervously. "This is my fault," she blurted out with a full mouth. "All of it is my fault."

The girl I was *before* meeting the Civella brothers would've tried to console her—tell her that none of this was her fault. But I had been toughened up a little bit. I had empathy for Vicky and recognized that her journey of self-growth and love started from a bad place. She was the reason we were in this mess, and I wasn't going to ease her guilt by telling her otherwise. I was, however, going to support her as she grew from this.

Anthony and William started whispering to one another, and my eye was drawn to a doctor walking toward us. I instantly stood up, my entire body on high alert.

"He's out of surgery," the doctor said once she was close enough. She had a couple of gray hairs peeking out through her cap and was wearing a mask. The sweat on her brow hinted that she had spent long hours working hard on Nick's butchered body. "I was a little worried about his abdomen wound, but you're very lucky it got his large intestine. The stab in his arm sliced across a major artery though, and it was difficult to repair. We gave him a blood transfusion and stitched him up the best we could. There is a portion of his shoulder that's missing. As if the flesh had just been carved out. He's going to require skin grafts for that area, but we were unable to do it during the surgery. He's lucky to be alive."

I nearly collapsed from relief. Vicky spoke first. "Can we see him?"

The doctor nodded. "He's getting moved to a room now. If you'll just follow me."

Anthony grabbed my hand and threaded his fingers through mine, giving me his strength. William stood at my back, ready to support me, but Vicky stayed where she was, shifting from side to side. "Maybe I should stay here," she said. "I might upset him or…"

I looped my arm through hers reassuringly. "Come on. Let's go see him."

Nick's hospital room was the size of his walk-in closet at the mansion. There was one chair beside the hospital bed that I currently occupied because Anthony was on a mission to take care of me. William stood by the door, answering phone calls from his men whenever they came in. There was a lead, last I heard, but that was an hour ago, and I was too exhausted to deal with the stress of finding the man responsible for doing this.

Anthony stood behind me, lightly running his fingers through my hair and scratching at my scalp in a way that made me want to fall asleep. If it weren't for the consistent beeping of the machines Nick was hooked up to, I probably would've passed out a while ago.

Vicky was sitting on the floor with her back against the wall in the far corner. She rested her cheek against her knees and would startle any time Nick groaned—which was quite often.

The doctors warned us that he might rest for hours. The sun peeked through the blinds and cast shadows on his skin. He had lost a lot of blood and needed time to regain his energy. But it was already the afternoon, and he still was asleep.

"Maybe you should go home and—" Anthony began.

"I'm not leaving him," I said in a calm tone. My voice was thick with sleepiness. "He'll wake up soon. Besides, I feel safer here with all of you."

I looked over my shoulder and saw Anthony puff out his chest with pride. "I will always keep you safe. This asshole will not hurt you," he growled.

"Nothing feels like the right thing to do," Vicky murmured. "I hate that we're even in this mess. I brought you all out here because I was too scared to just knock on the door. Mom and Dad would be rolling in their graves. They'd be horrified to know I couldn't come home."

Anthony's shoulders dropped. William pulled a toothpick from his pocket and started nervously chewing on it. "Nick made it clear that we couldn't go home. It's not your fault," Anthony said. "It's not my fault either."

William cleared his throat, as if he wanted to say something. The passive aggressive noise made Vicky snap her head up and stare at him. "Is there something you would like to say?" she asked.

William yanked the toothpick from his mouth and glared at her. "There are plenty of things I would like to say, none of which would be helpful right now." William snapped the toothpick between his thumb and index finger before tossing it in a nearby trash can.

Vicky, seemingly unfazed by William's temper tantrum, began to speak. "You see, William, that's your problem. Maybe if you spoke up for once in your life—"

William's frustrated ramblings interrupted Vicky's insult. "Maybe if for once in your life you came to me with your problems instead of relying on Nick, we wouldn't be in this mess. Maybe if he stopped acting on impulse. Maybe if—"

"What would you have done, William? Huh? You've had your head shoved far up Nick's ass our entire lives. I'm surprised that you didn't tell him about Juliet all those years. Sometimes, I think the only reason you didn't was because you were too scared of his reaction. I didn't come to you because you live in Nick's shadow. You're his lapdog."

William shook his head. "I would have helped you. If it were my doorstep that you showed up on, I would have helped you."

Anthony gripped my shoulder, as if touching me was

somehow holding him together. "You didn't help me," he said in a soft tone, so low that I was certain I was the only one that heard it. William said nothing in response to that. There was a stark difference between Anthony and Vicky. Vicky was not competing for my attention.

William started pacing the small room, making the four walls wrapped around us seem to close in. My breaths became shallow, and Anthony started massaging the back of my neck. "Nick should've never been at that club alone," William said. "He's cocky. Impulsive."

"What else is new?" Vicky replied sarcastically. "The jerk pushed us all away and went and got himself hurt. I hate that I even care."

Nick moved on the hospital bed, and I held my breath. He coughed a couple of times, the sound accompanied by a gasp and a groan. I imagined it hurt his wounds. The anesthesiologist warned us that he'd have a cough from being intubated. After a haunting cry, he ripped his eyes open. "I didn't ask for anyone to care," he rasped out melodramatically.

I would've rolled my eyes at the drama of it all if I weren't so relieved that he was awake. Vicky scrambled until she was standing. Anthony grabbed a cup of water from a nearby table and handed it to Nick. William looked into the hallway and waved down a nurse. As I watched everyone jump into action, I was reminded once more that this family was deeply interconnected. They moved as a team.

"That fucker stabbed me," Nick growled before weakly

taking the cup from Anthony's outstretched hand and taking a sip.

When he was done drinking the water, Anthony took the cup back, and I reached for Nick's hand. I just wanted to feel that he was alive and real. "The doctors couldn't quite figure out what you were stabbed with," Anthony replied in a playful voice. "All the voices in my head are taking bets over what it was. Stiletto? An ice pick?"

Vicky fought a smile. Leave it to Anthony to joke in a situation like this. Nick coughed again, then winced. I wondered if he needed more pain medicine.

"Where is that nurse?" William grumbled.

"He stabbed me with a bone," Nick growled. Anthony's face lit up like a Christmas tree. "A bone? What kind of bone? Did he sharpen it? Was it human, animal, synthetic—"

Nick held up his trembling hand to stop Anthony from rambling. "It was a human bone that he had sharpened to a point."

Anthony nodded enthusiastically. "Oh, that's sick. I want to meet this guy."

Vicky crossed her arms over her chest and let out a huff. "Are you going to ask for his autograph?" she asked Anthony in a snarky tone.

"I was thinking about seeing if he wanted to be interviewed for Juliet's podcast, thank you very much. I've never met a real cannibal before. I'll do a lot of things with dead bodies—but I draw the line at eating them."

I rubbed at my temples with my free hand, and Nick squeezed me gently. "We need to figure out where he lives,"

Nick replied. He was already in revenge mode. I could see the fire in his eyes.

"Already on it. Luca is confirming his location as we speak."

"Have you secured a safe house or headquarters?" Nick asked.

"Yes."

"Reinforcements?"

"On their way."

"No one can know I'm in here—" Nick said through clenched teeth.

"Already taken care of," William said. "We don't need your enemies knowing that you are weak."

I couldn't tell if Nick was proud of William for taking charge or annoyed by it. Nick looked around the room at each of us. William's shirt was wrinkled. Vicky had bloodshot eyes. I was two seconds from collapsing from exhaustion, hunger, and worry. Anthony was hiding behind a playful smile, but on the inside, he was crushed by what happened.

Nick looked down at our joined hands before addressing the room. "You all didn't have to be here," he said. There was a defensive lift to his words that made my heart soften a bit toward him. Nick thought he had to run the world all by himself.

"Of course we did," Anthony replied solemnly.

"As much as you want to get rid of us, you should know by now that it's impossible," Vicky chimed in.

I lifted his hand to my lips and kissed him. "I love you,"

I whispered reverently.

William remained quiet, but there was a stormy declaration in his gaze. I wondered if Nick could see the truth right in front of him. He was loved. His family was devoted to him. He didn't have to control loyalty, it was already there.

Nick seemed choked up, but not a single tear fell from his eyes. I expected nothing less from the ruthless mob leader. "How long do you think I have to stay here?" he asked William.

William let out a low whistle. "A few days at least. You have pretty major injuries. He also took a bite out of you," William added reluctantly. "They want to put a skin graft over the wound."

Nick's lip curled in fury. "I want out of here as quickly as possible. I'm going to kill that motherfucker."

chapter twenty-one
juliet cross

Anthony finally convinced me to go to the hotel William got us and rest. He had to practically drag me from Nick's hospital room, but admittedly, I was too exhausted to put up much of a fight.

Vicky stayed to talk to Nick. I wasn't sure exactly what she wanted to say, but I knew they needed time together to work through their issues. Vicky and I weren't completely healed from what she'd done, but she was working through her problems and trying to redeem herself. I was glad that she was making an effort. It also helped that Nick was practically strapped to the hospital bed, so he couldn't run away from whatever confrontation she wanted to have. I almost doubted leaving Nick with her while he was in such a vulnerable state, but Anthony assured me that nothing would happen.

I leaned on Anthony as we made our way to the hotel room. It wasn't safe for any of us to return to Vicky's condo since Norman knew where she lived.

The elevator doors opened, and Anthony scooped me up in his arms as if I were a rag doll. "You're so sleepy," he murmured while carrying me down the long carpeted hallway of the five-star hotel toward our room. I rested my head against his chest and picked the cotton collar of his shirt with my fingers.

"I just need a quick nap, and then we can go back to the hospital," I said quietly, my voice rough from the long couple of days.

"A nap. Some food. A shower. Maybe some new shoes, too. Vicky's sneakers are too big for your feet," he laughed. I had to steal some of her yoga pants and a crop top since she didn't allow me to pack a bag before leaving. William had taken it upon himself to go pick us up some supplies and promised to grab me clothes that actually fit.

"When did you get so bossy?" I asked in a soft voice.

"I'm just trying to take care of you," Anthony replied before gently setting me down in front of the hotel door. I reached for his hand just as he was about to dig in his pocket for the hotel room key card.

"You know I don't need you to take care of me, right?"

I asked.

Anthony cupped my cheeks with his hands. "Being obsessed with your wellbeing is better than my obsession with other things."

"Do you think maybe you use your obsessions to ignore the things that are really bothering you?" I asked. I wasn't usually so straightforward with Anthony. I'd always taken his lead, but not this time.

"I'm sure you're right," he reluctantly admitted while averting his gaze. I waited for him to continue.

"I just don't want to become another Band-Aid, Anthony. I love you too much for that."

He nodded. "It bothers me that Nick went alone to this club," Anthony said. "It bothers me that this creepy asshole is what I could have become. Who knows what I would have done if I let my mind continue down the path it was on before Nick sent me away?" Anthony pressed his forehead to mine. "It bothers me that I hurt you. That I kept hurting you. It bothers me that Vicky was gone. That our parents are dead. That I was kidnapped and abused and tossed in with a pile of cold, dead bodies. It bothers me that I'm the fuck up in our family. It bothers me that I'm nothing more than the clean up guy. It bothers me that I like being the clean up guy."

Anthony pulled away from me and yanked his hotel key card from his pocket before jerking open the door. I stood there in silent awe of his honesty, not sure what to say in return.

It seemed Anthony didn't want me to respond, he just

wanted to get it off his chest. He grabbed my hand and walked through the threshold leading to the extravagant hotel suite. The first thing I saw was massive floor-to-ceiling windows overlooking the ocean. In the living area, there was a large glass chandelier, leather seats, a dining table, and a collection of champagne that probably cost more than I made in a month at the funeral home. Well, I'd probably lost my job now. I didn't have my cell phone to check, but I was certain that there was an angry voicemail from my new boss waiting for me.

"I need to call Grams. She's probably worried," I murmured.

"William called her earlier. Said we decided to spend a couple days in Miami. She seemed excited that you were taking a trip and wants you to call her soon."

"Maybe after a nap?" I suggested. If I called her now, I'd probably break down and have to explain to her everything that was happening. I didn't want her to worry about me, not when everything was still so intense.

"I think that's a good idea." Anthony walked over to the glass window and instantly pressed his face up against it. The fog from his breath and the smudge of his fingers left marks all over the pristine glass. I fought the urge to giggle. "Gosh," he began before spinning around to face me. "William is truly losing his touch. This place looks like a two-star hotel. We weren't even greeted by a butler."

I licked my lips. "I suppose he's been a bit busy," I played along. "Capturing murderers and whatnot."

"But to forget the roses imported from Perth. It's just

so unlike him."

"I suppose we will have to forgive him for this shack," I said while looking around playfully at the fine furnishings and elaborate design. "But just this once."

"Agreed," Anthony replied with a posh uptick of his nose.

We both broke out into a fit of laughter that almost seemed to lift the weight from my shoulders, if for just a moment. But the relief was short-lived. My grin turned into a deep yawn. Anthony's playful expression dropped once more into seriousness. "Let's get you in bed," he said before clapping his hands together.

He started marching toward me but paused at the dining room table. I hadn't noticed it before, but there was a nicely wrapped box sitting on the tabletop. "Perhaps he hasn't completely lost his touch after all. Should we see what gift William left for us?" he asked mischievously. "I bet it's a golden dildo. You know how much I love dildos."

I laughed at his joke and slowly made my way over to the table to see what the gift was. The large box was a matte black with a blood red ribbon on top. I wasn't even sure how William had the time to buy something. We had all been so busy with the hospital, finding Norman's house, and all the other bullshit in between, that it surprised me.

My gut had this foreboding sense of terror. Anthony went to lift the lid, and it was on the tip of my tongue to tell him no. An eerie chill swept over my skin. Something about this felt wrong. Anthony tossed the lid to the side, and I looked over his shoulder to see what was inside. "A dinner plate?" Anthony asked. "Do y'all have some kink I'm not aware of?" He reached for the plate and picked it up. The plain white porcelain looked... "Dirty plates?" Anthony asked. "There's something red smeared all over it. Like steak sauce. Maybe William needs to come here and rest."

"Put that down, Anthony," I told him.

"What?" he asked. I ripped the plate from his grip and threw it on the ground. Porcelain shards scattered all over the tile floor.

I looked in the box once more and found a fork and knife. They looked...strange. Bleached white ivory carved to perfection. "Is that?" Anthony began. "Certainly it isn't—"

A sound in one of the connecting suite bedrooms made both of us spin on our heels. Anthony, seemingly recognizing the danger we were in, went into full alert. All the levity in his expression completely evaporated. I knew exactly where this gift came from. And it wasn't William.

Anthony held his finger up to his lips. Whoever was here already knew where we were. I eyed the front door. Anthony followed my gaze and shook his head. Was he thinking someone was out there, too? Was this an ambush? A trap?

Anthony wrapped his hands around my wrist and pulled me toward the window. He moved with calm certainty that seemed so unlike him, and in my frantic fear, I realized that *this* was the portion of Anthony's trauma that made him a survivor. I'd never seen him react like this, but it was interesting to see him process the situation in a matter of seconds.

Unlike him, my pulse was racing. My skin was cool as ice. The adrenaline coursing through my veins made my bones tremble with fear. I used to be disconnected from my reactions to terror. Now, it was all I could focus on. Finding my humanity had its consequences.

The sound of crunching glass under my shoes seemed as loud as a scream. I couldn't help but feel like either Norman or a collection of my worst nightmares were going to pop out of every dark crevice this hotel suite had to offer.

Anthony reached into his pocket and pulled out a switchblade. "Anthony," I whispered. "We have to get out of here." Instead of answering me, Anthony pushed me behind him, pinning me between the glass window and his hard body.

The front door jiggled. Fear made my eyes begin to water, and I grabbed Anthony's waist. Peering over his shoulder, I waited for whatever monster was on the other side. Time seemed to slow. I thought about Nick, about William. I thought about the broken relationships we shared and my dwindling chances to mend them.

Anthony flexed his muscles, raised his shoulders, and widened his stance. He was prepared to fight whoever was here.

Slowly, the door to the penthouse opened with a creaky groan.

I held my breath.

Waiting.

Waiting.

Waiting.

William strutted inside with one hand holding his phone up to his ear and the other full of shopping bags. "Answer your goddamn phone, Luca! I want those coordinates now," he said into the receiver. I instantly relaxed at the sight of William, but Anthony tensed even more. William's eyes scanned the room, and when they landed on us, he immediately hung up the phone. Without a word, he dropped the shopping bags in his grip and pulled out a gun. "What's going on?" he asked.

Anthony looked down at the shattered plate on the ground, then back at William before whispering, "We've had a guest."

A random creak from the hallway made me flinch. A gasp ricocheted out of my mouth, and Anthony snapped to attention, slicing through the air with his blade.

"Where is your gun?" William hissed at him.

From behind him, I could see the tips of Anthony's ears turn red. "I didn't trust myself to carry one."

What did that mean? Was he worried he would hurt someone else?

Or himself?

William clenched his jaw. I knew he was feeling the strain of being here. We only had a few men. Some had to stay with Nick, the rest were trying to find the killer. We thought we were safe, but...

"Stay here." I stared at William's back as he slowly made his way toward the source of the sound. He braced his hand on the bedroom door and pushed it open, gun raised, finger on the trigger.

Once he could see inside, he did a sweep of the room with his eyes before crossing the threshold and entering the room.

"I'm going to keep you safe, Juliet," Anthony promised.

I nodded and held onto him, straining my senses for sounds in the room.

I could hear a door sliding open. I was so attuned to every noise it made me tremble.

"Fuck!" William yelled from inside the room. "Fuck! Fuck! Fuck!"

My pulse spiked. Every nerve ending in my body was going haywire. "What's going on?" I called out.

Silence that seemed to stretch for miles answered me.

"William!" I screeched. "Answer me!"

"Come here. Norman is long gone," William finally said. Anthony let out a sigh of relief, but I still couldn't shake the fear from my bones. Had William truly checked everywhere? There were still more rooms in here.

Anthony guided me over to the room, and I was instantly slapped with a familiar stench. I lifted the collar of my shirt over my nose. It had been a while since I'd been around that rotten foul smell—since the night Anthony left.

"If you wanted to visit me, all you had to do was ask. Dinner at six p.m. Don't be late," William said. In his hand was a sheet of paper with blood red words scribbled on it. At William's feet was a sight that horrified me. Luca's severed head was sitting on the ground. His eyes and mouth were sewn shut, and his normally tan skin looked to be a mixture of green and pale.

I pressed the back of my hand to my mouth and felt my empty stomach roll. My reaction to seeing him was odd. It was like opening the gates to my humanity and letting the horrors of what I saw come flooding out. William dropped the letter and moved to comfort me. Anthony stared at my reaction, as if I were a puzzle he couldn't figure out.

I'd been numb for a while, but now I could feel the terror. There was no making sense of the gore and blood. I wasn't going through the motions anymore.

Anthony jumped into action when William crushed me to his chest. Ripping a sheet off the bed, he covered the severed head with it, hiding it from sight. I knew it was still there. "You're safe," William murmured. "The sound was just the head falling from the top shelf to the ground. We're going to leave now, okay? We'll go back to Kansas City and regroup."

I nodded as I clung to him.

William turned to his brother and barked out an order. "Clean that up. We need to bring him back to his family for a proper burial."

I pulled away and tried to steady my breathing.

Anthony let out an exhale. "I can't."

William froze. "Why not?"

Anthony stared at me for a lingering moment, a message in his gaze that I struggled to decipher. "That's not who I am anymore. I can't…" He let the words linger in the air, mixing with the stench of death that surrounded us.

William seemed to understand the words Anthony couldn't vocalize. "I'll send someone up to handle it. Let's go to the hospital." Anthony let out a sigh of relief. We needed to talk about this more, but I was too eager to leave. I didn't want him to completely change who he was for me.

"Let's go," Anthony gritted through clenched teeth before stalking out of the room.

William wrapped his arm around my shoulders, and we followed after him. I just wanted to leave this city for good.

chapter twenty-two
juliet cross

"Where the fuck is my gun?" Malice yelled. He was full of revenge and had violence coursing through his veins.

Vicky was sitting on the ground again, shaking her head in annoyance. "What are you going to do, Nick? Shoot up the hospital?" she replied with a roll of her eyes.

Nick swatted at the wires connected to him in fury. "I need to kill something. And I'm tired of this fucking place. I can wipe my own ass, thank you very much."

"They wipe your ass here?" Anthony asked excitedly.

"Do you have to make an appointment for that service, or should I get stabbed?" Nick's lip twitched, as if he were trying to contain a smile. I wondered how many times over the course of their lives Anthony would lighten the situation with his humor. Was it genuine or a coping mechanism?

"I've already spoken with a doctor back home that can have you admitted by the end of the day," William replied. "I also hired a nurse to travel on the private plane with us." He was distracted by a text that had just come in, not even looking up at his angry brother.

"I'm not going home until this guy is dead," Nick replied, his voice like steel. Somehow, I knew he would say that.

"Yes, you are," William replied, his tone bored.

"I think William is right, Nick," I said. "We should go back to Kansas City. We have more resources there."

William started aggressively typing on his phone while standing next to me. "We honestly should have never *left* Kansas City," he grumbled.

Vicky clenched her fists. For the last hour, William had made little digs at her nonstop. I was frustrated to be in this situation, too, but he needed to let off. Vicky honestly looked exhausted. When was the last time she ate? Luckily, it was Anthony's calm voice that replied.

"Coming home didn't feel like an option. Drop it, William," he said.

William stopped staring at his cell phone to sweep his eyes across the room. "If I were in charge, it would have been an option."

My mouth dropped open. This was the first time I'd

heard him blatantly take a stand about being in control of everything. Anthony grinned. Nick looked about ready to pull the IV needle from his arm and shove it through William's eye.

"But you weren't in charge. And you still aren't. I call the shots, and I'm not going to be running away from this asshole. If he's anything like Cora, then he is all talk and no game. He got lucky with me, but I'm willing to bet he's just as pathetic as his sister."

Vicky shook her head and hugged her knees to her chest. "He's nothing like Cora," she murmured.

"And what do you suggest we do, Nick? Storm his house with our men and take him out? We'd be walking right into a trap. You certainly aren't capable of handling an ambush right now," I jumped in. We needed to get the hell out of here and regroup.

"That is exactly what I'm suggesting," Nick replied before looking down at his hospital gown and letting out a guttural growl. "Fuck this place." He removed some of the monitors taped to his chest, making the machines go haywire.

I pinched the bridge of my nose as a nurse came running into the room. She had wispy gray hair, rosy cheeks, and eyes like fire. "Mr. Civella, if I have to tell you one more time not to take your monitors off—" she clipped with sass.

"I want to be released. Get me the release paperwork," Nick snapped back, cutting her off.

She arched her thin brow at him. "You want to be released? You just had major surgery. Do you realize you were stabbed five times?"

Nick squared his shoulders at her, but she didn't cower. Whoever this nurse was, she was a badass. "Yeah," Nick began. "I also had a psychopath take a literal bite out of my shoulder. But I want out of this hospital, out of this gown, and away from you."

She marched over to Nick and glared at him. If I didn't know any better, I'd say Nick was slightly impressed by her tenacity. "If you leave here without any medical supervision, your stitches could bust. You could have internal bleeding, and by the time you realize that you're dying, it'll be too late. Now, my colleagues worked very hard to bring you back from the literal dead, and I'm not going to sit here and let you ruin all of our hard work because you are a stubborn little child."

Anthony let out a low whistle. William looked like he wanted to take notes on how this nurse was handling Nick. Unfettered, Nick responded. "It's important that I get those release papers soon, Nurse Luan."

"I think I'm going to be busy for the next few hours. I'll get to it as soon as I'm able, Mr. Civella," she said before straightening her spine, spinning on her heels, and marching out of our room.

"I want to be her when I grow up," Anthony said the moment she was gone. Nick picked up a cup on his bedside table and tossed it at his brother. Luckily, it was empty.

"You are in no position to run an ambush," William said.

"I think you should listen to your nurse," I piped in.

Nick sliced his eyes over to me and glared. His look made me feel like I was betraying him. But William was right; going after Norman right now was a bad idea. We were tired. We only had a handful of men. We didn't know what kind of arsenal Norman had up his sleeve. "I know you want to get back at him but—"

"You don't understand," Nick growled.

I walked over to him and tried to grab his hands, but he flinched out of my reach, a wince on his face as he did. "Then explain it to us."

Nick looked side to side, as if the walls were closing in on him. "I couldn't move," he snapped. "He drugged me and…" Nick started scratching at his palms.

"It's okay to feel unsettled—"

Nick cut me off. "Unsettled? He stabbed me with the bone. I couldn't even fight back. I was helpless and just had to lie there and take it."

This time, it was Anthony that surged forward to comfort his brother. "You just want to feel in control again," he said tenderly.

Nick averted his eyes. I wondered if there was ever a time that Nick felt completely out of control. But these last few weeks, everything about his life had been spinning wildly out of his grasp. I was no longer under his thumb. Anthony spiraled. Vicky came back. William was challenging him. Norman was the bloody icing on a very rotten cake.

"I can't go home until he's dead," Nick said softly.

"We will get him," William replied. "You have to think

like a leader right now. We don't have the manpower. How are we supposed to protect Juliet and Vicky?"

Anthony stared at William for a long, long time. "I can protect Juliet and Vicky." He then crouched down to look at Nick, an unspoken conversation passing between them. I wished I had access to their thoughts. "Whatever you want to do, I support you. I know what it's like to try and go home after having your world completely ripped apart. If you don't handle this now, you might never feel normal again."

"This is insane. Juliet, talk some sense into them," William argued.

I cleared my throat before speaking. "I agree with William. We should go home."

Vicky, who had been quiet this entire time, finally spoke up. "He'll still find us there. I've spent weeks dodging this guy. The more time we give him to plan and act, the easier it will be for him to take us down—and he *is* going to take us down if we don't do something. I know that this is my fault and it's a lot to ask of you, but I think we should stay."

William threw up his hands and let them fall to his sides in exasperation. I felt the same way. Staying felt wrong. Every sense of self-preservation that I possessed was practically begging me to get the hell out of Miami and regroup. We had more resources in Kansas City. We had allies, guns, and the police in our pocket. This guy was unhinged, and we didn't exactly know how far his reach went. From what we already had gathered, he'd made some connections in the community. We needed to go back to our turf. We were untouchable there.

Miami made us feel…vulnerable. Normal, almost. This place stripped us of our titles and powers and forced us to stare at the dirt beneath our nails. We truly were just five broken people navigating a dangerous world.

"What do you know about him?" I asked Vicky. If Nick was determined to stay, then we really needed to lean on Vicky's insider knowledge of him.

She swallowed, the move making the tattoo on her neck dance. "I know he's obsessed with me. About a month after I let him free, he started sending me severed limbs, bloody notes, and other gruesome presents. They were always wrapped in a box with pretty paper and tied with a bow."

Anthony propped his fist under his chin as he listened. "He takes pride in his work," Anthony murmured. "He takes small chunks of the body until there is nothing left."

"What do you mean?" I asked. From the corner of my eye, I saw Nick flinch. I couldn't help but think of the messy heap of flesh taken out of his shoulder.

Anthony replied. "When I broke into the medical examiner's office to see if it was really Cora, she had chunks of flesh missing. I tried to see if he returned to crime scenes after the fact but never saw him, but the ME office announced an attempted break-in three days later. At first, I thought it was me. I was careful, but shit happens, you know? But this guy wasn't as good as I am." Anthony paused to wink at me. "Couldn't even get into the freezer room. The police released security footage of the guy and…"

He pulled out his phone and pulled up the article before

showing it to Nick. "Norman," he grunted.

"Is Cora's body the only one he's left behind? Or do they have others?"

"Cora's body is the only evidence they have that was useful. All the other victims were shredded to pieces. Hardly anything left." Anthony shifted his weight from side to side, like admitting this was uncomfortable for him.

"Norman hates Cora. He picks victims that look like her. Hell, he picked someone just for having a similar name," Vicky added.

"He wasn't done with her," I whispered. "Something happened and he had to leave her behind. I bet it's killing him that he can't finish what he started."

William cleared his throat. "This is all well and great, but it changes nothing. I don't know why we're wasting time even talking about this. Our best course of action is to go home."

Nick glared at his brother, and it was a look so full of anger that even *I* shivered. "Then go home, William. That's what you do, right? You run away."

William took a step toward Nick, his fist clenched at his side. "And you push people away," he retorted. "I think it's foolish to stay here. Once again, you're only concerned with your own vendetta, and you're too blind to think of everyone else's safety."

"Killing him protects all of us. Stop being such a coward," Nick rasped out before taking a sip of water. The heavy insult settled between the five of us like a weight on our chests. "Even though you're a pain in my ass, I need you here. You're my right hand man, and it's going to take all of us to do this."

William seemed surprised by Nick admitting this. I wasn't sure Nick had ever claimed to need his brother. "You want me to stay?" William asked. I couldn't tell if he was being genuine or not, because his tone sounded sarcastic.

"I want all of us to work together to take him down. I want to move past this," Nick replied before looking over at his sister.

Vicky nodded before speaking. "Together."

Anthony shrugged. "You're my ride home. As long as Juliet is safe, I don't really care about anything else," he said before looking at me.

I didn't know how to speak up, but I felt like it was my turn to convince Nick that this was a terrible idea. I felt conflicted, though. I refused to leave anyone behind. Looking at William, I let out a sigh. "I still think we should go home," I said. William smiled at my support. "But I don't want us to split up ever again. I will be where the majority is and support you however I need to."

If I had any hope of our relationship mending and being stronger than what it was before, I had to work with them all on this. Despite my hesitations, I felt a glimmer of hope. Vicky was back. Anthony was back. William and Nick still had a few differences to iron out, but they were close to finding a new way of thriving together. As much as I hated to admit it, Nick experiencing a little vulnerability might've been good for him. I fell in love with him because he seemed like a god among men, but it was his human vulnerabilities that made me want to pick his soul apart and understand him.

At the end of the day, these four siblings were simply struggling with a dark and devious world. They were taught to navigate death and power with cruelty.

William looked down at his shoes before meeting my gaze. "I guess we stay," he replied softly.

I opened my mouth, not sure what to say, but he left before I could figure my words out. I sensed his frustration and betrayal with every step he put between us.

"So," Anthony began, "I guess now we have to figure out how to steal Cora's body, huh?" When none of us answered, his brows dipped. "I mean, it's the only way, right? If Norman wants to finish what he started, I'm willing to bet he'll be a little reckless to do it. Probably won't be easy to get our hands on her, but I don't really know of any other bait that'll get him out of his comfort zone. Also since it's my plan, I would really like the opportunity to ask him what brains taste like. I went through a whole zombie phase, and I've always been curious."

I giggled. Nick clenched his jaw.

"He seems pretty obsessed with me," Vicky said. "I'm just saying, if you need bait—"

Nick interrupted her. "Absolutely not. You called us here to help, and we're going to help. Putting you in danger is not an option."

Vicky's eyes watered. I wondered if Nick realized how much she needed to hear that from him. I couldn't help but once again see that sliver of hope festering between us.

I was scared. But we were all together.

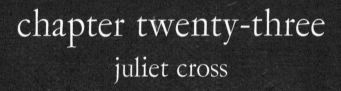

chapter twenty-three
juliet cross

I sat on the edge of the bed while watching Nick try to strip out of his clothes. I wanted to get up and help him, but also enjoyed watching his stubbornness play out. As he moved, he groaned in pain, and I knew without a doubt that he needed to be hospitalized. His determination to get out and get rid of Norman was going to rip open one of his stitches and push back his healing.

"Fuck!" he cursed before dropping his hands to his side. The fact that he was even moving right now was a testament to his tenacity. Nick didn't like looking frail. It was killing him to feel so helpless. Maybe he needed this moment. He had to recognize that some things were out of his control.

"Would you like some help?" I asked while openly observing him.

"Don't patronize me," he gritted back. I slowly stood up and sauntered over to him. The room was dark, aside from a small side table lamp on the nightstand. We rented a house in a Miami suburb under a fake name. Nick sent word back home for even more men to come here, and they were currently taking shifts walking circles around the perimeter. I felt relatively safe, but every noise had me flinching and checking over my shoulder.

Norman embodied every evil thing I had spent my life researching. I had read about sinister killers and all the many forms they came in. But it was terrifying to think that soon we would come face-to-face with the real cannibal. I wondered what made him this way. Was it his controlling sister? The trauma of being locked away and nearly dying? Or was it always something innate within him? A small flame that he fanned until it became a roaring inferno that tore through his psyche.

Nick wouldn't look at me as I reached over to unbutton his shirt. His pride would be the death of him.

We needed to replace the gauze on his shoulder, as he had bled through it. "I wish you would rest," I said softly. I wasn't trying to make him feel like less of a man, I just loved him.

"If you were my nurse, maybe I would've stuck around

that damn hospital," he murmured before slowly, slowly reaching up to brush my cheek with his thumb. Every movement had him wincing in pain, but still, he reached for me. I leaned into his touch, completely consumed with relief that he was still here, still pissing me off with his determined, controlling attitude.

Once his shirt was removed from his body, I gently walked him over to a chair and sat him down. "I'll fix your bandage," I said before retreating to the adjacent bathroom for the first aid kit.

In the bathroom mirror, I caught sight of my reflection and grimaced. I looked like hell. My hair was a tangled mess on top of my head. My clothes were a little small for me; I had to adjust them to fit, but it still didn't look right. I had bloodshot eyes and hollow cheeks. The strain of this world was once again killing me.

I walked back into the bedroom, first aid kit in hand, and resisted the urge to cry when I saw Nick. His shoulders were bent, and he looked unsettled. His face was fixed in a permanent wince. I probably wouldn't get any sleep tonight because I would be too consumed with watching his lungs move up and down as he rested. I did not like the fact that he was not being monitored in a hospital, but I also felt powerless to stop him.

He flinched when I gently touched his shoulder. "Let's clean this up, yeah?" I whispered.

It took everything in me not to throw up the moment I removed the bandages. How he was functioning right now was a miracle. I could see rogue teeth marks sharply carved into his skin. Puss and blood was draining out of it. What if it got infected? I made quick work cleaning the wound and dressing it, trying to go as fast as possible to alleviate some of the pain Nick was experiencing.

"Talk to me," he whispered. I sensed that he needed the distraction.

"I don't even know what to talk about," I said helplessly. "Things are weird between us. I'm mad that you left the hospital. I'm mad that we're staying here in Miami."

"I have to do this, Juliet," he said hoarsely.

I finished bandaging him up, then circled around to face him head on. Kneeling at his feet, I looked up into his bleary eyes and spoke. "You have nothing to prove to me. I know that you are strong, capable, and invincible."

Nick looked down at the carpet for a brief moment, and I wanted to crack open his mind to understand what he was thinking. "My dad taught me to never let an enemy live," he admitted.

I couldn't help but wonder if Nick felt like a failure. His parents put so much pressure on him to run their empire, protect his siblings, and follow all these archaic rules in his grab for power. Nick was a man molded by his father's teachings. He had to be hardened to handle the sort of life he lived, but it broke him.

"You're so beautiful, you know that?" he murmured. "I want to be mad at you. I want to punish you."

I reached for his hand, and he gently squeezed me. "So we're both mad at each other?" I asked. "Does that mean I should sleep on the couch tonight?" There was no way in hell I would sleep on the couch, but we needed to hash this out. We hadn't really had an opportunity to talk about all the things piled up between us like a mountain neither of us wanted to climb. If I had my way, I would just bulldoze through our problems to get to where he was.

"Stay with me tonight," Nick whispered.

I helped him strip down to his boxers, and we both made our way to the king-sized bed with lavish bedding in the center of the room. I helped him lie down before crawling onto the mattress beside him. I couldn't rest my head on his chest, but he threaded his fingers through mine and held me tightly. "I would do anything for you," Nick whispered. To some, the declaration would feel like an empty promise, but I knew how serious Nick was being. I was his greatest weakness. He turned his head to look at me, and I could see his gentle expression in the soft, dark room. "I want to marry you," he whispered.

I knew that he was being sincere, but the phrase still made me giggle. The pain pills must have kicked in. "You know you have to ask Grams first," I replied.

"I'm gonna work hard to be worthy of you," he then said.

"That's the thing, Nick, I never asked you to prove yourself. I just wanted you. I don't need the walls you're willing to build around me. I don't need your financial security. I don't need your protection or your gifts. I need your time and love and acceptance. I need room to breathe, and trust. More than anything, I need trust."

He squeezed my hand with what little strength he had.

I sensed that he would be falling asleep soon. "You could have all of it. All of me," he replied reverently. I moved to kiss him on the forehead. His words were sweet and believable, but only time would give us the opportunity to learn and grow in our relationship in a way that would make us healthy again.

"Go to sleep," I whispered.

And Nick obeyed.

———

I woke up to someone tapping me on my shoulder with their light finger. Tap, tap, tap. Slowly, I opened my heavy eyes, and the shadowed sight of Vicky standing over me made me gasp in fear. For a while, she was the headliner of my nightmares, and in my sleepy state, I almost forgot that we were trying to be better again—*trying* being the key word.

After placing her index finger to her lips, she smiled wickedly at me before nodding toward the door. I looked over at Nick and saw that he was sleeping peacefully—or at least as peacefully as he could, given the circumstances. His beautiful face was still twisted up in agony, as if he were trapped in a nightmare he couldn't escape.

With a sleepy sigh, I got out of bed and followed her out of the bedroom door and into the bright living room. I had to blink to ease the sting of the harsh lights. Anthony and William had left hours ago, before we fell asleep, and were still gone. The two of them were working on our trap to get Norman and eliminate him.

Vicky spoke cautiously to me as I yawned. "Sorry to wake you up, but Anthony wanted me to make sure you had dinner. I'm not sure you've eaten at all today."

She then pointed at a table full of tacos and Spanish rice. The sight of it rumbled my stomach, and my mouth immediately watered. "Thank you," I said, clearing my throat.

Vicky plopped down at the table and reached for a fork. Following after her, I felt trepidation at the prospect of spending an entire meal alone with her. There was something intimate about the ritual of meal sharing that had me feeling cautious. During our road trip, we remained silent for most of the time. Although I was hungry, I was unsure of whether I could eat a cordial meal with her. I wanted to trust her, but I didn't. I wanted to love her again, but I couldn't. I kept having to force myself not to be angry with her for Nick's injuries. It wasn't directly her fault, but her impulsive actions led to the giant snowball we were currently running from.

"I used to bring you tacos at Dick's, do you remember?" Vicky asked with a smile. She looked desperate to make eye contact with me and connect. "There was that taco truck you always liked." I nodded before picking up my food and taking a bite out of it. It was so damn good. An explosion of flavor bounced along my tongue, and I had to resist the urge to moan. I hadn't realized how hungry I was. It was hard to stomach food with the sight of Luca's severed head drowning my mind with fear. I welcomed the normal reaction to trauma, though. It was better than being numb to everything.

"You're welcome," Vicky said. I nodded enthusiastically, though there was still a reluctance in my chest. Being alone with Vicky felt wrong. She stared at me, waiting for me to speak again. But I preferred the awkward silence. At least then I was being authentic to myself. Forcing a surface-level conversation with Vicky just didn't appeal to me.

She cleared her throat. "So, how was Nick?" she asked.

I sat down my taco and stared at her. "He was in a lot of pain. I fixed some of his bandages, but he should honestly be in a hospital right now. I'm nervous for him. This whole thing feels really reckless. We should be on a plane back to Kansas City right now. I'm not even sure we should have come here at all."

Vicky's playful expression dipped into neutral territory. "You blame me," she said. "I understand why. I just had hoped that we were getting better."

I didn't know how to explain to her how I was feeling. Forgiveness came in waves. It was this back-and-forth thing I struggled with. Part of me wanted my friend back. There was a long time that I relied heavily on her. But then I remembered how it felt to be chained to that chair in the warehouse, the fire kissing my skin as I sobbed. I couldn't help but think of Anthony and his steady decline into madness instigated by her betrayal all those months ago.

But saying all of this out loud was like beating a dead horse. Vicky knew what she did. No amount of vocalizing my grievances with her was going to make this better. But forcing myself to feel something I just couldn't feel was wrong, too. Forgiveness was a double-edged sword, and I was still pulling the weapon out of my back.

Vicky searched my face with her eyes. Seeing her inquisitive gaze made me angry. She cleared her throat. "My dad used to tell me I was too impulsive for this business," she said. "He would test me all the time and ask me questions just to see how I'd respond. It didn't take long for him to realize I wasn't a good fit for this world. I got bored of chess. I searched for the easiest, laziest path to success. All my brothers had to kill someone before they were initiated. But not me."

I sat back in my seat, partly shocked that she was opening up about her life. Her past had always been a secret to me. She never told me about her brothers, her upbringing, her fears or her regrets. For so long in our friendship, all I ever heard was vague references to her parents. It was strange to hear her talk about her parents specifically.

"My brothers are good with their fists. He trained them to be murderers and conquerors. I was trained to be a manipulator. A desired plaything. Growing up, my greatest strength was my looks." The strap of her tank top slipped over her shoulder.

She grabbed a tortilla and tore a piece of it off, popping it in her mouth with a distant look in her eyes. "My mother wanted more for me. She knew what could happen to pretty girls in this world. She loved my father very, very much. But she didn't want the same life for me." I kept my mouth shut, too scared to speak and ruin the moment. I ached to learn more about the girl who became my best friend and then betrayed me.

"My brothers didn't get it, you know? They had their own struggles. Their own responsibilities. But when Nick became in charge, it got worse. I grieved my mother. She was the only person actively trying to get me out of here. Not only was I still expected to be a pretty face for the empire, but Nick was even more controlling than my father. I don't fault him for it. He was scared—and rightfully so. But it was like being buried alive."

"You wanted out," I said softly.

She let out a sigh and looked out the window at the night sky. From her spot at the kitchen table, she looked ethereal. "I didn't realize that at the time, but I leaned on you a lot to get a sense of normalcy and freedom. I was a little selfish about it, too. Our friendship wasn't about friendship, it was about escaping. It made me giddy to have a secret from Nick. It made me feel a sense of independence that I had never had."

What was she saying? Did this mean we were never really friends?

"Do you remember the podcast you did on women that snapped?" she asked me.

I nodded my head. It was one of my more popular podcasts. Society loved to hear about women completely losing their minds. Men did it every day, but when a woman finally broke, she broke beautifully. She was like this destructive storm barreling through everything in her path.

"I snapped, Juliet. It was ugly and vicious and painful. I regret going to Cora, but you have to understand—she felt like my only choice. I had tried to run away, and Nick stopped me. I had tried to rise above my status in this criminal world, but my father constantly reminded me that I was nothing more than a warm body for a man. I wasn't raised to feel like a princess. I was raised to feel like an asset."

"Did you ever care about me?" I asked her. I just needed to know. Back then, life was like holding my breath, and seeing her once a week was the one time I could gasp for more air. I was lonely and barely surviving.

"I cared. I still care. I love you. But when we were talking about my brothers and how you were demanding that they treat you the way you deserve, it made me realize that I was just as bad as they are. I made you meet me on my terms. I saw how lonely you were and did what I was trained to do—I manipulated you. It was fucked up. But I was so addicted to the feeling of freedom that I didn't care. I regret it, though. "

"Your brothers are learning. I think you could learn, too."

Vicky nodded at me. "If you want to know about my past, I'll tell you. If you want space from me, I'll give it to you. If you want to forgive me, I would struggle with feeling worthy of your forgiveness, but I would graciously accept it. Watching you teach my brothers how to love you made me realize that I want to learn how to be your friend."

"I'm trying," I said softly. "It just takes time. Are you

serious, though? I can ask you anything?"

She smiled. "Anything."

"Tell me about your relationship with your brothers. You were willing to kill them all just months ago. I'm trying to wrap my head around it."

Vicky nodded, the movement making some of her pale blonde hair fall from her messy bun. "They're all I have," she replied with a shrug. "Collectively, they aren't the family I would've chosen for myself. But they're the family I got." I wondered if that was why she found it strange that I actively chose them every single day.

She continued. "I tell everyone that I'm closest to Anthony, but it's a lie," she replied. "We were both family rejects—failures in our own rights. So our parents tossed us together while focusing on the children they could actually trust to lead their empire. It doesn't mean we were loved any less, they just didn't see the point in investing in relationships with us. Anthony and I understand each other, but between you and me, I'm actually closer to William."

"William?" I asked skeptically. It made sense. William had confided in Vicky when we first started dating. William was also the person Vicky trusted to introduce to me. I wanted to hear her perspective on it though.

"William cares about me, but he doesn't smother me. I feel like I can be myself around him. He's the big brother I can count on. It's probably why he's so pissed off that I didn't come to him when Norman started harassing me. I suppose I just look up to him the most out of all of them, so it's very difficult. My betrayal hurt all of you, but it was a different kind of hurt for William."

"And what about Nick? You wanted to talk to him today, what did you discuss?" I asked.

"Nick is an asshole," Vicky said with zero hesitation. "But I think I understand him better now. I used to think he was this invincible superhero. But now I think he's just scared. Scared to disappoint the ghost of our father. Scared to mess up and get us hurt. Scared to lose you. Scared of being alone. Everything he does is motivated by fear."

It was hard for me to picture Nick afraid of anything. He seemed so stone cold and unmovable. Like a proud tree with deep roots.

"And what about you, Vicky?" I asked. "Who are you? We're going to take down Norman tomorrow. Then, we're all going to pack up and try to go back to our lives. What life are you going back to?"

My question seemed to surprise her. I was practically hanging on the edge of my seat, waiting for her answer. "I'm going to go back to my freedom," she answered instantly. After all, freedom was all she ever wanted. It's what motivated her to do what she did to us. "But I'm also going to be a better sister and a better friend. Now that I'm out of this crazy world, I can see myself clearly."

She leaned over the table, staring me down. "The truth is, we're all a product of this fucked up world, Juliet. Part of loving them means loving their evil, too. Anthony almost killed you. Nick controlled you. William broke your heart. You've decided that they're forgivable. I just hope one day you can see that I'm worthy of it, too. It's not about being good or bad. It's about realizing that all we have is each other. We're better together. It just took being away from them for me to realize that."

It took a lot of balls to own up to what Vicky did, but my gut was telling me that she was being nothing short of authentic and genuine with me. Even though it was my base human instinct to hold a grudge, I felt like her honesty spurred us forward into a new reality. A new friendship. We would never be what we were, but maybe once we were out of this mess, we could be more.

chapter twenty-four
juliet cross

It was an eerie afternoon for a fake funeral. It was a dramatic production set in a run-down cemetery. Cora's final resting place was nothing more than a dilapidated plot and a plaque with the words:

Here lies a bitch who died.

The caption was Nick's idea. It bothered him that we were following through with so much ceremony for a woman who made his life a living hell. She would return to the earth the same way she lived—unremarkable, forgettable, and for the purpose of something much bigger than her. She was a scapegoat for greater things.

The owner of the cemetery gave us free rein of the land for a fat flat rate. He even let us use his morgue on the property. The place was cheap and falling apart, but also mostly off the grid. We didn't have to worry about anyone coming here to see what we were up to.

There would be no hopeful words whispered reverently, priest, or prayers said over her battered body tonight. Nick wanted to toss her into the ground like forgotten trash left on the side of the road. He wanted her body to crumble and contort when it hit the dirt just so she'd spend the rest of her life uncomfortable, not even at rest.

And then at sundown, we would wait for Norman to arrive.

The mortuary was a split-level brick home that looked like it had seen better days. The owner of the cemetery lived on the top floor, and the first level was the funeral home. Down a long, dark hallway was where he performed cremations and embalming. Dust covered every surface of the space.

"How much longer until the hole is dug?" Nick asked William. Vicky and I were sitting at a shaky table. I hadn't really spoken since we arrived. I wasn't sure what I could say. I didn't agree with this. And I didn't like feeling like a sitting duck.

William was staring at a brochure for caskets and didn't bother to look up when he responded. "Should be ready in about thirty more minutes. The night vision cameras are set up, and all the men know where to hide. Cora's obituary was published early this morning, and a statement by the police has been made that she is going to her final resting place. If he's watching, he'll know she's here."

I tapped my foot on the wood floors. William had pulled everything off. I was surprised he was able to get Miami police to turn over Cora's body. His efficiency impressed me. His effectiveness and professionalism both helped Nick and also irritated him.

I was feeling great about things until William continued. "But, of course, we threw this idiotic plan together in a little over a day. We don't have a ton of manpower, and this guy will probably know we are here waiting for him. It's a stupid trap, and I can't wait for it to fail so we can all go home."

"If it fails, that's on you," Nick gritted.

"Right," William continued. "The plans that work are yours, and the ones that fail are mine. How could I have forgotten?"

I sensed that Nick was in pain. He refused to take any medicine and risk not being aware for tonight's job, but he could barely walk. I wasn't sure what he thought he would be doing tonight. Most likely, one of his men would capture Norman, and Nick would shuffle out there to put the final bullet through his skull.

"I still don't know why we had to do this at night," Anthony said. He was pacing the floors by the front door, arms crossed over his chest. Every few minutes, he would tug down on his beanie.

His discomfort was unusual for me. Anthony typically thrived in places like this. But not once did he crack a joke or ask to take pictures of the crematorium. He hadn't even opened Cora's casket to look inside.

Anthony was trying to change, and this experience felt like putting an alcoholic in a room full of expensive whiskey.

The sun was setting outside, casting a hazy glow over the tombstones. There was going to be a storm tonight. William sighed and rubbed his cuff link. "So if he doesn't show up, can we go home?"

"He'll show up," Anthony murmured.

"What makes you so sure?" William asked. Nick closed his eyes. He was breathing hard. In and out. In and out. I didn't care if I had to drag him to the private jet and duct tape him to a seat. We were going home after this. I wanted a doctor to look over him soon.

"It's an obsession," Anthony croaked out. "I understand him."

"You're nothing like him," Vicky said in a soft voice, trying to reassure her brother. I appreciated her saying that to him. Maybe if Anthony heard it enough, he'd start trusting himself with me again.

William's phone pinged, and he cleared his throat. "Hole is ready. Let's get this over with. The asshole isn't coming. Just another sleepless night chasing bullshit."

William stood up and Nick slowly stood, too. His limbs shook as he did. "I'll go with you. I want to say goodbye to the cunt."

"You're in no position to walk—"

"I said I'm going!" Nick roared, cutting off William.

"And I'm tired of hearing you bitch about this plan. You're either in or you're out, William. I can do this without you if necessary."

William's brows raised. "Oh, you can, huh? You can barely walk, Nick. And were you going to organize this clusterfuck? Find a cemetery about to go under that would let us pay them a lump sum so we can do shady shit on their property? Or were you going to call the newspaper and put an obituary in last minute? Ask me how I got the body, Nick."

Nick looked so pale. He could barely stand up. "William," I whispered in warning. "Enough, please."

William looked at me, the ice in his stare making me bristle. "I'm going. You all obviously have this handled. I've done my part."

"William!" Vicky yelled as he stormed toward the door.

He stopped and glared at her. "Leave me the fuck alone, Vicky! Shit was better when you were gone," he said with a steel voice before marching out the front door toward his car.

Vicky shook her head but didn't seem fazed by his words. "He's such a drama queen," she replied. "He'll be back."

"Once I'm better, I'm going to kick his ass," Nick grumbled.

"Orrrr," Anthony interrupted. "You could, you know, like, thank him for helping you."

Ignoring Anthony's quip, Nick carefully walked over to the door. I got up, ready to help him should he fall. "Stay," he demanded while pointing at me. "I'm fine. I'm going to make sure they dump her body and come right back. I want to do this alone."

I shook my head. "We can come—"

"I said alone!" Nick yelled. "I just...I need to..."

Anthony looked at Nick. "Are you chasing flies, Nick?" he asked.

Emotions crawled up my throat like an exorcism, and I was suddenly brought back to the night I ran away with my thoughts and had a complete mental breakdown. The guys had been there for me, swatting at imaginary flies like they could beat the demons in my mind by sheer will.

I hated that Nick wanted to do this alone, but also understood it.

Nick stared at his hands. "I don't swat at flies, Anthony. I strap bombs to their chests and watch them light up the sky like fucking fireworks," he murmured before shuffling out the door.

The moment the door clicked shut, I moved from my spot to the window so I could stare at Nick's back as he walked toward the burial plot about fifty feet away. "He's going to rip open all his stitches," I murmured to myself.

"I'm sure we could find a needle and thread around here somewhere. The morgue is probably stocked with stuff," Vicky replied sarcastically. "I also brought the first aid kit. It's around here somewhere..." From the corner of my eye, I saw her stand and start searching around for it.

I moved to continue staring at Nick's back. He wandered slowly across the cemetery, none of his men daring to help him for fear that he would flex his authority and prove to them just how capable he was with a skilled bullet lodged between their eyes.

Anthony moved to linger at my back, and I felt his hot breath feather down my exposed neck. "He'll be okay," Anthony whispered.

I spun around and faced him. "You sure have a lot of patience and understanding for the man that sent you away."

Anthony grinned. "I don't blame him for sending me away. I needed to work on some things. And right now, he just needs to fight his demons. Just as he has given me space to process my own shit time and time again, I'm giving him space to do the same. Have grace for him."

I cupped Anthony's cheeks. "You're too good, Anthony," I said.

He grabbed both my hands and lowered them with gentle caution. "I'm not," he whispered. I was about to ask him what was wrong, but Vicky's shrill scream stopped us both in our tracks.

Anthony spun around as her shattering plea was cut off abruptly and became muffled. I jumped into action and moved beside him to see what was happening, just as a shadowed figure started dragging Vicky down the hall. Her legs kicked and slipped as a towering man pulled her by the armpits. There was duct tape over her mouth, but her wide eyes expressed the fear she felt.

I thought we were secure? William had the perimeter checked twice.

She reached for us as she slipped into darkness. The picture frames that lined the walls fell down, and the glass shattered around her. Anthony sprang into action and chased after them. I took an extra moment to open the front door, lean over the threshold and let out a bone-chilling scream.

"Help!!!"

I didn't even wait to see Nick's reaction. The night sky was settling over the cemetery, and the sounds of struggling bodies spurred me forward. My feet slapped against the wood floors of the funeral home, and I pumped my arms while running toward where Anthony, Vicky, and the shadowed man disappeared. A loud boom surrounded me, shaking the walls loose of dust and dirt as I fell down. It sounded like a fucking cannon going off.

My palms hit the floor, and I forced myself up, ignoring the sharp sensation of glass digging into my skin. I then stumbled down the long hallway and through the building, my skin breaking out with goose bumps as I went. My heart raced in time with my feet, and a blanket of pitch black covered my vision.

At the entrance of the morgue, I ran into something solid and yelped out in pain as we both went crashing to the ground. Anthony cursed. I cried out as my skin scraped against the concrete. "Get out of here," Anthony hissed while helping me up.

Somewhere in the echoing room, I heard Vicky struggle against her duct tape gag. Her moans were nothing but muffled yelps.

"I'm so glad we could all meet," a calm voice said from the darkness.

I gripped Anthony's arm, the terror coursing through me making me squeeze so hard that my nails nearly punctured his skin. "Show your fucking face," Anthony shouted.

"As you wish," Norman replied before flipping on the lights. My pupils screamed from the quick invasion of brightness, but I quickly scanned the room in search of Vicky.

The cremation machine with its metal doors and impressive touch screen panel was on the far side of the room, and right in front of it, a man wearing a sweater vest and slacks was standing there. His nimble fingers were wrapped around a sharp knife that he held to Vicky's neck. She kicked and thrashed, desperately trying to get away from him, but her harsh movements made him slice at her soft skin. She instantly became compliant when she realized how easily he could cut at her jugular.

"It's nice to meet you, Anthony," Norman said before licking his lips and staring at us. "My sister told me stories about you."

"Shut the fuck up," Anthony said before pulling his switchblade from his pocket and aiming at Norman. "How did you get in here?"

Norman licked his lips. "I'm used to waiting in quiet, dark places. No one even knew I was here. If you spent less time bickering and more time putting your brains to good use, maybe you could have prevented this. Cora made it sound like you were invincible. But you let your differences distract you. Lucky me, I suppose." Then, Norman simply smiled at both of us while using his free hand to reach behind him and turn on the cremation machine. A loud bang indicated that the metal cage full of fiery inferno had kicked on. "Cora said you reminded her of me. She said they tossed you into a pile of cold bodies and you felt at home," Norman said. The way he spoke made my skin crawl. It was lifeless. The monotone nature of it had creepy undertones, like speaking with evil.

"Let Vicky go."

"I can't do that. Vicky won't ever be free in this body. She's like me." Norman crouched lower until his face was level with Vicky's. I watched in horror as he dragged his tongue along her neck to lick up the blood there and moaned. She tried to get away, but the sharp knife cut into her skin again, making more blood drip down her chest.

Anthony took a step forward, spurring Norman into action. The crazed man stood up and dropped the knife to yank Vicky's hair, forcing hot tears of terror to stream down her flushed cheeks. The room was growing hotter and hotter.

"I thought you wanted Cora," I began, trying to buy us time. Where were Nick and his men?

Norman looked at me, cocking his head to the side in an assessing way that made my stomach flop in disgust. "I'll have Cora. I'll consume every bit of her until she's nothing. She'll pay, don't you worry. I just couldn't let my little pet suffer anymore."

Norman lifted Vicky up. She was sobbing hard, but I couldn't hear her cries for help because of the tape. The only evidence of her distress was the way her wide eyes leaked tears. Her legs trembled. Her chest heaved up and down.

Anthony took another step closer, his knife raised, as Norman pressed a button to open the door to the cremation machine. Heat and fire escaped from the door in heavy waves. I flinched from the intense, overwhelming blaze. Anthony put his knife in his mouth and lunged for Vicky's feet, attempting to grab her and pull her away from the psycho trying to put her into the fire. She thrashed and punched at Norman, who seemed unfazed by her movements. He was impossibly strong, his bones like steel.

Anthony grabbed his knife and moved to stab Norman, but he moved out of the way and kicked Anthony's hand, sending the knife scattering across the floor. Anthony followed it with his eyes, momentarily distracted enough for Norman to take advantage of it.

Lifting his foot up for leverage, Norman slammed down his boot on Anthony's face. His boot landed with fierce efficiency, knocking Anthony off of Vicky. A splatter of blood scattered along the white tile from Anthony's nose, and I moved to help him, but Norman screamed, "Stop!" I froze in place, paralyzed by my fear. Anthony moaned. Where the fuck was Nick or William?

Norman then hoisted Vicky up and started edging her toward the fiery entrance. Her hair singed, and smoke filled the room. Anthony tried to get up but fumbled. "No!"

I screamed while looking around the room for something I could use as a weapon. I curled my hands into fists and decided to fight for our lives just as Norman shoved Vicky headfirst into the fire.

My heart stopped. Time slowed. The crackling flames groaned.

It was a hissing sort of silence that would haunt me for the rest of my life. She didn't scream—she couldn't scream.

Her lower body twitched as he continued to shove and push.

Burn, burn, burn.

I had a moment of hesitation but then ran at him. Weaponless. Hopelessly determined to save Vicky. Lunging at his tall body, I knocked him over enough to loosen his grip on her body.

Norman and I rolled on the ground. His hard body was a heavy weight against mine as I threw punches in every direction, not even sure if my hits were doing anything. He got the upper hand and pressed me into the concrete, shoving his thigh between my legs in the process. In the corner of my eye, I saw Anthony scream while trying to pull Vicky from the fire.

Her limbs were still.

Too still.

Baring his teeth, Norman inched forward, his beady eyes trained on my neck as he did. I flailed and kicked. Hot smoke filled my lungs, and my vision grew hazy.

"I love when they fight," Norman said. "I'll free you too, lovely."

He went to bite at my jugular but was shoved off of me. Anthony stood over me like a raging angel of death, fire building like wings behind him.

I crawled on the ground toward what I could see of Vicky's shoes. The room had become so clouded with smoke that the bleached white sneaker was all I could see.

Fire. So much fire.

Anthony tackled Norman to the ground, and I army crawled away from the scuffle. We needed to get out of there. The dilapidated building didn't even have working fire sprinklers. Soon, this entire place would be engulfed in flames from Vicky's body.

I was in survival mode, my processing abilities so dulled by fear and adrenaline that I almost didn't realize what I was crawling toward.

The charred skin.

Her burnt clothes.

Muscle and meat exposed.

Blood, so much blood.

Flames consuming the air around her.

Legs that occasionally twitched from the misfiring nerves.

A smoky stench that smelled like burnt hair and vomit.

Vicky was dead.

One minute, she was alive.

The next...

I screamed.

And screamed.

My throat was dry.

Heat caressed my body like a numbing kiss.

I'd met my threshold of pain.

"Juliet!!!" Anthony screamed.

My skin hissed, and I realized my shirt had caught fire. Anthony had been wrestling with Norman but shoved him off before running to me to help me strip out of my clothes. A side door opened, creating a vacuum of smoke as Norman fled. Anthony tore the clothes from my body, my exposed skin stinging with protest, and Anthony yanked my sports bra off while shoving me toward the open door.

"Vicky!" I sobbed.

Anthony threw me over his shoulder, and he ran until the chilled night air greeted us with relief. It was like cutting the zip tie that was around my lungs. Men surrounded us as I heaved in air. My heart was this half-beating thing that mourned, oh, it mourned.

"Move!" William bellowed before taking me from Anthony. Nick was barking orders but was barely standing. He tried desperately to get to me. Time ticked slowly, and when his hand landed on my arm, I cried out. "Where were you?"

"Norman set off a bomb at the gravesite," William said. "It went off when you screamed. Nick was far enough away that it only knocked him out, but four of our men…"

I couldn't even process all the death. "Vicky!" I sobbed while holding my head.

I hated fire. I hated how the smoke wrapped around my naked body, stinging my skin with defiant embers. I hated the smell of burnt flesh, the ashes heavy on my tongue, my charred soul like splinters deep in my chest.

"She's dead, Juliet," Nick whispered. "There's nothing else you can do—"

I shoved him away from me and sobbed hard and recklessly. Dragging my bleeding feet across the concrete, I walked toward the fire. Heat licked at my cheeks. Sirens off in the distance cursed my ears.

"Dead, dead, dead," Anthony whispered while rocking back and forth.

William was the only one to stop me from jumping into the flames. He wrapped his arms around me as I cried out. I hated him for saving me, for loving me.

All of this started because I made a choice. Because I fell in love. Because I was a lonely girl clinging to dangerous men.

She was dead because of them.

chapter twenty-five
anthony civella

Hello there. I'm Anthony Civella.

I'm sorry, my mind is a crowded place right now. I'd pull you up a seat, but there just isn't any room. Oh. Good. Yes, just stand in the corner next to the dead homeless man I found three years ago. *Howdy, Jacob. How are you? Say hello to the wife for me.*

Racing heart. I need to focus. I know what I have to do.

Sometimes, the unalive call me Wrath. I suppose you can call me that if you'd like. I'm kind of going through a bit of a rebranding right now. Gentle, gentle, gentle.

Can you all shut the fuck up? I'm trying to focus. Oh, you're curious about what's next? You should know by now that I'm a ticking time bomb about to go off. Isn't sanity fickle? Don't answer that, friend.

I'm gripping the steering wheel. Madness or maybe anger is like shockwaves making it hard to drive. It's dark outside. My phone is ringing. Too much going on. Too many sounds. Too many thoughts pouring through my mind.

Don't you hate it when people won't stop talking? Shut up, I'm trying to listen!

"Hello?" I answer.

"Where are you?" William asks. "Juliet is asking for you—she needs you, Anthony. Now isn't the best time to go fucking crazy."

He acts like I have control, guys. Hilarious. "William, this is why our whole group thing is perfect. I need you to be there for her right now. I'm currently on a safari through the Florida wilderness."

William curses. "Fuck, Anthony. She's not asking for me. She wants you. Can't you just be normal for once?"

My spine tingles. "Ooh, you sound like Dad."

"Vicky is dead, Anthony!" William screams.

Shhh, it's okay, guys. He's just angry. He doesn't mean it. He doesn't know what I've set out to do.

Vengeance. Vengeance. Vengeance.

"I'll be there soon. Stop calling me," I say before hanging up the phone.

It was probably shitty for me to just walk out of there to let Nick and William deal with the aftermath. *I know, I know.* There were so many dead bodies just waiting for me to greet them. Love them. Bury them. My poor friends, now one with the earth. Bloodied. Battered. Beaten and bruised.

My phone is ringing again. *Would you mind putting it on silent for me? Thanks. Actually, let's just toss it out the window. Okay. Goodbye, cellphone.*

I tighten my grip on the steering wheel. I laugh to myself. I force my eyes to dry up. No time for tears. Only anger.

So maybe you're wondering where we are headed. Maybe you're mad at me for not staying with Juliet. Maybe you think I've lost my mind. How can I lose something I so clearly have—all of you here wouldn't exist without it.

Florida is a swampy cesspool. It's humid. I hate it here. Norman shared his address so freely. If I lived in a hut surrounded by alligators, I'd be embarrassed. You know what I love about my sister? She's never embarrassed. She walks into a room and owns that shit, you know? She's always telling me that I've got to accept myself.

Acceptance is such a funny concept. How can you accept something inevitable? Acceptance only means something if you have a choice. If it happens to you, it's just existence. Living. Breathing.

I drive down the winding road. Mosquitos that are practically the size of my hand hit my windshield. Splat go the bloodsucking motherfuckers. I'm going to kill him today. Have you ever killed someone? It's easier than you think. Bones break. Veins burst. Eyes pop out. Guts spill. Necks snap. We're a painfully vulnerable species. It doesn't take much.

I turn on my high beams while pulling into his drive. There is no point in hiding. I want him to know I'm coming for him. Do you think he feels fear? I get scared sometimes. Are you with me? Let's do this together, okay? I'll end his life. You look him in the eye so we never forget.

I get out of my car.

I lean against the driver's side door.

Be quiet, everyone. The show is about to start. Get your popcorn.

Norman walks outside like he's been expecting us. Look at that smug grin. Do you think if we cut his mouth from his face, we could sew it back on in the shape of a frown? I hate his smile. He was smiling when he killed Vicky, you know.

"Alone, Anthony?" he calls out.

It's okay, friend. Don't listen to him. Just because he can't see you doesn't mean you aren't there. "I'm never alone. I hope you're ready to die, Normy."

"You're mad about Vicky. I get it. One day, maybe you'll understand," Norman says.

There's a gun in his hand.

I just brought the switchblade I got for my thirteenth birthday.

I don't trust myself with guns, you know.

Norman has blood on his cheek.

Does it belong to Vicky?

"Why are you here, Anthony?"

Do you think Norman and I are similar? Certainly I'm saner than he is, right? I'm fishing for validation here, friend. The least you can do is tell me I'm not on the same level as a fucking cannibal.

I suppose we could stay here and talk to him more. But I have a purpose for being here. We have a purpose. I'm going to kill him.

"Norman, Norman, Norman," I say while spinning my switchblade between my fingers. "You're never going to be free. I'm going to lock you up and keep you in my basement for all of eternity."

Would you mind holding this? It's a box of grief. Hold it tight to your chest for me so I can do what needs to be done.

Trapped. He's going to be trapped. Norman has the decency to look slightly uneasy.

I get in my car and put it in reverse. He watches me. He watches me. He SCREAMS. *Are you paying attention? This is the crucial part. Norman is about to die. Sit up. Open your eyes. Pay attention.*

Back up, back up, back up. The wheels groan as I pull back like a slingshot. He grips his gun tighter. I put the car in drive. He aims. I duck before slamming on the gas.

Gunshots. Shattering. I'm chomping on glass. A screaming engine pushed to its limits. Sloshing swamps. I drive the car forward and slam into his shady hut that has seen better days.

The ceiling collapses. Walls cave-in. Norman's gun goes

off again. Whoosh, by my ears.

Is everyone okay? Yes? Good.

I get out of the car. The smell of leaking gas fills my lungs. I love it. Inhale deeply, guys. Get high off the fumes. Dizzy freedom.

VICKY IS DEAD.

Crunching under my foot.

Stab the bastard.

VICKY IS DEAD.

Slay the dragon.

VICKY IS DEAD.

I find his body shoved between the wall and the hood of my car. He has blood pooling from his mouth.

I lift my knife.

It's time to go, guys. There's only room for me here now. I gave you my madness, and you threw it back at me. Goodbye, friends.

Vicky is dead. Slice.

Vicky is dead. Splat goes the mosquito. Splat!

Vicky is dead.

epilogue
william civella

I held onto Juliet like we were on a sinking ship. I tried to be her life raft, but she kept asking for the weights holding her down.

"Has Anthony called back?" she sniffled while clinging to my shirt. The expensive Italian button-up was soaked with her snot and tears. I brushed her hair with my fingers.

"Not yet," I whispered. Disappointing her hurt worse than my own sense of betrayal. He left. He just left without a word. Did he even care about Juliet—about us?

"How is Nick?" she croaked.

I eyed the bandages on her stomach. She had some burns there, and I was scheduled to put more ointment on it in the next hour. "He's fine. Should be released from the hospital by morning. I told him you'd call soon."

Nick was surprisingly compliant when the paramedics said he needed to be looked at. Guilt was a nasty disease, yeah? I bet he couldn't look at Juliet right now. Couldn't face the consequences of his actions.

He was the reason Vicky died.

He was the reason Anthony had gone AWOL.

He was the reason for every ounce of pain and suffering our family had endured, and I'd had enough.

"I'm glad you're here," Juliet whispered while nuzzling me. "I just can't believe she's gone."

My chest could have been cut open right then and there, and it still wouldn't have hurt as much as reality did. Vicky wasn't perfect, but she was our responsibility to protect. Nick fucked up too many times to count. She was dead because of his negligence and pride. Fuck his control.

I leaned down to kiss Juliet's forehead. More tears streamed down her cheeks, and I wanted to catch all of them in a bottle and drown my brothers in her sadness.

It was time for a new era.

New leadership.

A new fucking *king*.

I would be the heir to my father's legacy.

I was in charge now.

The End

**Grudge, the final book in the Malice Mafia saga releases March 2022.

author's note

I feel like I owe you an explanation. When I first wrote Malice, I had every intention of making it a standalone.

I never imagined you would love these characters as much as you did. To say I've been shocked by the response would be an understatement. I'm so incredibly thankful that you've taken a chance on these characters. I wish I could consensually hug each and every one of you for taking a chance on my book.

That being said, I read the reviews and heard your pleas. You felt there was more story to be shared, and I don't ever want to let you guys down. So, I picked up the loose ends and ran with them.

But in my own way, of course.

I wanted Vicky to be understood. Not necessarily redeemed. Not even liked. But understood. None of these characters are the hero of the story. But I wanted to show that they all have painful, traumatic origins that have shaped them into the villains they are today. Some of you might not like that I brought her back, but it felt authentic to the characters. Juliet couldn't just demand more from her relationships with the guys, she had to take a hard look at her friendships, too.

Thank you for reading. I have so many plans for the final book in this series. Wrath was about Anthony accepting and adapting to his trauma. Grudge is about William owning up to his power. Nick is on the path to healing, too. Even if it isn't what you expect.

Thanks for your patience with this series. Thanks for your love. Thanks for every review and kind word.

Love,

Cora

acknowledgements

This book would not have been possible without the support and love of Christina Santos and Christine Estevez. I could not do what I do without them.

I would like to especially thank Rita Reese, Katie Friend, Meggan Reed, Savannah Richey, Lauren Campbell, and Claire Jones for beta reading. Thank you for the late night messages, encouragement, and calls. I am so thankful for each of you and truly appreciate all the hours you put into reading my messy manuscripts.

I am grateful to all of those whom I have had the pleasure of working with during this book. I'd like to especially recognize my editor, Helayna Trask. She always takes the time to dive into the worlds I create and make sure they are perfect for you all. I would also like to thank all the dedicated members of The Zone and Cora's Crew.

Ingram Content Group UK Ltd.
Milton Keynes UK
UKHW010659050623
422889UK00005B/607